SOFIE METROPOLIS

Sofie Metropolis

TORI CARRINGTON

A TOM DOHERTY ASSOCIATES BOOK

NEW YORK

SOFIE METROPOLIS

This book is printed on acid-free paper.

A Forge Book
Published by Tom Doherty Associates, LLC
175 Fifth Avenue
New York, NY 10010

www.tor.com

Forge® is a registered trademark of Tom Doherty Associates, LLC.

ISBN 0-765-31240-9
EAN 978-0765-31240-2

Printed in the United States of America

0 9 8 7 6 5 4 3 2

We dedicate this book to our sons,
Tony Jr. and Tim,
our own personal Greek-American heroes.
Upon touching sand, may it turn to gold.
Yia esas!

ACKNOWLEDGMENTS

There are many to credit for Sofie's existence. We extend our heartfelt gratitude to, first, our sons, Tony Jr. and Tim, who walk the colorful path that is Greek-American life with grace and beauty every day. You both are an endless source of inspiration.

Our younger son, Tim, for taking two seconds to do what we had spent days struggling to do, namely, come up with Sofie's last name, Metropolis. Maybe we should have spent those days at the beach with you in Greece.

Our dear friends Teresa and Mike Medeiros (You!); Christine and Richard Feehan and the entire family for, well, making us feel part of the fam; Karen Drogin aka Carly Phillips, Leslie Kelly, Julie Leto, and the rest of the '65 Club, Temptresses, TrailBlazers, and Ex-RomExers because you all rock big time! Denise Lynn Koch and Maumee Valley RWA for providing a local support system; RWA for providing a national one. You all have the stuff of which the greatest heroes and heroines are made!

Our agent, Robert Gottlieb, of Trident Media Group: You really are a god among men. And Jenny Bent, Alex Glass, and Kimberly Whalen: A body couldn't wish for better cohorts-in-crime.

Melissa Ann Singer, Linda Quinton, Natasha Panza, Anna

Genoese, and the gang at Tor/Forge, new friends who immediately felt like old friends. Thanks for helping make Sofie a reality!

To Brenda Chin, for showing us our wings then shoving us off the edge of the damn cliff.

Everyone at *Romantic Times* BookClub, especially Kathryn Falk, Carol Stacy, and Giselle Hirtenfeld-Goldfeder, for giving voice to the romance genre and promoting all that is wonderful in the world. And for reminding us that, in the end, it's all about the friends we make and the joy we share.

The late Vaggelis and Kostoula Karayianni and Carl J. Schlachter Sr., and our sisters and brothers in Greece and here, the late Penelope Psali, Ekaterina and Georgios Fragkopoulous, Andreas and Lambrini Karayianni, Theonesis and Dina Karayianni, Victoria and Alfon Tsilias, Thotheres and Georgia Karayianni, Carl J. Schlachter Jr., Jamey Schlachter, Stephen Schlachter, and all of our nieces and nephews. You are the shoulders we stand on.

Our niece and nephew Dina and Manolis Karayianni, who call Queens and Astoria home. And Lucienne Diver, who lives in the heart of Astoria with her husband, Pete, and son, Ty, and helped us hear the "wind chimes" of Astoria Park as well as letting us bug her whenever we're in need of details only someone who shares a love of Astoria can give.

Everyone in Astoria. Being Greek means you're "home" whenever and wherever you cross paths with another Greek. No question is unwelcome, no subject taboo. *Zeto E Ellas!*

And last, but certainly not least, our Friends. More specifically, Barbara Hicks, Morgan Leigh, and every last member of our fan-run ToriCarringtonFriends e-mail loop. Thanks for "locking us in the closet" when we're under deadline, giving us the Big Cucumber to keep us grounded, and generously sharing virtual chocolate with us when it's time to celebrate. . . .

Break out the chocolate!

SOFIE METROPOLIS

One

THERE ARE TWO KINDS OF people in this world: Greeks and those who wish they were Greek.

At least that's the maxim to which my grandfather Kosmos subscribes. Me? Well, I suppose maybe we all are divided up into two groups. But I don't think it has much to do with ethnic makeup, because let's face it, we're all pretty screwed up no matter where our parents, grandparents, or forefathers hail from.

The first group is made up of those who follow the road well traveled. Maybe because they're afraid of losing a heel, getting a run in their stockings, or, worse, disappointing their families. Then there are those who take an alternate route—or perhaps even forge a path all their own—so focused on the road twisting and turning before them they don't have much time to think about what kind of shoes they're wearing, much less what anyone else is thinking.

I know the difference between the two groups because I used to belong to the former. Now I'm happy to say I'm a card-carrying member of the latter.

I used to be Sofie Metropolis, waitress and good Greek daughter—not necessarily in that order. Now I'm Sofie Metropolis, PI.

Has a nice ring to it, doesn't it? Sofie Metropolis, PI. I definitely like the sound of it. Even though I won't be legally licensed for another three years (the result of some hokey New York State law). And even though some might argue that my abilities as a private investigator rate somewhere between amateur sleuth and pet detective. Of course, it doesn't help that I'm not anything like my own idea of what a private investigator should be. When I think PI, I think Philip Marlowe, James Garner in *The Rockford Files,* or VI Warshawski. Or, at the very least, my Uncle Spyros, who's nobody's idea of what a PI looks like but has made a passable living at it for the past thirty years.

Anyway, Uncle Spyros is to blame for my quitting my waitressing job three months ago and hiring on at his detective agency. All because he asked me one simple question: "What do you want to do with your life, Sof?"

Maybe it wasn't so much the question itself, but the mud puddle I was knee deep in the middle of when he asked it.

But where Uncle Spyros is to blame for my professional woes, the rest of my family is responsible for my personal instability, no matter how much I love them.

You see, three months ago, on the day I was set to marry a good Greek boy, just like any good Greek girl eventually does, I caught my groom schtupping my maid of honor in a back room at St. Constantine's Greek Orthodox Cathedral. It was then that I realized that good was overrated. I'd spent so much time trying to be good, trying to live up to others' ideas of what good was, that I never stopped to ask myself what I wanted, good, bad, or otherwise. Which is why Uncle Spyros' question will be forever burned into my brain.

So I nixed the groom and kept the wedding gifts—the biggest

being the six-unit apartment building my family bought and couldn't exactly return for store credit. A lot of the other gifts still sit, unwrapped for the most part, in a corner of my bedroom on the top floor of my biggest gift. From time to time I pop open one of the bottles of reception champagne, then unwrap one or two of the gifts that don't look like toasters. My mom thinks it's bad etiquette that I don't return the gifts. Me? I figure since everyone knew about my groom's extracurricular activities but me, I deserve a little slack. Besides, most of the gifts are from his family. And since he's threatening to sue me for the cost of the two-carat engagement ring I fed to the garbage disposal . . . well, let's just say I'm glad I arrived early on that fateful day, or else I might even now be married to the lousy skirt-chaser.

Still, after all this, my mom, Thalia Metropolis, never gives up on the idea that someday I'll get married. Someday as in tomorrow or the day after that. You know, so I can produce more little Greek children who'll suffer from their own cultural identity crises.

And in case I needed a reminder of that, a prime example of what my mother thinks of as groom material sat on her plastic-covered sofa, staring up at me with a goofy grin. He was Greek. Of course. And he looked like he could do with a good salon referral. Preferably one that included body waxing.

I'd stopped by my parents' house to see if my brother, Kosmos, or my maternal grandfather—also Kosmos—were around so they could help me carry the mammoth area rug in the back of my Mustang convertible up the two flights of stairs to my apartment. It was a Saturday morning and a hot spring day in June and I'd gone into the city to do a little shopping at the Chelsea Flea Market. And I'd spent the half hour—sans traffic—driving back to Astoria in the northwest corner of Queens wavering between shopper's high and guilt.

Of course, right now all I felt was exasperation. The guy in front of me on the couch hadn't blinked. And I'm pretty sure I was scowling.

"Sofie! I was just telling Themios that you might stop by." My mother came in from the kitchen carrying a tray of the standard: Greek coffee, glass of water, and something sweet. In this case the sweet was *koulourakia,* my mother's version of a Greek vanilla cookie that turned rock hard five minutes out of the oven and was inedible unless you first dunked it into the coffee.

I looked back at Themios.

Sometimes it seems my mom always has another potential groom hanging around—you know, on the off chance I might stop by (which happens often, because I only live a block away and, yes, I admit, every now and again I get a little homesick. But that's between you and me). My mom recently read that you could have your hymen surgically replaced and wants to schedule an appointment for me yesterday. You know, so she's not ashamed on the rare occasions I go to church. Oh, and for the guys like Themios that she's always trying to fix me up with because, you know, no man wants a girl who's "been around."

I can see it now. Sofie Metropolis: PI and born-again virgin.

"Themios Kokotas, I'd like you to meet my daughter, Sofie." Mom put the tray down and leaned closer to me. "You could have cleaned up a bit."

I was wearing jeans, a black Lycra T-shirt, and a pair of Skechers slides. Comfortable, but not exactly groom-nabbing material. Not that I intended to nab any grooms in the near or far-off future. I stared at Themios. Especially not this groom.

"She's older than I thought," he said in Greek.

I squinted at him. He couldn't possibly be implying that I wasn't the right bride material?

"Is Grandpa around anywhere?" I made a point of asking my mother in English.

"Funny you should say that," she said, sitting down on the far end of the couch and motioning for me to sit between her and the human Chia Pet. I ignored her. "He stopped by earlier looking for you."

I headed for the kitchen where my grandfather always hangs out.

"Only he left straight after." My mother put the coffee, water, and cement cookie down in front of Themios. "And before you ask, your brother's not here either. He went to some sort of seminar or another downtown." She smiled at her guest. "My son's going to be a doctor."

That's doctor as in Ph.D., not physician, but try explaining the difference to Thalia Metropolis.

And that's my brother. Always expanding his mind and making me, his older sister by a year, look like an even bigger idiot. It was all I could do to graduate from high school eight years ago while he was now a year away from a double doctorate in psychology and education.

Don't get me wrong. I'm proud of my little brother. But sometimes I think he stays in school just to get out of working at the family restaurant.

"I've really got to go, Mom." I aimed what I hoped was a smile in Themios' direction. "It was really nice meeting you. I hope you enjoy your visit to the States."

"Visit? I've been here twenty years."

Oops.

I bent to kiss my mom's cheek and swiped a cookie at the same time.

She caught my arm in a death grip. The kind only mothers know how to give.

"I've got something else I need to talk to you about." She slid a glance toward "our" visitor. "Something about Mrs. Kapoor."

I held my breath.

"And Efi's upstairs. She's got another one of those . . . things in her face. Her eyebrow this time."

Efi is my nineteen-year-old sister, and she recently developed a fetish for needles. When she's not piercing something, she's tattooing it. Mom keeps telling me to do something about it, but beyond running a chain through Efi's many piercing rings and fastening her to the radiator, I haven't a clue.

"Tell her I'll call her later." I extracted my arm from my mother's grip and dove for the door and sanity.

Being twenty-six and single in a Greek family isn't easy. I think it's one of the reasons why I'd agreed to marry Thomas-the-Horny-Toad Chalikis in the first place. Sure, he was a cheating bastard, but could he carry my rug up to my apartment?

Sometimes I think it would be better if I just packed up and moved to someplace like . . . I don't know, Omaha, maybe. Being in a place where everyone knows your business (especially the wince-worthy groom story and the honeymoon I took by myself that I spent drinking worm shakes—long story) is more than a challenge. I stopped outside the front door and bit into the *koulourakia* with my back teeth, looking around the neighborhood in question. But then I ask myself: Where would I go? I mean, this—Astoria—is it for me, you know? No matter how many issues I have with my neighbors. Or how many questionable men my mother tries to match me up with. This is home and these guys, all of them, are my family.

Well, okay, except for maybe Mr. Romanoff down the block. Everyone thinks he's a vampire. Oh, and my mom's Bangladeshi next-door neighbor and best friend Mrs. Kapoor, who's forty years overdue for a new pair of glasses.

I stuffed the rest of the cookie into my mouth, then waved at Mrs. K even though I couldn't see her. For all intents and purposes she couldn't see me either. But she seemed to have some sort of Sofie radar that let her know when I was around in case, you know, I was getting into some kind of trouble. Again.

I climbed into my 1965 candy-apple-red Mustang convertible. Well, okay, the car's really more bondo gray than red and looks like she belongs in a scrap yard, or at the very least like a prime candidate for a car version of *Extreme Makeover*. But I see through all her imperfections to the hot mama that lies underneath. And as you know, any hot mama needs a hot name. In this case, I'd christened my car Lucille. I'd even tried to break one of the bottles of my reception champagne over the front fender when I bought her a couple months ago. After several failed attempts I'd settled for pouring the bubbly over the hood.

I could already tell it was going to be a scorcher. Not just the day, but the summer as a whole. And where there are hot temperatures, wicked thunderstorms are sure to follow. I eyed the sky and the bruised clouds creeping in from the west. It wouldn't dare rain before I got this rug home.

I took a sip from my ever-present portable cup of Nescafé frappé then started up Lucille.

Everywhere you looked people in the neighborhood were watering, clipping, and trimming the flowers and foliage lining their narrow front porches, washing the cars parked in their narrow driveways, or sitting on their porch chairs to watch others work. I knew that a couple blocks up on Broadway the Greek sidewalk cafés would already be filled—mostly with Greek men gathered for coffee to unwind and share any interesting gossip they'd picked up during the week. (I know this because my father and maternal grandfather own rival cafés kitty-corner from each other and I've worked at both of them, although never at the same time because of an age-old feud between the two most important men in my life that began long before I was born.) I took a deep breath. I was in luck. The wind was blowing just right and I caught a whiff of the *souvlaki* stand at 32nd Street and the Greek patisserie churning out *tsoureki* (braided Greek sweet bread) a couple blocks up from there, reminding me of more of the things I liked about the neighborhood.

If Astoria is the American equivalent of Athens, then Broadway is the *agora* or city center. An all-inclusive neighborhood where Greeks are prominent, but aren't the only game in town. I don't know how people in Omaha live beyond what I see on TV, but I don't think they can walk two blocks to the south and enjoy an Indian dinner, or see a Muslim community center snuggled up against a Catholic church.

I drove down the one-way street away from my apartment building and hung a right. The route would take me by my uncle's PI agency sandwiched between a fish store and a Thai restaurant on Steinway. I figured that since I was presently the only full-time investigator—however unlicensed—working there it might be a good idea to check in with Rosie, the office manager, to see if there were any potential clients.

I spotted a guy outside the office window, a hand shielding his eyes from the morning sun. He tried the apparently locked door, then went back to the window.

It looked like I was the only one, period, working at the agency this morning.

I pulled up behind a ten-year-old white Cadillac bearing a Giants bumper sticker and one of those crown air fresheners in the back window, and cut the engine. The Mustang coughed and sputtered before finally going silent.

"Who you looking for?" Frappé in hand, I got out of the car.

In his mid-forties with a receding hairline and a slight cushion around the middle, he looked like any one of a hundred guys from the neighborhood. I took some comfort in knowing that in ten years Thomas-the-Toad would look the same. "I'm looking for the PI."

I stuck out my free hand. "Then you've found her. Come on in."

The outside window read SPYROS METROPOLIS, PRIVATE INVES-

TIGATOR in gold and black stenciled letters, so I could understand the man's squinty-eyed look. Uncle Spyros owned the place and would until I qualified for a PI license. Or maybe that should be *if* I ever qualified, because I hadn't made a solid decision one way or the other on my new vocation beyond liking the sound of the initials after my name.

Anyway, right now it was my uncle's name that brought people in. No matter how strange the people.

To date I'd worked on a missing iguana case, investigated the chef at a nearby bakery on behalf of a silent partner who was convinced he was skimming (which he was—out of the display case. Given his girth, his appetite ate into an interesting percentage of the profits), and an uncomfortable number of cheating spouse/lover cases. But if it had been my name on the window, I was sure that the only work I'd have gotten would have been the iguana case.

I could only hope this guy would offer up something interesting. That didn't include scaly pets that liked to hide out in neighbors' mailboxes.

I unlocked the glass door and led the way into the gloom just beyond, switching on the overhead light. The place probably hadn't been painted since the 1970s when my uncle first opened up shop, and the once-psychedelic green walls now fell somewhere between pea green and baby-poop brown. Half of the front room was occupied by two desks—the battered metal one to the right was mine—and a line of dented filing cabinets. Faded posters, maps, and old calendars were pinned to the walls. Three doors opened to the back. One was the bathroom, which was little more than a closet with running water. The other two rooms were offices, one belonging to my Uncle Spyros, the other to his one-time full partner, now silent partner, Lenny Nash. Lenny looked older than dirt and was just as responsive. I wasn't sure if that was because he couldn't hear anyone or if he just plain didn't care, but I was relieved that he didn't seem to spend much time at the office. Ever since I was a kid, doing some odd jobs for my uncle, Lenny had reminded me of Ebenezer Scrooge before his ghostly visitors.

My cousin Pete, Uncle Spyros' oldest son from his first marriage, hung around sometimes, usually when he needed cash, and took over his father's office when he wasn't around. Which was often lately.

At any rate, a few questions told me the new client's name was Bud Suleski, and for some reason he looked a little nervous talking to me. I explained to him that my uncle wasn't available on account of he was semi-retired. (Actually, he was in Greece just then, but I like to make it sound like I'm running the place and that Uncle Spyros is only a phone call away.)

"I think my wife's screwing around."

I was pretty sure I winced.

So much for this case being different.

I put coffee on to brew. Even though I always carried around my own, the smell of the ancient coffeemaker helped chase away some of the musty odor of the old building caused by lack of attention and decades of cigarette smoke, though no one had smoked there since the city's smoking ban went into effect. Activity also gave me a minute to get my thoughts together. Call me crazy, but every time someone came in with a cheating spouse case—which was way too often if you asked me—images of my own ex with his tux pants bunched down around his ankles came back to haunt me. It wreaked havoc on my nonexistent love life. And made sleeping next to impossible.

"And you want me to catch her in the act," I asked.

"Yeah. Yeah, I do."

The door opened, letting in a rush of fresh air and office manager Rosie Rodriguez.

Rosie is a Puerto Rican dynamo who, even when she isn't moving, looks like she is. Her breasts easily comprise a full third of her body weight and are always displayed to what Rosie refers to as their "utmost flattering degree." She has cheek dimples the size of plates and can disarm you with her surprisingly sweet smile or scald you with curse words that haven't even been invented yet, depending on which side of the bed she woke up on. Uncle Spyros hired her a year ago for, I thought, reasons having to do strictly with her physical assets. But when I'd hired on at the agency, I discovered that Rosie's best features were above the neck and had nothing to do with her dimples. She's smart as a whip, takes crap from no one, and ceaselessly seems out of breath, giving her voice a high-pitched quality that only adds to her disarming personality.

She stopped in front of me and waggled her finger. "You're not gonna believe this." She made a tsking sound. "You know old Mr. Romanoff down the street from your parents? The tall, creepy one that's whiter than my grandmama's underwears? You know, the vampire? Well, supposedly he's got a nephew visiting."

I knew Rosie would get around to her point sooner or later. But with a client present, I wished it would come sooner. "Rosie, meet Bud Suleski."

"Hey." She spared him a glance, popped her gum, then turned back to me. "Anyway, ever since this nephew showed up, no one's seen the old man, you know? It's like he just up and vanished or something."

"People don't vanish, Rosie."

Mr. Suleski spoke up. "I had a cousin disappear once." He shrugged. "She showed up eight months later, in Ohio of all places, and married to a deadbeat from Minnesota, but she disappeared."

Rosie and I stared at him.

Rosie turned her back on him and gave me an eye roll. "Anyway, I told the neighborhood you'd look into it."

"What?"

Rosie shrugged, poured herself a cup of coffee, then stuck her gum to the rim before taking a sip. She gestured with her hand. "Come on, Sof, the guy could be stuck in his freezer in the basement or something. Or cut into little pieces and stuffed into Tupperware containers."

It wasn't all that long ago that I would have taken great advantage of the opportunity to dish about the neighborhood vampire and his visiting nephew, preferably over a healthy helping of *galaktoboureko*—a Greek custard pastry—at a Broadway café. But beginning the day I started at the agency it seemed everyone had a missing cousin, an old flame they'd lost track of, or a pet they'd lost two years ago, and could I do them a favor and find her or him or it? At first I'd been excited that people sought me out. Until I figured out that "favor" meant no money would be changing hands.

Now I asked Rosie, "Why don't you look into it?"

She gave an exaggerated shudder. "Because in addition to all I have to do around here, I have that baby shower thing I'm putting together for my sister Lupe. Anyway, you know how I am about vampires."

No, I didn't, and I wasn't sure I wanted to either.

I sat on the corner of the desk I had inherited and crossed my arms. I'd watched Uncle Spyros do this countless times while growing up and I found it helped my concentration. And probably made me look like I knew what I was doing. Which never hurt.

"Do you have kids?" I asked Suleski.

He blinked.

"You know. Those humans that look like adults only smaller?"

"Two. A boy and a girl. Nine and seven."

The same age as my cousin Helen's kids.

Realizing I'd moved on, Rosie sighed and booted up an antique computer she always swore at in a way that could singe a body's eyebrows clean off.

"And if I do this? Catch your wife in the act, I mean? What are you going to do with the information?"

"Say, you want the job or not?"

I didn't want the job. But I needed the job. If only to use it to talk Spyros into a fresh coat of paint for the office and maybe a new computer for Rosie.

"Talk." I picked up a pad and started taking notes.

Two

IN THE PAST THREE MONTHS I've come to understand that owning my own apartment building is both a blessing and a curse. A blessing because the building is mine, free and clear, so I'll always have a place to stay. A curse because I'm not particularly good at collecting rent.

Mrs. Nebitz across the hall from me in 3B is great. She pays her rent on time, every time. The only problem is that Mrs. Nebitz has lived in the same apartment for the past forty-five years and her rent hasn't risen significantly since she first moved in because of the city's strict rent stabilization laws. I could easily get three to four times the rent for the place in today's market.

But I guess in the end everything evens out because she's a great neighbor. Quiet, considerate, and she brings me brisket and knishes and doesn't bother to check whether or not I've eaten the gefilte fish she sometimes gives me (a dish she makes that has to do with a few fish I saw swimming in her bathtub last April right before Passover).

Then there are the three hard-partying DeVry students in 2B

who told me they were looking for a place for a month or two until they found a bigger apartment but show no signs of moving on. I can never catch all three of them home at the same time, and whoever I do catch inevitably tells me one of the others has the rent, making trying to collect it a full-time job. So much so that I haven't had the time to try to collect this month's rent yet, and the month's already half over.

Of course then there's the working mom in 2A who got laid off two months ago and has been having a hard time stretching her unemployment check. Her daughter, Lola, is nine and looks like an angel, but is evil incarnate. Anyway, I haven't the heart to ask Etta Munson for more than she apologetically gives me, which is only about a third of the rent.

I won't say much about the one-room basement apartments 1A and 1B because I'm pretty sure they're illegal, which appears to be the norm in the city, except to say that the young black couple in 1B has lived there for over two years and 1A can't seem to hold a tenant (the rest of the tenants have a running bet on how long the old Indian guy—think dot not feather—who moved in last month is going to make it).

Still, despite all this, I get a little rush whenever I pull up in front of the rectangular, brick structure, built about seventy-five years ago and solid as a rock. And today was one of those rare days when I actually got a parking spot right in front. There are solid wood floors throughout the building, and it's the floor of my living room I planned to cover with the area rug I bought with money I really didn't have at the Chelsea Flea Market.

I eyed the rolled rug in question. It was sticking out of the backseat. Good thing I had a convertible or I would never have gotten it home. Even though I had no idea how I was going to carry the eight-by-ten stretch of heavy Persian wool up the three flights to my apartment alone.

I looked up the block to my parents' house and wondered if my grandfather had dropped by again. Or if I should give him a call and have him come over.

Then again, maybe not.

The last time Grandpa Kosmos helped me out with something I'd ended up minus my favorite pair of K-Swiss and a mysterious, itchy rash on the back of my calf that had stuck around for three months.

I thought about the cheating wife case I'd just taken on as I grabbed the end of the rug and gave it a tug. So being Sofie Metropolis, Private Investigator, wasn't all it was cracked up to be. So what? Experience told me very few people found their lives and/or careers fulfilling. And I'd certainly held dumber jobs. My three-week crash embalming course at my Aunt Sotiria's funeral home when I was nineteen sprung instantly to mind. Still, even that job had had its benefits: At least I'd gotten to see dead bodies. I'd just figured out fairly quickly that I didn't want to see them on a regular basis.

After much puffing and tugging, I managed to work the rug halfway out of the convertible and watched as the end drooped to the ground. Yes, that about summed up the other area of my life right now. My love life was completely limp. Limp? It would take some major action just to boost it up to limp. At this point I'd settle for a small rise.

Or at least a stupid rug that could maintain a stiffie.

Of course, after what happened three months ago, I haven't exactly been interested in anything having to do with stiffies or the opposite sex, which, it could be argued, are one and the same. Until recently. Recently my body had begun letting me know that it still had certain parts that required other moving parts to work properly.

I crouched down and worked the rug over my left shoulder, then stood up. I could do this. All I had to do was take tiny little steps in my Skechers slides and I'd be in my third-floor apartment rolling this baby across my bare living room floor in no time.

I took two steps then wavered, my foot halfway up the curb.

Then again, maybe not.

A window opened overhead.

"Hey, Sof! Need a hand?"

I looked up while keeping my head firmly against the rug to brace it. A better man would have just come down to help me. A better man might even have brought more help. But Don Meyers wasn't a better man, he was a business school student. And sometimes I wondered if he was a man, period, no matter how well he filled in jeans and a T-shirt.

"Why, does it look like I need help?"

He shrugged, then closed the window.

That was the three DeVry business school students in 2B for you. How they managed to tie their shoes in the morning was a mystery to me.

Drugs. It had to be drugs.

I negotiated the curb and stumbled toward the dozen steps leading to the front door.

My cell phone picked that moment to start vibrating. Recently I'd started to feel a little thrill at the sensation, but not right now. I was going to get this thing up to my apartment, and I was going to get it up there now.

A brief spurt of a siren sounded on the street behind me.

I was beginning to think that someone didn't want me to have this rug.

My load slid from my shoulder onto the sidewalk.

"What do you got there, Metropolis?"

I turned to face Pimply Pino, a kid who'd always sat in the seat behind me at St. Demetrios and who was no longer a kid or pimply, but was no less irritating than he used to be. Especially since he now wore an NYPD police uniform and had a tendency to hike his pants up in a way that made even me wince.

I motioned toward the rug. "Pino, you're just in time to help me get this rug up to my place."

He leaned over and tried to peer inside the roll, using his night-stick to poke at the limp rug. "I got a call you were hauling around dead bodies."

"What?"

It wasn't hard to figure out who had put in the call. I stared up the street to where Mrs. Kapoor's curtains fluttered.

Mrs. Kapoor was the one who'd caught me flashing my nonexistent breasts at Johnnie and Jason Petros when I was seven.

Now she was calling me in for dragging around dead bodies.

I crossed my arms over the chest that hadn't grown much since I was seven and watched Pino continue to poke at the rug with his stick. I caught myself staring at the long, thick, stiff length of the billy club.

Oh, I needed help. Big time.

I squinted at Pino. "You're never going to forgive me for sliming your chair in fourth grade, are you?"

His answer was a deadpan stare. "I think the question is are you ever going to live down having sucked back three bug and worm shakes on that show before blowing the chance at fifty grand when they stuck you headfirst under water?"

That lousy reality show I did in L.A. when I was supposed to be lounging on the beach with a piña colada and a husband. Why did I have the feeling I'd be hearing about that low point even when I was eighty?

"If I were carting around a body, don't you think I would be try-ing to get it away from my apartment instead of into it?"

Pino blinked at me as if the idea hadn't occurred to him.

"Mind if I take a closer look?" he asked.

I motioned toward the rug. "Go ahead. Although I don't know how much closer you can get short of unrolling it."

Another idea I had apparently just planted in his head.

I watched as he pulled at the middle of the three ties holding the rug closed and pulled my vibrating phone out of my pocket.

My mother.

Figured.

Mrs. Kapoor had probably called 911, then Thalia.

"What are you doing dragging dead bodies around?" my mother asked.

"I'm not dragging dead bodies around. I bought a rug."

"Oh. Anyway, that's not the reason I called. I told you I had something I wanted you to do for Mrs. Kapoor."

Only my mother could get a call about my transporting dead bodies around and call me for a different reason. I only hoped it didn't have anything to do with the human Chia Pet.

"Mrs. Kapoor's dog Muffy has gone missing and I told her you would find him."

I squinted at nothing in particular. I'd known I'd live to regret the iguana rescue. "Are you telling me Mrs. K sicked Pimply Pino on me and I'm supposed to help her find her dog from hell?"

Pino's head jerked up from where he inspected the rug.

This wasn't happening.

"Is that how I raised you? To disrespect your elders?"

I hated that my mother still had the ability to make me feel guilty.

Pino had rolled the carpet out so it covered the steps to the door.

He waved his nightstick. "Okay, we're clear."

"Ma, I've got to go. You know, so I can take the dead body up to my apartment before I have to get back to work."

"Work? What work? Don't tell me you're still doing that private eye stuff."

I wasn't sure which bothered me more: that my mother had accepted my dead body reference at face value, or that even after three months my family hadn't accepted my new vocation.

"Talk to you later, Ma."

I pressed disconnect, then stepped backward to watch the window above me as I said "noroms" into the mouthpiece—morons spelled backwards, because the three guys didn't even rate a known word—and the line instantly began to ring.

"Yo," Don said as I watched Pino get back into his cruiser and drive away looking disappointed that he hadn't been able to pin anything on me.

"What do you think about knocking twenty bucks off your rent?" I asked.

AT JUST AFTER SUNSET, I pulled into a spot in the far corner of a Wendy's parking lot facing Queens Boulevard, my target a fleabag motel across the street whose neon sign was missing the "n"; the red sign read o VACANCIES. The bored housewife I'd been following for the past four hours apparently had decided to take up a hobby that didn't include carpooling, play dates, or transporting her two kids to soccer games. I watched as Mrs. Carol Suleski went into the motel office, then came out moments later and walked toward Room 7. She knocked, then the door opened briefly to reveal a man before Mrs. Suleski went inside and the door closed behind them both.

Once, just once, I'd like one of my clients to be wrong. I'd like to follow a suspected cheating spouse and find out the only thing they were having a love affair with was a shoe store.

I squeezed off one more shot then put down the high end Olympus camera I'd borrowed from my younger brother—well, okay, in this case "borrowed" meant I had snuck into his room and lifted it three months ago while he was at some class or another and he had yet to discover it missing. The equipment rounded out my full PI gear, which included a can of industrial mace, an expandable baton, a PI badge I had tucked into my purse, and a 9×19 Glock it had taken me two months of target practice to get used to that I had locked in my glove compartment where I hoped it would stay.

Of course I'd gotten all the equipment when I'd thought my job would be much more exciting than it was turning out to be.

At any rate, it looked like Mrs. Suleski and friend wouldn't be going anywhere for a while. I debated the wisdom of shutting off the car engine, seeing as it would make more noise shutting down than it did running. (Lord forbid I ever had to be quiet while following someone or I'd be in trouble.) Deciding that the nonstop traffic on the ten-lane Boulevard of Death would disguise the sound, and that I couldn't really spare the gas anyway, I turned the ignition key and reached for the plain white bag on the passenger seat. Ah, dinner. Actually it was the first thing I'd thought to eat all day—*koulourakia* aside—so it could really be called breakfast-lunch-dinner. I opened the bag and took a deep breath of the contents. *Souvlaki.* The Greek equivalent of Wendy's, except instead of a bun there was pita and rather than a beef patty and cheese there were grilled morsels of pork and a thick cucumber-yogurt sauce packed full of garlic. But in the end it was probably as good for me as a burger, despite the yogurt and slices of tomato layered inside.

I figured that things should be going like gangbusters in Room 7 by the time I finished the *souvlaki* and I could maybe sneak across the street and get a few shots between the crack in the curtains.

"Sofie, luv. I don't know if it's illegal, but eating food other than what the restaurant serves while sitting in their parking lot is at the very least bad manners."

The deep Australian accent broke the *whoosh-whoosh* of traffic on the busy boulevard and made me jump in my seat. Good thing I'd left the top down or else I'd have probably hit it.

Porter . . .

Or, more specifically, Jake Porter. One of the many great things the country of Australia has bestowed on the world. Yep, him and koala bears. Who could want for more?

At nearly six foot five, Jake was the epitome of tall and handsome, even if his longish sandy brown hair knocked him out of the dark category. I think he's a bounty hunter or something but I can't be sure. He's the type that creates mystery because there probably is no real mystery. Except in his case it works. Anyway, I'd run into him months back while working one of my first cheating spouse cases. Since the meeting had come on the heels of my broken engagement, I hadn't been much in the market for a man, but if I had been, Jake Porter would have fit the bill. Forget that he filled out his jeans better than any ten men put together; he had a cocky, flirtatious . . . macho way about him that should have turned me off but didn't. And there was that whole man-of-mystery bit that made me squint at him a little harder and caused my palms to itch. I wasn't sure what his angle had been on that case months back, but he'd claimed a starring role in my fantasy life, which seemed to be gaining momentum lately.

Of course now that my ex was slowly disappearing into the murky distance of the past, that physical condition I was becoming more and more aware of shifted into overdrive at the mere sight of the sexy Australian. Oh, Jake Porter would probably all too willingly take care of that condition for me. And very satisfyingly at that. The problem was that my brief experience with him dictated that he didn't stick around longer than it took me to recover from the shock of seeing him.

Porter's mouth curved up in a sexy-irritating half grin. I idly wondered if he always looked like he needed a shave and pondered what that prickly stubble would feel like against the inside of my thighs.

A blonde tottered up beside him and took his arm. His thickly muscled arm, which bore a black tattoo of some Chinese character or other that the short sleeve of his white T-shirt didn't quite cover.

"What was that?" Porter asked me.

I'd been about to ask what he was doing there, but no longer had to. The blonde answered my question and then some.

"Jake-y, are we going to the motel or not?"

I had never considered myself a knockout, but I thought I rated somewhere between presentable and pretty. At the very least screwable. While my thick, curly dark hair probably looked better before I attacked it with the hair dryer and countless hair products every morning, I'd been told my olive green eyes were downright naughty.

Of course, it didn't help that the guy who'd told me that was standing next to my car with a woman whose dress was at least two sizes too small and still managed to look good.

I quirked a brow. "Jake-y?"

His grin widened. "You know, I could fix this little filly up for you if you like, Sofie. Fool around with a few things under the hood. Smooth out some of the bondo. Have her purring like a happy Sheila in no time."

I suddenly couldn't breathe. I was too busy casting myself in the role of Sheila.

Porter rested his hands against the door and squinted toward the motel. "You on a case?"

I turned my head toward the building in question and took another bite of *souvlaki*, although I questioned my ability to swallow just then. I reached for my frappé. "Some of us do have legitimate paying jobs."

Funny, I'd completely forgotten that the last time I'd seen Porter he'd mucked up things for me but good. Strange what effect blondes in tight red dresses have on jogging the memory.

The blonde leaned in a little closer. "Christ, Sofie, is that you?"

I stared at her, thinking she looked a lot like the women Uncle Spyros paid to be process servers. Because of the ploy, the agency had a ninety-nine percent success rate. Men nearly always opened the door thinking they might get lucky, and women did because they thought they might get some really good gossip out of the conversation.

"It's me! Debbie. You know, Debbie Matenopoulos? We went to St. D's together. I was two years behind you."

Like I really needed to be reminded that I was not only unattractive, I was old.

"I didn't recognize you without my glasses," Debbie said. "How in the hell are you doing?"

And so ensued a three-minute conversation that I really could have done without just then, mostly because she was with Jake and I wasn't.

Finally, after sharing a story about her sister closing down her hair salon and her losing her cosmetology license, Debbie fell silent, stepped back, and laid claim to Porter's arm again. "It was great seeing you, Sof. Tell your brother Koz I said hi."

I promised I would, then reached for my purse. "Here. If either you or your sister need some extra cash, the agency might have something for you." I handed her two business cards.

"Oh. Sure. Thanks." I wasn't amused when she tucked them into her cleavage.

I looked back at Porter to find him squinting at me.

"What?" I asked, irritated. "Don't you have a motel room to get to?"

His grin widened even as a light of recognition brightened his eyes.

Ouch.

I wasn't even going to think about what I'd revealed with that simple but loaded question.

Porter leaned his forearms against my door, then reached for my face. I stared at him, horrified and—yes, I realized—a little hopeful. But he merely wiped something from the corner of my mouth. He considered his cucumber-yogurt-sauce-covered thumb, then licked it clean. "That reminds me that I could go for a little grub myself."

I wondered why he was looking at me as if I might offer myself up as a quivering buffet of female flesh even as I jabbed my finger toward the fast-food restaurant. "They're still serving."

He winked at me, then stood back up, allowing Debbie to re-stake her claim on his arm.

Oh, yeah. I'd forgotten. He already had a willing buffet.

"See you later, mate," he said.

I watched as he made his way across the busy street toward the motel. *Mate.* Wasn't that Aussiespeak for "friend"? I slowly sipped from my frappé straw, then took another too-large bite of my *souvlaki* even as I prayed for Debbie to fall in her red stiletto heels. No such luck. The pair disappeared into Room 8.

I glanced at my watch.

Oh, shit! I'd nearly forgotten I was there for a reason. Damn sexy Australians.

Stuffing the uneaten *souvlaki* back into the bag, I wiped my hands against my jeans, then grabbed the camera, hurrying along the same path those before me had taken—or as fast as I could, anyway, considering I had to wait for the light to change on the corner and still had to dodge traffic as I crossed the ten lanes. Just outside Room 7, I crouched down and moved over to the crack in the curtains. Adjusting the camera lens, I slowly inched my way up and began shooting away.

Unfortunately it appeared someone inside the room had the same idea.

Only he wasn't holding a camera, he was holding a gun.

And the shots he aimed through the curtains? They included real bullets . . .

Three

ONE MINUTE I WAS DELIVERING the photographic proof of infidelity my client wanted, the next I was promising never to take another picture again—allowing, of course, that I survived the encounter. I supposed being shot at had that impact on a person.

The zoom lens of the Olympus shattered and the camera flew from my hand, landing in a mess of broken parts at my feet along with the glass from the busted window. A mess I covered as I flattened myself against the spotted, cracked cement of the sidewalk.

Oh, boy . . .

A hand clamped onto my arm. I screamed.

"Get the bloody hell up," Porter said.

I blinked him into focus.

He yanked me to my feet, then hauled me off to the side of the window out of view of the shooter within.

I wasn't completely convinced I hadn't been hit, and I was afraid whoever had shot at me wasn't done; still, I registered that Porter was dressed. I don't know what I expected to see. His tux pants bunched around his ankles, maybe?

I moved to look in the window and Porter yanked me toward him. Up this close I was reminded of how very tall he was. And how damn fit to be eaten.

"I, um, think I'm going to go now," I said.

His blue eyes darkened. "And here I thought things were just getting interesting."

Was he talking about between us?

No, I was pretty sure he was talking about the shooting.

I think.

I started sprinting back toward the corner and the stoplight, the prospect of dashing straight across Queens Boulevard mid-block akin to the prospect of standing upright in front of that motel window. I'd no sooner stopped than I turned around and headed back toward the motel.

"Back for more, luv?" Porter asked, holding what looked suspiciously like a gun as he flanked the door to Room 7.

Another gunshot.

I dropped to all fours and crawled until I could grab my camera. Correction: my brother's top-of-the-line demolished Olympus.

Oh, he was going to kill me for this one.

Of course, right now my brother would have to stand in line.

Another shot rang out and I wasn't positive but I thought it came from Porter.

I was halfway back across the busy street, nearly getting nicked by a Camaro making a right, when I realized I was crouched like a terrified duck whose wings had been clipped or, even worse, like Charlie Chaplin minus the cane and mustache.

Oh, that was sexy.

And would inevitably be something else no one would ever forget if someone I knew spotted me.

I stood up on my uncooperative knees and scrambled the rest of the way to my car.

Had I just been thinking about how I wished my job were a little more exciting? At least as interesting as my stint at the funeral home?

Of course, working at my Aunt Sotiria's hadn't required the presence of my own dead body.

And the thought of Aunt Sotiria fixing my hair in a beehive for the viewing sent an additional shudder running down my back.

I added Lucille's squealing tires to the sound of the traffic on Queens Boulevard and raced west toward home.

What in the hell was that? I'd been tailing a woman whose life had been even more boring than mine, then *bam!* I was getting shot at.

It didn't make any sense. No sense at all.

I eyed my speedometer and forced my shaking foot off the gas pedal, the world only slightly beginning to shift back into focus.

And when it did, I realized I'd just run from what was possibly one of the most thrilling moments of my life.

Well, aside from sex with Alex Nyktas on top of the Empire State Building when I was nineteen.

I crossed two lanes over to the curb and pulled to a stop, ignoring the blare of more car horns.

"I think my wife's cheating on me."

Such innocuous words, said by Mrs. Suleski's husband just that morning.

But there was a hell of a leap between cheating *on* someone and shooting *at* someone.

Namely me.

I looked both ways on the boulevard, then did a U-ie at the next intersection, nearly sideswiping the side of a cargo van. I read the words on the side. Was it really from the flea market I'd gone to just that morning? I hadn't known they delivered . . .

Within moments I was pulling back into the Wendy's parking lot and staring at the broken window across the street.

No sign of Porter.

No sign of the shooter.

No sign of Debbie.

No sign of the police.

No, wait!

The door to Room 7 opened, then Porter appeared.

Only I was pretty sure that the rug he was carrying over his right shoulder was indeed a dead body . . .

NOT MANY THINGS CREEP ME out. After all, I had downed those three bug-and-worm shakes on that reality show three months before without ruining my lipstick. But, of course, the feel of little bug legs getting caught in my teeth was a long ways away from bullets whizzing by my head.

By the time I'd crossed Queens Boulevard again, Porter and whatever he'd been carrying were gone, and the door to Room 7 stood wide open.

I wasn't sure how I felt about that. Especially since I hadn't thought to get my Glock out of my glove box. If I was going to be shot at again, it would probably be a good idea to do some shooting back.

There was a rumble of thunder. The sky was the color of the bruise I was probably going to have on my right elbow. Rain. Great. That's just what I needed now.

The heavens opened up. I stared across the street at where the top on my Mustang was down, then sighed and ducked through the open motel room door.

Leave it to me to jump from the rain straight into a firing range just so I wouldn't get my hair wet.

My heart felt like it was beating in my throat. I swallowed hard and took in the empty room. Well, empty but for the motionless pair of men's shoes I spotted on the floor sticking out from the other side of the king-size bed. Shoes that could only still be on feet, given the way the wingtips pointed toward the water-stained ceiling.

Oh, boy.

Part of me wanted to book out of there. But a bigger part urged me to move in for a closer look. Essentially the same part that had egged me on when I heard Thomas-the-Toad's zipper open on my wedding day.

Well, at least I knew this guy wasn't going to be causing me any trouble—his eyes were staring at the general area his toes were pointing at on the ceiling and the red stain on the front of his white dress shirt was going to be hell to get out. Not that I thought the guy would mind, because hey, things like that tended not to be important when you were dead.

I edged around him, not daring to blink in case I had gotten any details wrong and he reached for my ankle or something. I caught myself nodding. Definitely not the guy who had let Mrs. Suleski into the room. That guy had had blond hair while this guy's hair was dark.

Speaking of Mrs. Suleski . . .

Even as I bent over the body, I took in the rest of the cramped confines of the room. An empty closet without a door stood off to the left and to my right was the bathroom, one of those opaque windows on the back wall. The shower curtain was open and since the door lay flush against the inside wall there was no place for anyone to hide there. The bed was without a bedspread but was made, and a knock against the base found it solid.

No Mrs. Suleski.

Nothing but the dead body I was much closer to than I would have preferred to be.

A dead body I should probably be paying closer attention to.

Rule No. 5: Observe everything in the immediate area. I heard Uncle Spyros' voice in my ear.

Since the dead body was the only thing in the immediate area, I narrowed my gaze on it.

Or rather him.

The guy was maybe in his mid-thirties. Built. Receding dark hair. Brown eyes. He wore a dark suit, white shirt, and black tie, no jewelry that I could see, only a watch—one of those cheap kinds you can buy on the corner for five dollars on a good day. I gingerly patted one suit jacket pocket, then moved to the other. Something stiff in that one. I stuck my fingers inside, making as little contact as possible with the body itself, and slid out a plastic card key bearing the name of a hotel in the city, but nothing else.

Okay, now came the hard part. I closed my eyes and pushed at his right hip, checking his trouser pockets, both front and back. Then I did the same with the other hip.

Nothing but pocket lint and a crisp, brand-new fifty-dollar bill that I automatically put back. I don't know why. There was always the possibility that a mini duplicate of the guy was out there somewhere who might need the cash. Because he or she certainly wasn't going to get anything more out of him.

I let out the breath I'd been holding and rocked back on my heels. This wasn't normal PI stuff, but since my job was to watch Mrs. Suleski, and Mrs. Suleski was presently nowhere to be found, the dead body was my only opportunity to figure out what was going on and where I might find her.

Besides, I still didn't like that I'd been shot at.

Okay, no ID, no wallet, no clue as to who the guy was. I palmed the card key as I studied his right hand, then his left. Both were noticeably empty. I leaned in a little closer, taking note of a small tattoo on his right hand between his thumb and index finger. Was that a heart with a dagger through it? It was vaguely familiar but I couldn't think of why just then.

I drew back again. So if this wasn't the guy who had let Mrs. S into the room, who was he? And, more important, what had he been doing there? Had poor, hard-working Bud's domestic diva decided one extra man wasn't enough and gone for two?

If that was the case, who brought a gun to a ménage à trois?

Not that I was a major expert in this area, but hey, even I knew: whips and chains, go, guns, no.

Police sirens sounding in the distance and getting closer jerked me out of my dead-body-induced trance. I got to my feet with a little help from the bed, then walked back out the open doorway and ducked off to the side, away from the broken front window from which the thick, white-backed curtains now fluttered. The hard, pounding rain soaked through my T-shirt and made my Skechers soggy.

The first squad car pulled up at the curb in front of me. And, of course, Pimply Pino would be the one to get out, sliding his nightstick home as he approached.

"Twice in one day. I must have pissed off the gods but good this morning," he said, coming to stand in front of me.

His smart-ass remark was all the impetus I needed to slip the hotel key into the back pocket of my jeans. "At least this time there's a real body involved." I jabbed my thumb over my shoulder. "In the room over there."

A couple more squad cars joined Pino's and I stood as far out of the rain as I could as they trampled inside the room, probably mucking up any trace evidence that remained. *CSI* was one of my favorite shows and I imagined Marg Helgenberger shaking her pretty red head.

"Okay, where is it?"

I squinted at Pino, which wasn't really a good idea because Pino wasn't particularly attractive in normal view. Squinting only made his bad complexion look worse. No, he no longer had zits. But he did have craters I could park my Mustang in.

"Where is what?"

"Very funny, Metropolis. The body. Where's the body?"

I nearly knocked him into the street in my hurry to stare inside the room. The shoes were noticeably missing.

As was the dead body they'd been attached to.

Correct me if I'm wrong, but just as dead men can't talk, neither can they get up and walk.

I shuddered even as my gaze fastened on the now open bathroom window. Uncle Spyros' oft-repeated favorite rule trailed through my mind:

Rule No. 1: Learn how to think like a detective.

Obviously I still hadn't gotten that one down.

WHY IS IT THAT EVERY time I cross paths with Jake Porter, something strange happens?

It was nine o'clock and I was back at my apartment in a pair of dry jeans and an Adidas T-shirt, rubbing my hair with a towel and staring out at where my Mustang was parked halfway up the block, the top up but a good inch of rain still soaking the interior carpet. The radio I'd turned on told of more rain to come as I switched on a light then tugged on the cord to close the mini-blinds.

Immediately my cell phone began vibrating on the hall table. I reached for it just when it was about to pulse right off the edge.

My mother. I'd hoped it was Pimply Pino calling to tell me my body had turned up. Well, not *my* body, *the* body. Beyond calling

Bud Suleski and asking if his wife had shown up, I didn't know what more I could do to figure out what had happened.

I considered not answering Thalia's call. After all, I had that missing dead body and a sexy, mysterious Australian to think about.

If only there was a way to contact him . . .

"Hi, Ma."

"Where have you been? Aklima and I have been waiting all day."

The light. I'd turned on the light next to the window, alerting my mother and her neighbor Mrs. Kapoor of my return.

I should have stayed in the dark.

"Sorry, but I was out on a job watching a dead body disappear."

A pause then. "So long as you're all right, come on down to Mrs. Kapoor's so you can get more details on Muffy."

I massaged the area between my eyes, wondering if it were possible to get permanent creases at age twenty-six. Muffy the Mutt. I'd forgotten about Mrs. Kapoor's missing dog from hell who had a taste for Sofie flesh.

I wanted to beg off for tonight, but I had promised I'd look into the missing dog.

Key word being "look." Frankly my life would be a lot easier if the dog stayed missing.

I stared at where the rug I'd bought that morning sat like an extra large devil dog on my living room floor.

"Fine. I'll be right over."

"Good. I'll tell Aklima to put some tea on."

"That's okay, I don't plan on stay—"

Not surprisingly, my mother had already hung up.

Four

MRS. KAPOOR'S HOUSE SMELLED EXACTLY the same whenever I visited, like a combination of curry and cinnamon. The mixture seemed to coat the inside of my nose so I smelled the scent long after I left. It took me all of two seconds to figure out that Mrs. Kapoor and my mother weren't the only ones there as I heard the third member of their trio, Mrs. Quakenbos, raise her voice from the kitchen. I kissed my mother on the cheek as she ushered me inside the house and closed the door to prevent my escape.

"You're soaked."

"It's raining, Ma."

"What, you don't have an umbrella?"

Sometimes I think Thalia missed her calling as a Jewish mother. Then again, from what I can see, there's not much difference between a Jewish mother and a Greek mother. Well, aside from the icons of saints in the front room.

Mrs. Kapoor didn't have Greek icons, however. She instead had a Hindu shrine. Or what I guess constituted a shrine, anyway.

There was a statue I think she called *Darshana,* about a foot tall surrounded by fresh flowers, fruit, and some kind of food that Mrs. K sometimes fed us and we only pretended to eat because we had no idea how long the food had been sitting there. This shrine was in the corner of her living room and looked . . . well, strange.

I'd once asked her what it signified, why she felt it important to have a small altar in her house, back when I was about eight and Mrs. Kapoor used to babysit for me and Koz for an hour or so after school before my mom came back from the restaurant. And she told me she performed a daily *puja*. She didn't get much further than that because, well, the word was too similar to the Greek word *poutsa,* which means penis, and at eight years old anything having to do with the human reproductive system was cause for major hilarity.

"Your grandfather's still looking for you," my mom said, giving me a nudge down the hall.

"One crazy old person at a time."

That earned me a stare that I had the good graces to wither slightly under.

"There's nothing wrong with my coffee cake," I heard Mrs. Quakenbos saying as Thalia pretty much shoved me toward the back of the house and the kitchen. "It always sells out at the church bake sale."

"More like they probably throw it out, you know, in case the church should be sued for damages to people's dental work," Mrs. K fired back.

One final shove put me in the middle of the shouting match, pretty much the same one Mrs. K and Mrs. Quakenbos had been having for all twenty-five years they'd been friends. Their disagreements usually had to do with Barb Quakenbos' cooking skills, or lack thereof. But rather than the arguments curbing her desire to cook—or at least spurring her into taking a class or two—she merely seemed to make more of the inedibles that sat on our dining room sideboard around the holidays for about a week, untouched, before my mom threw them out.

"Sofie's here," my mother said.

The other two women blinked at me as if they hadn't seen me enter. I gave a little wave, wondering why I always felt I was two feet high whenever I was around them.

And why I knew far more about their sex lives than I was comfortable with.

A half hour later we were all still seated around the kitchen table, a plate of coffee cake untouched while crumbs were the only remainder of my mom's offering of *karithopita*, or walnut cake. Mrs. K somehow managed to make even regular tea spicy. I stared at my still full mug, wishing I could ask for water or something to wash down the syrup from my mom's cake, but not daring to. Wishing even more that I'd thought to make a fresh frappé.

That morning Mrs. K had let Muffy the mutt out for his (yes, I said "his"—seems Mrs. K hadn't had a full grasp on Muffy's sex when she first got him and thus he'd remained a male Muffy even after his sex became apparent) morning "tinkle" and when she'd gone to let him back in he was gone.

It was still raining so I couldn't check out back for any little doggy holes the Muffster might have wiggled his fat little body through. Instead I took my mom's and Mrs. K's word that there were no obvious means for escape. And, besides, Mrs. K pointed out, the Jack Russell terrier would never run away. He had everything he wanted here.

While I doubted that was the reason the mutt stuck around, since Muffy had been a part of the Kapoor family for five years and had never gone missing for longer than it took to nab Mr. Newman's *Queens Chronicle*, pee on my mom's rosebushes, or bite me whenever the mood called for it, I conceded the point.

This appeared to be a clear case of dognapping.

The question was who the hell would want to take the white-and-brown-spotted terror—I mean terrier?

I forgot about not drinking the tea and took a hefty sip that nearly choked me. Did she put curry in everything?

"You've checked the streets, of course," I said quietly.

The three women stared at me as if I'd just suggested they try wearing their underwear on their heads.

Then Mrs. Quakenbos gasped and slapped a hand over her mouth. "What an awful thing to say."

I grimaced. "Just covering all the bases."

For all any of us knew, Muffy the Hellhound had zipped across the street to tear apart Mr. Newman's newspaper and been run down by a street cleaner.

Then again, that was my own personal fantasy.

I checked my cell hoping for a call from Pino about my missing dead body. Nothing.

"What did you do, Barb? Burn yourself?" Mrs. Kapoor said, ignoring my question and taking hold of Mrs. Quakenbos' hand. I'd noticed earlier she had a bandage on the right side, the meaty side. "You got this cooking, didn't you? And for what?"

"Is anyone going to answer my question?"

Mrs. K waved at me. "Muffy isn't dead."

"How do you know that?"

"Because I would know if he was."

I thought of the shrine in the other room and decided it better not to argue that point either.

I looked at my watch. Nearly ten. Not late by any means for me, but still I felt like it should be five A.M. two days from now, considering all that had happened to me in the past few hours.

I figured disappearing dead bodies had that impact on a person.

I sighed. "Okay. Tomorrow I'll start with the animal shelter and ask the neighbors if they've noticed anything funny."

"They haven't," my mother said. "Noticed anything funny, that is. We already asked."

"It won't hurt to ask again." I stood up. "Now if you'll excuse me, I have a missing dead body to think about."

The three women started talking again as if I'd never been there, much less had just mentioned a dead body, missing or otherwise.

I did an eye roll and quietly let myself out.

BACK AT THE COMPOUND ALL was quiet, if maybe not well. The students in 2B had their music down to a reasonable level, audible only when I passed their door. I could hear the news channel through Mrs. Nebitz's door—something about a soggy weather front hitting us—and my rug was right where I'd left it, sitting in the middle of the floor, when I unlocked the three deadbolts and pushed the door open, a bag from the Chirping Chicken in hand. I tripped over the rolled-up rug on my way to turn on the lights, hesitating only slightly as I wondered who else might call when they saw I was back home. Deciding my mother had probably done as much damage as she could for one day, I turned on the lamp, put the bag down on the table, then started stripping out of another set of soaked clothing on my way to the bedroom for something dry.

Call me stupid, but I personally think there should be a law against it raining on a Saturday night. Rain was meant for Mondays, a day that normally sucks anyway.

But it was a sacrilege to rain on a Saturday night in June.

Not that my Saturday nights are any different than any other night, mind you. At least not lately. But still . . . if it weren't raining, I could go up on the roof and contemplate the world from my little corner of it. I could go for a ride in Lucille with the top down, letting the warm wind clear the cobwebs from my mind and ease the wrinkles from my forehead.

I could be doing anything but be stuck at home in a two-bedroom apartment I was supposed to be living in with my new groom but instead was rattling around in by myself surrounded by furniture we had both chosen and my family had paid for.

After leaving Mrs. K's, I'd given in and called the Suleskis' house, only I hadn't gotten an answer. Which helped me not at all in figuring out what had gone down at the motel. It was all I could do not to call Pino through the 114th Precinct to see if he'd turned anything up. But I wasn't up for another cool reception from a guy who was a walking advertisement against pimple popping.

I held my soaked T-shirt in my hands, chilly in nothing but my jeans and wet bra, and stared at the mammoth black leather Barcalounger Thomas-the-Toad had chosen and that stuck out like a sore thumb in the jewel-toned room. I crossed to stand beside it and gave the chair a nudge with my knee. It didn't budge. I bent over and leaned my shoulder against it, putting some muscle into it. Still nothing. I stood back and gave the recliner a kick, then wondered what had made me do something so dumb while my big toe smarted.

I hobbled to my bedroom, ignoring everything but my dresser as I changed my clothes, again, then padded back through the living room and into the kitchen.

I'd never gotten to finish that *souvlaki* earlier in the car, and there aren't very many things worse than cold *souvlaki*. Especially after being shot at and having dead bodies disappear on you.

But now that I'd put a little bit of time between me and what had happened, I was beginning to regain my grip on things. Well, as much as I'd ever had a grip, anyway. And one activity that was good no matter the weather was a couch picnic with a charcoal-broiled bird from the Chirping Chicken as the main attraction.

I threw open the refrigerator door and stared at the contents. What was great about a couch picnic was that you didn't have to worry about presentation or plates or glasses. You grabbed whatever containers held food—in my case there were always a lot of left-overs from my mother who always cooked like she was expecting company—and a beer or a soda or whatever beverage was available, then you laid it all out on the coffee table in front of the television, utensils optional.

I grabbed a fork and a beer and four of the closest containers, closed the fridge door with my bare foot, then dumped it all out onto the coffee table in the other room next to the chicken bag.

Now, all I needed was something good on TV and I was set for the night.

Well, if I could stop thinking about the dead guy's vacant eyes and slack-muscled expression, anyway. I shuddered.

I did some channel surfing even as I opened one of the containers. *Dolmathakia.* Mmm. While I never quite mastered the art of making the stuffed grape leaves myself—or should I say I didn't have the patience to master it—I loved when Mom made them. I passed on the Greek-language cable channel NGTV, found no *Seinfeld* reruns, then settled on Larry King, who was just going into a commercial. I prayed he had someone interesting on, someone who couldn't even spell politics, much less speak on it. It was a longstanding custom in the Metropolis household that weekends were politics-free zones. Sure, you could watch the news, but try talking about anything even remotely political and you'd find the closest available food stuck into your mouth.

I filled my own mouth with a stuffed grape leaf, happy to carry on the tradition.

Lemon juice sluiced down over my chin and I caught it before it could splat against my third clean T-shirt in so many hours. I was looking for something to wipe my hand on when a knock sounded at my door.

I froze. My mouth was full of *dolmathes.* My chin was wet with lemon juice and my left hand held a small puddle of the same. My right hand held a chicken leg.

Just then I caught a reflection of myself in the television screen, which had gone blank between commercials. I looked like death warmed over. Worse, I looked like a single white female who had nothing better to do with her Saturday night than pig out and watch TV.

Another knock.

I uncrossed my legs, put the remainder of the food back into the container and power chewed even as I dashed into the kitchen to rinse my chin and hands.

My visitor was knocking for a third time when I opened the door with the dishtowel I still held.

For a moment I both feared and hoped it would be Jake Porter. Feared because when bad stuff happens, it tends to happen a lot in a short period of time and Porter's appearance just as I was at my worst would be par for the course given the day's events.

Hoped because, well, a part of me still wanted to be Sheila, Queen of Astoria to his Australian He-Man.

Of course, his being the only one who held the answers to the questions crowding my mind followed quickly on the heels of the other two thoughts.

"It's about time you opened the door."

I stepped back to allow my grandfather Kosmos into my apartment.

My family didn't so much visit as they commandeered my place whenever they came over. And I had little doubt that my five-foot-four-inch maternal grandfather registered everything in the apartment with one glance . . . up to and including the hefty piece of cake left over from my cousin's name day yesterday. I'd dragged a pickle over it last night, leaving a green trail through the white frosting.

"Your mother didn't tell you I was looking for you?" Kosmos asked, having taken in his fill of the room, offering his left cheek for me to kiss.

"Mmm. At least five times."

"So why didn't you call?"

"I figured you'd catch up with me sooner or later if you kept trying."

He muttered something under his breath that resembled Greek profanity but with a traditional, strange Greek twist. Something along the lines of doing some really icky things to a goat.

"Good, you've fixed a *trapezi*. I have the munchies."

Trapezi means "table" in Greek but the meaning is more literally "set the table," as in for dinner.

And somehow it struck me as odd that my *pappous* had the munchies. It conjured up images of him hitting the street corner in search of some ganja, then smoking a joint on the stoop before coming up to my apartment. Not something I wanted to think about just then even if I wouldn't put it past the old man.

"Actually, I was just finishing, *Pappou*."

Pappous is the Greek word for "grandfather," or you could use the more casual and direct *Pappou*. The similarity of the word to the American Indian word *papoose*, which means baby, was the source of much rolling-on-the-floor hilarity when I was five years old. Now I avoided saying the word in mixed company because I was tired of explaining the Greek meaning.

"Nonsense. Get a couple plates and glasses and another beer. I'm starved."

I knew my grandfather hadn't come over to eat, but wherever there were Greeks there was sure to be a table full of food no matter the time of day or night. It was a wonder that we all didn't look like Weebles, wobbling but never falling down.

So I played the role of good granddaughter and got the things he'd requested from the kitchen along with the napkins I'd forgotten earlier and another fork.

He rubbed his large, dry hands together. "Good. I always think better on a full stomach."

"Funny, I have trouble thinking of anything at all when I'm stuffed."

He waggled a finger at me, his heavy Greek accent somehow always pronounced when he was about to impart some particularly wise advice. "Ha! That's because you eat until you're stuffed rather than just full."

I found myself staring at Thomas-the-Toad's recliner, focusing all my pent-up hostility on the chair.

Don't get me wrong, I adore my grandfather. We have more in common than any other two members of the family. Not in terms of experience, but rather in our wicked sense of humor and our wry take on life in general. More often than not I nodded through anything he said, and he did the same to me. And we both laughed at the same crude jokes when everyone else cringed.

Yep, me and Grandpa Kosmos were on the same page.

Well, except when it came to my almost groom, anyway. My grandfather thought I should have gone through with the wedding then made Thomas' life a living hell for the rest of his years.

After all, Kosmos had said, Thomas had only made one little mistake.

The way I saw it, a mistake was forgetting to put the toilet seat back down. Schtupping my maid of honor was a capital offense.

I wondered if I could take the chair apart and throw it piece by piece out the window.

"Anyway," my grandfather said, moving food from the containers onto his plate. I poured the beer into the glasses and took a long slug from mine. "I want to hire you to do something for me."

"Hire?" I lifted a brow. "As in pay me?"

"Mmm. This is an official job."

"Meaning I can't let on to the rest of the family what it is."

He grinned, looking more than a bit like a mischievous imp with a craggy face and sunburst wrinkles on either side of his bright brown eyes. "Exactly."

"Gotcha." I crossed my legs and leaned forward. I liked when Kosmos and I shared secrets. It inevitably drove the rest of the family nuts. Especially my father (long story that involves that feud that began before I was even born). And that alone was worth its weight in gold. "What is it?"

"I want you to find something I lost a long time ago."

I scrunched my face. Kosmos was far from a pack rat. His one-bedroom apartment above his café down on Broadway was almost Spartan it was so devoid of clutter.

"What is it?"

"A war medal."

I recrossed my legs and chewed thoughtfully on a stuffed grape leaf.

Stories. While all families have them, my family seemed to thrive on them in a way that was almost like living inside a book.

"Larry King. Turn it up."

I blinked to find that Larry's guest was, indeed, a political pundit. I grimaced, remembering that the rule was only that you couldn't discuss what was featured, not that you couldn't watch it.

Damn. Now I didn't dare turn the channel without risking Kosmos' wrath.

Or a struggle for the remote control.

"By the way," he said, "you don't look so good."

I was pretty sure I grimaced. "Thanks. I hate the rain."

He looked at me and I braced myself for another bit of that grandfatherly advice I was so fond of. Name a situation, any situation, and Greeks usually had a philosophical take on it. I think it's fused into our DNA.

"There are three things you need to learn in life, Sofia," he said, using my given name. "First, to learn how to dance like you're alone even in a group of people."

His attention strayed back to the television set and despite my initial lack of interest I wanted to know the rest of his personal philosophy.

"Second," he said without prompting and without looking at me, "you need to know how to love like you mean it."

I concentrated on pulling apart the chicken on my plate. How did you love like you didn't mean it?

"And third . . ." He was looking at me again, chucking me under the chin until I looked back. "You need to learn to laugh at the rain." He pointed his gnarly index finger at me, then bounced the end against the tip of my nose. "Learn how to do those three things, and you'll be happy, always."

Right.

"When's the last time you saw it? This war medal," I asked, considering the physical characteristics of Larry's guest instead of what he was saying and ignoring my grandfather's advice. Botox. Definitely Botox.

"Forty-two years ago."

I stared at him. "You're kidding."

Kosmos shook his head. "Do you think you can find it?"

"I don't know. It depends on . . . well, a lot of variables." I squinted at him. How, exactly, did you learn how to laugh at the rain when your wet underwear gave you an inescapable wedgie? "I didn't know you were awarded a war medal."

Something like that would have made for a very good story in our family.

Kosmos shrugged. "It's not something I like to talk about."

My brows inched up even higher. "There's not anything out there you don't like to talk about." Example number one: The three secrets to a happy existence that would probably keep me up that night and that I would never achieve because my lot in life was to be perpetually unhappy.

He patted my knee and motioned for me to eat, an automatic gesture he probably didn't realize he was making. "Shows what you know."

Yes, I guess it did show what I knew. Or rather what I didn't know.

And in some strange way I was looking forward to finding out why my grandfather had never said anything about it, and what other things he had neglected to tell me.

He was looking at me. "Your mom said you also needed something?"

I looked at the rug I'd picked up and the cursed recliner, then turned back to him and smiled . . .

Five

I'D DONE A BACKGROUND CHECK on Jake Porter the very first day I'd met him and had come up with zero, zip, zilch, nada. But after a Sunday filled with church, dinner at my parents' house, and absolutely zero luck getting through to my client, Bud Suleski, I went to work Monday morning loaded for bear. My previous failure to turn up anything on the mysterious Australian didn't stop me from not only doing another search on my own but enlisting Rosie's help as well.

"Believe you me, if he's alive, I'll find him," the perky Puerto Rican said from her corner of the office, clacking away on her ancient computer. "No man can look that good and not rate a mention somewhere. He's a real piece of head, that one."

This and Rosie had only seen a smear of a photograph I'd taken three months ago in which Porter had been little more than a handsome blur (I was ignoring the head mention—I wasn't altogether sure I wanted to know what that meant). I hadn't intended to snap the shot. I'd been tailing my first cheating spouse and it was only after having the roll of film developed that I realized Jake had stepped into the frame. Although not far enough in to get a good likeness of him.

I didn't think much of it at the time. Considering the motel event, however, I was beginning to wonder if there existed any clean shots of the mysterious Jake Porter.

"Speaking of film developing . . ." I said and reached for the bag I'd brought along with me.

Rosie looked up from her computer monitor. "Who said anything about film developing? Did you hear anyone say anything about film developing? I didn't hear no one say nothing about film developing."

I put the bag on her desk. "I did. Just now. See what you can do about salvaging whatever shots you can from this roll."

She opened the top of the paper bag and stared at the contents. She immediately handed the bag back. "Uh-uh. There's a demolished camera in there."

I put it back on her desk. "With a few exposures that might have made it." I turned toward my desk and said more quietly, "And see what they can do about the camera."

"See what they can do? They can throw it away, that's what they can do." She put the bag down and concentrated on her computer again. "Kosmos is going to kill you."

Tell me about it.

During the summer of his freshman year at Columbia, my brother had worked part-time for Uncle Spyros rather than put in time at the family restaurant. And, of course, his first day on the job my parents surprised him with the top of-the-line Olympus—you know, so he could have the very best in order to do his job. It didn't matter that Kosmos had been a process server and errand boy and had absolutely no use for a camera. And my pointing out that he didn't need it had fallen on deaf ears and made me look like an envious older sister. Which, of course, I was.

Kosmos works for Uncle Spyros, he gets a camera. I work for Uncle Spyros, I get a hassle.

At any rate, Kosmos had played around with the camera for about two days before he'd tucked it away in his bottom drawer, where it had stayed until I'd borrowed it three months ago.

It only stood to reason that now would be the time he would look for it, though. And while my brother and I had always indulged in our share of healthy sibling rivalry, I didn't want to sabotage my new career with this latest development. I could just hear my mother now.

"You'd never get shot at at the restaurant. At the restaurant you're safe. And you wouldn't have broken your brother's camera." As if when I saw the bullet coming I had purposely shoved the camera out and said, "Here, hit this!"

If luck was on my side, I'd be able to replace the camera before Kosmos or my parents ever caught wind of what had happened to it.

The computer blipped "no records found" again and I reached for my frappé. Not that luck had been on my side lately.

The front door opened, letting in Pamela Coe along with a cloud of expensive perfume. Both went straight to Rosie. A couple moments later Josh Pruitt followed on her heels, looking all of twelve when in reality he was thirty-one. They were both among Uncle Spyros' top process servers, Pamela with a one-hundred-percent success rate, Josh with a ninety-nine, and that only because a woman he'd served had set out to rob him of his "virginity" and when he'd left, well taken care of and his glasses slightly askew, he'd found the summons still in his back pocket.

Serving court summonses and other legal documents accounted for a good percentage of the agency's income. Uncle Spyros had fifteen servers on call; they were paid well for successful deliveries.

Another good percentage of the agency's income came from being retained by at least thirty businesses, large and small, that needed background reports on new hires and occasional checks on current employees to make sure they weren't having financial problems that might spur them to skim from the company or find other, innovative ways to use the company for personal profit.

As for what Uncle Spyros' silent partner did, I couldn't be sure, on account of, well, he was so silent. All I knew is that when Rosie had been showing me the ropes in the beginning, I'd watched her enter a five-figure amount in the income ledger, the only label, in all caps: LENNY NASH.

Over the years there had been a series of junior investigators hired on to do the legwork for the remainder of the business the agency did. Like getting the goods on cheating spouses and, more recently, finding lost pets.

I caught myself grimacing at this one. The whole iguana thing had come about completely by accident and, I'd hoped, would only be a one-time event. Since then I'd received no fewer than five calls from people looking to enlist my services to find their furry or scaly loved ones. Five calls only I knew about, and had refused, and no one else would find out about if I had anything to say about it.

Muffy the Mutt aside.

Speaking of which . . .

I picked up the extension on my desk, getting the 411 on area animal shelters. While there were countless private shelters, the most likely public one he would have been taken to or picked up by was on Linden Boulevard in Brooklyn, maybe by way of the receiving center in Rego Park. I gave them a description of the hellhound. Yes, they said, they had two like that. One was dropped off last week, the other yesterday.

I straightened in my chair. Could this really be that easy?

"I'll be by later this morning."

"There's a cop for you on line one," Rosie told me as she handed sealed envelopes to Pamela and Josh.

I picked up, knowing it could be none other than Pimply Pino. (I really had to stop thinking about him that way, lest I slip up and accidentally say it aloud again. But a more than a decade-long habit was hard to break.)

"What can I do for you, Pino?"

"How did you know it was me?"

"ESP." That would probably give him something to chew on for a while. "Did you find my missing dead guy?"

"You probably only thought he was dead. But that's not why I'm calling."

I entered a new search string into the computer. "Oh?"

"There's an unclaimed car parked at the motel and I wondered if you knew who it belonged to."

"Why would you think that?"

"Because the guy was parked in the owner's slot and didn't move it and nobody else registered at the motel is claiming ownership."

"That still doesn't explain why I would know anything about it."

"Because it's something you would do."

"Ha ha. What's the owner's name?"

"Harry Brooks."

I entered the new name into computer. Nothing. "Just Harry? Not Harold or Herrick or something?" What other names could be shortened to Harry?

"Just Harry."

The computer spat its standard response back at me. "No records found."

"No, I don't know him."

"Fine. Call me if something jogs your memory."

I hung up the phone, then leaned back in my chair. Missing body, left-behind car . . .

My hand immediately went to my back jeans pocket. Only the jeans in question were back at my apartment.

The phone rang and I snatched it up. "Metropolis."

"Where the hell is my wife?" Bud Suleski barked at me.

NOW NOT ONLY WAS I missing a dead guy, I was missing a cheating spouse. Not exactly a banner couple of days as far as my career as a private investigator went.

After getting Rosie to promise she'd keep trying to dig something up on Porter—just what the hell had been in that rolled-up bedspread anyway?—I went back to my place and searched for the hotel card key I'd lifted off the missing dead guy. Of course, he hadn't been missing when I'd taken it, merely dead, but that wasn't helping me any in trying to figure out who would want to take his body. And what somebody had done with Mrs. Suleski.

Since driving into the city on any day was a trial in patience, not to mention expensive when you factored in thirty- to fifty-dollar parking rates if you couldn't find street parking (and I never found street parking), I left my car at home and hopped onto the W train at Broadway. As the elevated train car bumped and raced along the rail, my nose nearly immune to the scent of watered-down cleanser, I stared through the train window at Astoria's rooftops and tried to fit the puzzle pieces together.

Pieces that the sexy Jake Porter had one too many of tucked into his tight jeans pocket.

I stared down at the card key I held, something playing along the fringes of my mind.

Of course! Why hadn't I thought of that before?

I fished my cell phone out of my purse and dialed 411 for the second time that morning, hoping to do what I needed before the train went underground at the East River.

"Debbie!" I said when I was put through to Jake's motel date.

"This is Sofie Metropolis. Remember? We ran into each other the other night?"

"Yeah, Koz's older sister."

My back teeth set tightly together.

"OhmyGod," she said in that one-word way only native New Yorkers knew how to do. "What a coincidence. You are so not going to believe where I'm standing right this second."

I resisted the urge to press my thumbs into my eye sockets until I heard a satisfying pop.

She said, "Your office."

"Get out of town."

"No, seriously. I got up this morning, scoured the want ads, only to discover that if I haven't already applied for every job in there, I was unqualified for them. And I was getting my stuff ready to take to Pappas Cleaners and—*bam!*—your card fell right on my foot. It's a sign."

A sign that she shouldn't be sticking business cards into the front of her dresses, maybe.

Debbie's voice dropped an octave. "Say, where did you find this person?"

"Rosie? What's the matter with Rosie?"

"She's PMS-ing or something. If I had her job I'd be a much nicer person."

I tried to swallow my laugh but failed.

"Sorry," I said. "Once you get to know her you'll think it's part of her charm."

"I doubt it."

"Anyway, the reason why I'm calling is . . ." God, how did I put this in a way that didn't give me the type of information I wasn't looking for? "Jake Porter. Do you know how to get in contact with him?"

Silence. Well, except for the sound of Rosie's mouth going a million miles a minute in rapid-fire Spanish in the background.

"It depends," Debbie finally said.

"On what?"

"On whether or not I'm gonna get a job out of this."

"You're hired. Now tell me how to get in touch with Porter."

THE GOOD THING ABOUT DOWNTOWN is the amount of walking you do. The bad thing about downtown is the amount of walking you do. Hoofing it is a way of life for us New Yorkers, but when you figure in a dew point of one hundred percent edging the heat index up to over ninety degrees, and the air quality is similar to the consistency of lentil soup, well, walking held absolutely no appeal for me just then. Of course, it didn't help that the shopaholic in me demanded I hop off the subway at 53rd so I could hit Saint Gill's on Madison Avenue, a whopping fifteen blocks uptown from where I needed to be and between subway stations. Forget missing dead guys and missing spouses, I needed, on a level I was loath to confront, the killer purple Prada handbag that had been on sale for seventy-five percent off. I knew without looking into the store windows as I passed that my hair was a wild ball of frizz and that my fresh black shirt and khaki green cargo pants were wilted against my skin like a canned grape leaf. Not exactly the type of physical presence that inspired confidence.

Then again, it didn't matter what I looked like. What did matter was the brand spanking new picture of Andrew Jackson in my pocket. And if he wasn't pretty enough, then the portrait of Grant usually appealed to everyone.

So carrying a bag that felt heavier with every step, I turned the corner from Fifth onto 32nd, catching sight of the Holiday Inn Martinique, the hotel featured on the dead guy's card key. I was three stores away when I ducked into the doorway of a Korean grocer. Not because I'd gotten a sudden craving for *kimchi,* but because someone very familiar was getting out of a squad car and addressing the famous singing doorman of the hotel.

What in the hell was Pino doing there? Wasn't this way out of his jurisdiction?

I squeezed my shopping bag to my stomach as if it could hide me better than the fruit stand to my right.

Probably after calling me he'd put a bulletin out to area hotels looking for Harry Brooks. And probably the Martinique had called him back.

Great.

I looked back down 32nd Street. The hotel had to have another entrance. Surely the city fire marshal insisted on it. But there was nothing I could see from there.

I stared around at the flow of people, hoping to blend in and sail right past Pino and into the hotel without being seen. I was scanning the area across the street and behind me when I thought I caught a glimpse of someone else I recognized.

Jake Porter.

Curiouser and curiouser . . .

I stumbled closer to the curb as I visually followed the hunk in jeans across the street and earned a shrill car horn blast for my efforts.

As I hastened back away from the curb, I reminded myself curiosity had also flattened the cat.

Curiosity also quadrupled my desire to get inside that hotel to see what Harry Brooks was about. But in order to do that I had to get there first. Before Pino. Before Porter.

A shoulder-high cart full of Korean goods propelled by someone I couldn't see began to roll by me. I crouched down and moved along on the inside of it, nearly colliding with a smoker outside the hotel catching a cigarette—and pretty certainly gaining a singe spot on the back of my head. Then I ducked through the hotel's revolving door and made a beeline for the front desk and the clerk who stood far off to the right, out of eyeshot of the doorway.

I decided I liked the friendly way she looked at me and picked the portrait of Grant rather than Jackson. I slid the fifty across the desk along with my PI badge and asked which room Harry was in. Without batting an eye she typed in the name and told me.

The eighteenth floor, penthouse level. Great. It didn't even look like the hotel had eighteen floors. It couldn't be on the second floor, could it? No, his room had to be on eighteen.

"Ma'am, you need to take the other bank of elevators," the girl crossed to tell me when I edged around the front desk toward the elevators to the left.

I turned around to see where she had indicated. She meant the elevators closer to the front door.

Double great.

Not only could I still make out Pino talking to the singing doorman—it appeared the big Irish-Italian was serenading him—there was some kind of convention going on and at least a hundred people were waiting for one of the three metal death traps. So I instead headed up the stairs, all eighteen flights of steep marble, that went up and up like some kind of half spiral to the penthouse level, all the time looking behind me to make sure Pino and/or Porter weren't nipping at my heels (I nixed the idea of looking straight down the staircase for fear vertigo would clutch me in its ugly grip and give falling at someone's feet a whole new meaning).

I'd finally gone until I'd run out of stairs and could climb no more, and stood panting within an inch of my life, clutching my bag to my chest. I was known to smoke here and there, mostly to counteract the smell of others smoking around me, and unfortunately there were a lot of those, since smoking seemed to be as

Greek as baklava and ouzo. Right then I vowed not only never to put another butt between my teeth, but to buy one of those little battery-operated fans so I could blow others' smoke away from me. I'd read somewhere that a celebrity of some caliber had been known to do that, and I figured if it was good enough for them, it was good enough for me.

I stared at the signs posted on the walls and followed the one for Harry Brooks' room. I quickly discovered that the room in question was, of course, at the end of a long hall, adding to the mileage I had accumulated that day. A housekeeping cart sat outside, although it appeared the maid was in the room next door.

I could only hope she hadn't cleaned Harry's room already. The best stuff for a PI to find usually lies in the garbage cans. And if the maid had emptied them . . .

A couple feet away from the door, my cell vibrated. I pulled it out of my pocket and looked at the display. My mom. And she probably wanted to know what I'd done to find Mrs. K's pride and joy. Which was next to nothing.

I grimaced and put the phone back into my pocket without answering.

Looking over my shoulder, I inserted the card key into the locking mechanism, discovered I'd put it in wrong, and turned it around.

Presto.

I opened the door and stepped quickly inside . . . only to find myself facing two dark-suited men in mirrored sunglasses.

"FBI, miss. Please step away from the door."

Oh, shit.

Six

FBI.

I had Porter and Pino at my back.

And two FBI agents at my front.

And here I'd thought the downslide my professional life had taken as of late couldn't get any worse.

Ha.

"Step away from the door, miss," the other agent repeated—you know, in case I hadn't heard the first one.

And that's when I saw my out. *I hadn't heard.* Or hadn't understood, more accurately. And I was pretty sure my shocked expression would back up my claim.

"Signomi, kirie, ala nomizo anixa lathos porta. Signomi . . . signomi . . ." I told them I must have opened the wrong door and began backing closer to the very door they were trying to get me away from.

While I knew a bit of Spanish, so, it appeared, did everyone else. So I'd learned early on to draw from my Greek roots to get me out of certain sticky situations. Okay, so usually this only got me out of talking to telemarketers, or having to spend time with the Jehovah's Witnesses that came a-knocking, or paying overdue charges on DVDs when I went to the shop in Jackson Heights where they didn't know me and didn't know Greek. But I couldn't see why it couldn't work here, now, when it really mattered.

There were three stages people went through when they heard a foreign language they didn't know. First they tried to place the tongue. Next, they tried to place you. And third, they realized it really didn't matter what language it was or where you were from— they had a job to do.

I prayed I'd be long gone before the agents reached stage three.

I grabbed the door handle and backed straight into the house-keeping cart, nearly dropping my bag in the process.

"Den xero ti simveni etho kai den thello na xero." Which was true. I didn't know what was happening and I didn't want to know, either.

The only thing that would halt my steps would be if they drew their guns. And of course they wouldn't do . . .

In unison they both opened their jackets and reached for their guns.

My "oh shit" changed quickly to "oh fuck."

I grabbed the cart and shoved it toward the door, then booked down the hall. The long hall that led to the elevators and the eight-een flights of steps.

Oh, this was going to be good. Not only was I running away from FBI agents, I was most surely going to be caught by them. And then what did I say? Sorry, I thought you were somebody else? And just who might that be, maybe? Certainly not the dead miss-ing guy from whom I had stolen his hotel card key.

Well at least I was now fairly certain that Harry Brooks of the left-behind car and the dead guy were, in fact, the same guy.

Once, a long time ago when I was still wearing a retainer at night and felt like Jaws from one of those old James Bond films, and watched as Jenny Beckos became the object of the all seventh-grade boys' attention, I wondered if it were possible to cash in your bad luck cards for one, brilliant burst of good luck. It seemed every culture had their idea of just such a plan. Karma, yin-yang, be good, be rewarded (unfortunately some religions believed this didn't happen until the afterlife and I didn't want to think about that just now. Not considering that one wrong move and I might find myself in that afterlife).

Just as I rounded the corner, ready to fly down the stairwell without a glance at the two elevators to my left, one of the elevators dinged and right before my very eyes stood an empty, inviting cubicle.

Huh.

I nearly tripped over my own feet scrambling for it before the doors could close.

In I went, punching the DOOR CLOSE button along with the first-floor button as if my life depended on it. And that just might very well have been the case considering the guns that had been pointed at me.

Whoosh, the doors closed.

In that one moment I'd never been happier that I didn't cash in those luck chips so long ago in order to be Jenny Beckos for a day.

But as I stared at the lighted LOBBY button, I thought it was a pretty good idea if I didn't relax too much. After all, Pino could still be in the lobby. And the agents upstairs might not be alone.

And somewhere around here Porter was roaming.

Porter, with whom I needed to have a long conversation, but now wasn't exactly the right time for that.

The doors opened on six to let a couple in. I tried to contain my gulp as I discreetly punched the CLOSE DOOR button as soon as they were inside.

Almost to the lobby . . .

Just as the elevator light indicated the third floor, I pressed the button for two.

The doors opened and I dove out . . . running headfirst into a group of people wearing hobbit costumes.

Seems I'd run from one surreal situation straight into another. The difference being that these Tolkien lovers probably didn't have guns they wanted to point at me. At least I hoped they didn't. Then again, their weapons of choice would be swords if I remembered my Tolkien correctly.

I headed right, passing the stairs and anyone who might be coming up them, and started down a long, irregular hall chock full of people, some wearing costumes, some not. Tables against the wall were filled with what appeared to be free giveaways. As I passed, I pocketed an Aragorn chocolate bar that made me think of Viggo Mortensen not at all. Well, okay, maybe a little, but only because of the yum factor. The hall made a right and another left and before I knew it I stood at the bank of elevators that would put me behind the front desk downstairs.

Okay.

I made my way into the middle of the group waiting in front of the elevators and looked around. If this was the hotel's convention area, then it only stood to reason that there would be . . .

Bingo.

A door without a plaque or a number opened revealing a waiter balancing a tray of glasses of ice water.

I made my way to that door and ducked inside. A few mazelike moves and I was down the employee stairs and within moments found myself standing on 33rd, up one block from where I'd entered the hotel.

I fought the urge to punch a fist into the air in victory. I *knew* there had to be alternate access. And no matter how haplessly, I was ecstatic I'd found it.

Not about to chance circling back to the subway station at the front of the hotel (the one I should have gotten off at originally, but no, I'd had shopping to do), I hailed a taxi and told him to take me to Central Park, where I could catch up with the W train.

Once I was finally, safely in the subway car, clutching my bag from Saint Gill tightly to my chest as an afterthought, rather than from any real fear that someone might take it from me, I closed my eyes and tried to slow my heart rate.

Well, that little visit was revealing, wasn't it? Only not the way I'd intended. Rather than finding out who Harry was beyond the missing dead guy, I'd discovered I wasn't the only one who wanted to find out.

Had I known just what I had been leaving myself open for when I'd asked for an exciting case two days ago, I might instead have put a sign in the window advertising services as a pet detective.

"LISTEN, SOF, HE'S A GHOST."

Rosie hit me with this the instant I walked into the office feeling much like the wilting spider plant that sat in the front window . . . and probably resembling it more than I wanted to admit just then. I walked to the corner where I went about making myself a frappé. Two teaspoons each of Nescafé instant coffee and sugar and an ounce of refrigerated water, then I snapped on the lid of my travel cup and started shaking the mixture into a froth. "Who's a ghost?" I took off the lid and added a couple ounces more cold water and a couple of ice cubes. Sometimes I poured in a little milk but since there wasn't any in the small, ancient fridge, I stuck my straw into the mixture and took a fortifying sip.

"Porter."

I collapsed behind my desk. "Define ghost. Ghost as in spook or ghost as in white-sheet-rattling-rusty-chains ghost?"

"Spook? You talking government agent?" Rosie swiveled her chair to face me, making me regret not just directly asking what she'd meant. "Why would you say 'spook'?"

The girl needed to get out more. She lived a little too vicariously through me.

I rested my forearms on my knees. "So you're saying he doesn't exist?"

Rosie popped her gum. "Not so far as I can see. There's nothing out there on the guy. No driver's license, no credit cards, no house, not even a friggin' high school diploma. Now what's this about the government?"

I waved her off, already having turned to face my desk. On the top was a small pile of pink message notes. The first was from my mother. Written in large letters was simply CALL. Apparently she'd given up on my cell phone (she'd called twice after the train had emerged from the subway onto the elevated track across the river and I'd ignored her). The next three notes were to call Bud Suleski, my client for all intents and purposes even though it had been easy to forget that everything happening was the result of a simple cheating spouse case. I'd gotten off the phone with him quickly earlier, promising a call back. Instead, he'd apparently called me three times. No, wait. Seven times. On the third note Rosie had stopped using new message slips and instead had started putting check marks for calls.

"Speaking of weird, when you going to check out the vampire?" Rosie asked.

I blinked, certain I'd heard her wrong. "Excuse me?"

She gestured animatedly with her left hand. "Romanoff, the creepy guy down the block from your building. You know, the one whose even creepier nephew showed up the instant he disappeared?"

Oh, yeah. The unofficially official missing persons case Rosie promised I'd check into. For free. "Never."

Rosie made a face that looked entirely too cute on her. "You're kidding, right? I mean, everybody's 'specting you to do something."

"Everybody is not 'specting me to do anything."

Rosie gave me a dramatic eye roll and sighed against her chair. "Okay, maybe not *everybody* everybody. But I wanna know what happened to the scary old man."

"So go find out."

She shook her head. "Uh-uh. I don't want to know that bad. Anyway, I got that thing I told you about today."

"What thing?"

She returned to her computer, squinting at the screen while her mouth worked on her gum. "You know. That thing with my sister. Lamaze." She aimed a two-dimple smile at me. "I'm going to be there when Yolanda's born."

Yolanda. They'd named the unborn child already. Bad luck in Greek culture where a baby was called Baby or Beba until they were baptized, which sometimes didn't happen until they were a year old. Of course, unless the child was the third or after, there was usually little mystery about what it would be named because the first two children were almost always named after the paternal grandparents. Except in my family's case. In a bid to win over my grandfather Kosmos, my parents had named me and my brother after my maternal grandparents.

It hadn't made a bit of difference. At least that's what my grandfather said, even if I did see a little twinkle in his eyes every now and again when he called me or my brother by name. It didn't matter that there were already two other Sofias and one other Kosmos in the family, my cousins from my mother's sister and brother.

Anyway, if forced to choose between childbirth and checking into dusty old rumors about vampires on our block, I'd definitely choose the latter. But that was just me. And, I'm sure, it was something my mother prayed about every Sunday at church. It was an endless source of martyr material for her that she still didn't have any grandchildren to spoil. Why this responsibility fell solidly in my lap was beyond me. Why couldn't Kosmos get married and have a few grandkids? Oh, I forgot. Kosmos, the professional student, was still in school.

But enough for the sorry state of my personal life. My professional one was currently giving it a run for its money.

I really needed to try and get a handle on this Harry guy, scare up that missing dead body. And, oh yeah, it might be a good idea if I could get a line on Bud Suleski's missing wife.

"I'm going to pop over to see what my mom wants."

"The vampire's on the way."

"There's no such thing as vampires."

"Uh-huh. That's what that Lucy girl said and look how she ended up."

Who in the hell was Lucy? She wasn't referring to the Lucy in *Dracula*? I held up my hand to ward off any further cryptic messages and left the agency. I had enough to worry about without adding Rosie's neurosis to the list.

I PARKED DOWN THE STREET from my apartment building and cut the engine. The interior of the Mustang still smelled mildewy, the rainwater from yesterday not having completely evaporated what with the high humidity and all. Of course, it didn't help that it had begun to sprinkle yet again, or that the seal around the Plexiglas back window let in water that accumulated in the vinyl pocket behind the back seat designed to hold the top when it was down, water that sloshed whenever I drove and sometimes took on the consistency of pond scum if I didn't clean it out quickly enough.

I looked up at my apartment building, then farther down the street at my parents' and Mrs. K's houses. I'd learned a long time ago that things didn't go away just because I wished them gone (this rude awakening came when I'd been getting my first real kiss from Alex Nyktas and my first menstruation started later that same day. I'd been wearing white shorts and looked down to find they matched my red-and-white striped top too closely).

But it was beginning to rain, so I had an out.

As if on cue, my cell phone vibrated.

I sighed and pulled it out of my pocket. "Hi, Ma."

"Hi, Ma? All day you don't return my calls and all I get is a 'hi, Ma'? I've been worried to death."

More like Mrs. K was bugging her to death, but I wasn't up to arguing the point.

"I'm coming down now."

"Good. You can have that talk with Efi while you're here. Don't forget your umbrella. It looks like rain."

I sat staring at my cell phone, hoping the sprinkling would stop and I could get down to my parents' no wetter than I had to be. I had an umbrella around the apartment somewhere, but I could never remember where I put it and found it only when I didn't need it.

Of course, it stood to reason that when it came to my life, it didn't merely rain, it poured. Immediately after calling a halt to my wedding three months ago, I'd been heartbroken but had known I'd done the right thing. Until my ex-groom's family started making noises about suing for half the value of the apartment building. After all, it had been meant as a wedding gift, they'd argued, and Thomas-the-Toad was entitled to half.

That was a deluge I wasn't sure to forget.

And was a large part of the reason I'd kept the wedding gifts from his family. Wedding gifts I wished I could be upstairs opening right now instead of going down to my parents' to face God only knew what. So long as none of the remaining gifts shocked me as much as the one from my paternal grandmother. Transparent thong panties with red lips all over them was not what I'd been expecting to find in that particular box. Especially since it had been *Yiayia* who used to take me shopping for what cousin Helen called granny panties. You know the type. Yards of white cotton that stretched from under your breasts and sagged nearly to your knees?

Speaking of *Yiayia* . . .

I reached into the back seat and grabbed the plain brown bag there, then opened the car door.

To my surprise it stopped sprinkling. Not only did it stop sprinkling, but a ray of sunlight speared the thick dark clouds.

Two miracles in one day. Maybe going to church yesterday had done some good. Well, aside from the points it had gained me with my mother, who had made me wear the blue dress.

Energized by the display, I began climbing from the car . . . only to be halted by the appearance of someone in front of the bumper. A very handsome, hunky someone that I'd been trying to figure out a way to call for the better half of the day, since I'd gotten his phone number from Debbie.

Porter.

"You don't mind if I take a look under the hood, do you, luv?"

His question was a little more than my mind was capable of handling just then . . .

Seven

A HALF HOUR LATER, I still hadn't managed to convince myself that Porter was actually tinkering around under my hood.

Make that under the hood of my car.

Of course, all the questions I'd had for him vanished the instant I allowed him to lift Lucille's hood. Something about a man who knows his way around a woman—I mean a car—is beyond hot.

I clutched the paper bag and the bottle it held tighter while I watched him from my parents' sidewalk. From this angle I had a perfect view of his behind, while he sprayed something somewhere then inserted a donut-shaped cylinder-type thing that I knew was an air filter, about the only thing I could identify when it came to car engines. Well, that and the oil stick.

"So, tell me, what did they say?"

I glanced up to find my mom standing in the doorway. In the wake of Porter's mysterious appearance, given my desire to keep him in sight for as long as possible, I'd decided to question the neighbors about Mrs. Kapoor's dog. My mom had been right: No one had noticed anything. They'd spotted no suspicious, flattened white-and-brown fur scraps in the road, had no garbage that had been torn into, and could speak of no missing newspapers. Even Mr. Newman had grinned when I'd asked him if he'd seen anything, apparently enjoying Muffy the Mutt's disappearance almost as much as I was.

Of course, the one house I avoided like the plague was the vampire house. Was it me, or did there always seem to be a dark cloud hanging above the old Gothic-style structure? A kind of mist clinging around the shrubs that made me think of distant Romanian mountaintops and, yeah I'll say it, creatures of the night.

I cleared my throat and answered my mother. "Nothing. No one's seen anything."

"By the way, has anyone said anything to you about Mr. Romanoff?" my mom asked. "Aklima and I went over there today but no one answered the door. Not even that creepy nephew of his, what's his name."

I made a face and tried to pry my gaze from Porter's backside before my mom could catch what I was doing.

"Who's that man under your hood?"

Too late. I only wished I didn't shiver at the suggestion that it was my own personal hood Porter was working under. Although I don't think my mom would have been half as casual if that had been the case. Rather her response would have included some brow-scorching Greek profanity and some physical violence by way of a broom to the backside. Seriously.

I waved my free hand and started up the walk. "Nobody. Anything new from you on the Muffy front, you know, evasive neighborhood vampires aside?"

"No. But Aklima did find Muffy's favorite blankie missing."

Muffy had a blankie? I didn't even have a blankie. Well, I did.

Until *Yiayia*, who's lived with the family since I was five, used it as a mop.

"And you're avoiding my question."

"No, I'm not." I kissed her cheek as I passed. "I'm just not answering it. There's a difference."

I stopped just inside the door. There, on the plastic-covered couch, sat another candidate for groomship.

Ugh.

While younger than the guy the other day, this one had a hair problem as well, but instead of having too much, he needed to find some. His head was as shiny as a bowling ball and my mind was filled with the image of spit-shining the very top. I tilted my head. Actually, given his better-than-average looks, the idea wasn't so bad. So long as I could get a written guarantee that my mother wouldn't be sending out wedding invitations the next day. I couldn't imagine myself wearing sunglasses at breakfast to cut down on the glare from my husband's head.

I sighed and bypassed the living room in exchange for the kitchen.

"Sofie, aren't you going to say hello to our guest?" Thalia hurried after me.

"No."

I opened the refrigerator, poked around, and came up with a piece of feta cheese and a black olive. I closed the door and leaned against it. When I was stressed, I ate. And I was definitely stressed.

"And he's not our guest, he's your guest." I looked toward the stairs. "Efi in her room?"

"Where else would she be? She refuses to meet Mitsos as well."

"And Kosmos?" I asked about my brother.

"Downtown."

Good. That meant he wasn't home to find out his camera was missing and I wouldn't have to tell him it was broken.

Broken? The thing was demolished.

"At least come say hello." Thalia tried to fix her motherly death grip on my arm and I skillfully sidestepped her.

"Maybe later." Which meant, in effect, never. If I had to stay in the kitchen until food ran out—and considering how well stocked the Metropolis pantry was, that could be weeks, if not months—then I would.

"Sofie . . ."

"Do you want me to talk to Efi or not?" I asked, although I still had no idea what I was going to say to my nineteen-year-old sister beyond "how's it goin'?" and "is that a prong from one of Mom's forks in your head?"

Thalia gave a long-suffering sigh and gestured limply with her hand. "Go on. Only don't encourage her any more than you already have."

"Me? How do I encourage her?"

"Last time you told her she looked nice. That's encouraging her."

I lightly shrugged. Truth was, I thought the navel ring was pretty cool. If not for my own phobia of anything associated with needles (I even hated to change my earrings), I'd probably be Efi.

Well, except for the tongue ring. The tongue ring gave me nightmares. You didn't do things like that to an organ so central to the enjoyment of pizza.

My mother gave a long-suffering sigh—my life seemed to be punctuated by them—and finally left the kitchen.

My grandmother looked at me from where she was stirring a pot of something on the stove. I handed her the bag I held. She smiled and slid it into the deep front pocket of her black housecoat, probably sewn in to hold contraband, then returned to her pot.

I climbed the back stairs to the second floor, rapped briefly on my sister's door, then entered despite the sign outside warning trespassers not to enter under penalty of death.

Efi was lying crosswise on her bed facing away from me, her computer mouse pad at her left hand, her headphones on, her butt as narrow as it had been when she was six and resembled a little boy more than a little girl. I shook my head. I knew she ate. I often witnessed her stuffing her pretty face. I just didn't understand how she managed to keep so thin when she didn't seem to possess more energy than it took to power up her computer.

I lay across the double bed beside her, making sure I was on her right side because messing with her connection with her computer was truly a capital crime.

"Hey," she said, looking at me as if she'd been expecting me. Which she probably was, since Thalia had been after me for days to talk to her.

I immediately located the latest addition of metal to her face—a tiny bar through her right eyebrow.

This when, when I was sixteen it had required a major battle for me before I was allowed to get my ears pierced. Once.

By sixteen Efi was on a first-name basis with Bruno, the owner of the tattoo shop down on 31st, who personally saw to all her cravings for metal.

Why my mother hadn't tackled my sister to the ground and forcibly removed some of the piercings yet was beyond me. Maybe Thalia Metropolis was finally feeling her years.

Or maybe after me she'd just given up.

Efi removed her headphones and I could hear the tinny sound of alternative pop music pumping through them. Last month she'd given me a CD of Linkin Park and I'd bought her one of Nina Simone. I don't think either of us has listened to the other's CD yet.

"So what's up?" I asked, ruffling her short, dark, purple-streaked hair the same way I always had.

And she shrank away and scowled at me the same way she always had.

I'd been seven when Efi was born and my favorite pastime when Mom and Dad had brought her home had been to pretend she was mine (unlike my reaction to my brother, which included but wasn't limited to my stuffing half a dozen donuts into his mouth when he was three months old, nearly choking him, and giving him countless swirlies when he got older, during which I sometimes waited too long to let him up).

What I'm trying to say, I guess, is that I have more maternal than sisterly feelings toward Efi. Truth is, since she'd come so much later than Kosmos and me, my parents hadn't taken as much of a hands-on approach with Efi as they'd taken with us. So I liked to think I filled a bit of that gap, even if lately I'd been busy with my own life.

I grinned at Efi. "Given the magnetic field that computer monitor creates, I'm surprised you're physically capable of moving yourself from in front of it."

"Ha ha."

I looked at the computer screen in question. While I didn't know a lot about computers, I knew enough. With a deft move of her left hand, Efi collapsed the screen. But not before I could see she was logged into at least three separate chat rooms, was viewing a Web site dedicated to Gothic jewelry—including different eyebrow and tongue rings—and was writing an email that began, "My One & Only Love."

I squinted at the main screen that held a picture of a tattooed cat—could they really tattoo cats?—and mulled over that one.

"So how's life treating you lately?" I asked as casually as I could.

I hated it when Mom interfered in my love life. What surprised me is that I even wanted to meddle in Efi's. I mean, hadn't I learned the hard way what it was like to have someone try to offer up advice you weren't in the least bit interested in hearing, much less taking?

Efi stared at me. "Life's treating me fine."

"Everything going okay at the restaurant?"

"Everything's going fine."

So she was in one of those "fine" moods.

Okay, fine.

She shifted slightly. "Well, except that Dad wants me to take out my eyebrow ring while serving. I've explained that if I take it out this early on I might not be able to get it back in."

"I can imagine his 'so?' reaction to that one."

All in all, Dad was pretty cool. He didn't say more than he had to to get his point across. And he usually didn't say anything, period, when you caught him off guard. So unlike my mother, who spoke—or screamed—first, and apologized later. Well, she didn't so much apologize as she changed her opinion without any mention of her earlier, hastier take on the situation. Which was okay. At least she was flexible enough to actually change her opinion.

But Dad . . .

I rolled over to stare at the ceiling. Six months ago Efi had painted her room royal purple and had painstakingly applied fluorescent stars to represent the summer sky. Frankly, I didn't get it. You wanted to see the stars, you went outside at night. But to each their own.

"Let him grumble for a little while," I told Efi. "He'll get over it soon enough."

Efi lay her chin down in her arms. "I know."

And after having lived nineteen years in the Metropolis household, she probably did know. In fact, it wouldn't surprise me in the least if my wise if a bit odd younger sister knew more than I did about our family. If only because I'd spent so much more time reacting—much like my mother—than I did thinking about how I should react.

But that was me. And I was here to talk to Efi.

"Have you given any more thought about taking computer classes?" I asked.

Efi sighed. "I already know all that stuff."

"I know that you know but without the paper to prove it, nobody else knows."

"Toilet paper, you mean."

I snorted. Our brother, king of the paper degrees, would choke on air at that one.

I turned my head to study Efi's profile. Even without makeup the girl was breathtakingly pretty, slightly hooked nose and all. She had flawless olive skin, creamy green eyes, plump, pouty lips, high cheekbones . . . essentially everything everyone else went to a plastic surgeon to get.

And everything I wanted but didn't have.

I'd hate her if I didn't love her.

"So how are things on the boyfriend front?"

I watched as her face reddened.

While I'd always been the boy-crazy one, Grandpa Kosmos sometimes joked that Efi wasn't sexual enough. She seemed content to sit in her bedroom all day and do whatever it was she did on her computer, aside from teaching herself the complex programming techniques she had used to create an awesome Web site of her own that attracted more than fifty hits a day . . . whatever that meant (I'm fairly sure it means she gets fifty visitors a day).

She shrugged in answer to my question.

I rolled back over so that my shoulder and hip were in direct contact with hers. I gave a little nudge. "So does that mean things are okay?"

She looked at me from beneath her thick lashes. "How are things with you?"

Ask a stupid question . . .

I must have scowled because Efi grinned in elfin satisfaction.

"Bitch," I muttered.

"Nag."

I gestured toward the computer. "Let's just say I'm nowhere near using the words 'My One and Only Love.'"

Okay, so I took some pleasure in watching her grin slowly vanish.

"Yes, I saw that." I leaned closer and lowered my voice in case my mother had a glass pressed to the door . . . or worse yet, to the wall of my brother's room next door. "Who is he?"

Efi shrugged again, nearly hitting me in the chin with her bony shoulder. "Nobody. Just somebody I met online."

The words made me shudder. Mention online meetings and images of perverted dirty old men with jagged yellow teeth, along with stalkers with binoculars, exploded in my mind. Not that I had had experiences with either, mind you, online or otherwise. Strangely enough, I'd done all right without ever having owned a computer outside the agency.

I repositioned myself, my new vantage point giving me a view of the purple carpet on the other side of the bed. A series of glossy photographs of blond girls about Efi's age were spread out there.

I hiked my brows and stared at my sister. "You're not considering hitting for the other team, are you?"

Efi snatched a picture I'd picked up out of my hand.

"You sound like Grandpa Kosmos."

She was right. Kosmos had suggested once or twice that Efi might be, well, a lesbian. The word was whispered so quietly you almost couldn't make it out and was usually followed by so much solemn head nodding by him and whomever he was speaking to that you'd have thought someone had died.

Of course, he'd never brought it up to me. Because he probably caught on that I'd laugh him straight back to Greece.

Not that I had a problem with the possibility of Efi being bisexual or even homosexual. Let's just say that I'd caught her doing some flashing of her own when it came to the neighborhood boys throughout the years and had been instrumental in arranging her first date when she was eleven with Noah, the little Jewish boy a few blocks up. I'd driven them both to the movies and they'd both come out of the theater looking like they'd discovered a few things about the opposite sex they didn't know existed before and were now ready to slow down a little bit.

If Efi was a lesbian, surely she'd have gone to the movies with Noah's sister Sharon. Which would have been far easier because Mom could have taken her then and there wouldn't have been any of the hush-hush, big-secret cloud surrounding the outing.

I picked up another of the pictures of the blond girls, thinking one of them actually looked like Sharon Sonnenfeld. "So what's with the photos? I mean Colin Farrell I can understand . . ."

Efi snatched the photos away from me and gathered the rest of them up and put them under her stomach, where she promptly lay on top of them. "Jeremy wants to see what I look like."

"Ah," I said, as if what she'd said made perfect sense. "I'm sorry. Am I missing something?"

"Jeremy . . ." she said, waving her hand.

"Your online One and Only Love," I helped.

She glared at me. "Oh, just forget it."

"Jeremy wants a picture of you and . . . and . . . you're not thinking of sending him one of these?"

"Why not?"

"Well, because I think it would be better for you to find a shot of the ugliest girl you can find and send that. You know, lower his expectations. If he still has the hots for you then, *bam!* You know he's made of the right stuff."

She considered me for long moments.

I shrugged. "Unless of course he's hound material himself."

She clicked her mouse. Was she ever without that mouse? A picture of a completely hunky guy with blond hair and Aegean-blue eyes popped up.

Wow.

"You can say that again."

I hadn't been aware I'd said anything, but hey, it was my thought anyway so why argue the point?

"Who's to say he's not doing the same thing you're considering doing and this is a shot of a guy from an Abercrombie ad?"

Efi's head flopped against her hands again and she groaned. "Because I know him, that's why."

I stared at the picture again. There was no way she could know this guy. Guys like this didn't exist. At least not when I was her age. Hell, not at my age either.

I thought about Jake Porter and amended that.

"He ran track for AHS a couple years ago and I've seen him at football and baseball games and stuff."

"But he hasn't seen you . . ."

She shook her head. Well as much as she could while it was still fused to her arms.

I rested my hand against her hair to ruffle it again, only I held it still instead, feeling the soft strands against my palm. "I think you should send him a picture of yourself," I said quietly. "Start with the lies now and you'll never stop. A relationship built on lies has nowhere to go but down."

"You really sound like Grandpa Kosmos now."

I smiled. Yes, I did. Imagine that.

"At the very least, you'll know you've been accepted or rejected because of the truth."

"And if he does reject me?"

She was all big doe eyes and worried frown.

I pressed the tip of my nose against hers. "Then I go over there and breaka his kneecaps."

A small laugh. Then a bigger one. "You can't do that."

"Try me."

We both seemed to realize simultaneously how close we were to hugging and perhaps even saying how much we loved each other, so naturally I scooted away from Efi and she did the same, both of us clearing our throats and focusing on the computer and the shot of yummy Jeremy still on the screen.

"Was there anything else?" Efi asked.

I pushed from the bed and straightened my T-shirt. "Nope. That about covers it."

I turned toward the door, hearing the sound of my mother scurrying down the hall.

I paused at my sister's black-painted dresser and picked up her senior class picture. Sans purple streaks, her hair softer and not so spiky, she was better looking than those countless blondes she thought were so pretty.

I pulled open the door. "Oh, and no more piercings or tattoos or else you'll have to answer to me," I said loudly, convinced my mother was standing at the top of the stairs.

I tossed the frame to the bed and whispered. "Send him this one. He'll love it."

I met Thalia at the end of the hall. "So?" she asked.

"All taken care of."

Of course, I wished I could say the same about the other half-dozen messes littering my life at that moment. Not the least of which was the sexy Australian under my hood down the street.

I took the stairs two at a time. That was one mess I was looking forward to cleaning up. Sort of . . .

Eight

IT WAS DARK BY THE time I walked back down the street toward Jake Porter's primo behind where he was still under the hood of my car. Which was good for two reasons. First, because it meant my mom and Mrs. K would have a hard time seeing what was going on. Second, because I thought I looked better when the sun was turned down low. Especially considering how many times I'd melted in the muggy summer heat that day.

"So what was in that bedspread the other night, anyway?" I leaned against the body of the car and crossed my arms as if I'd just climbed out from behind the steering wheel instead of disappearing for an hour between moves.

Jake grinned at me over the raised hood. Or at least I was pretty sure he was grinning. While a nearby streetlamp seemed to shine a spotlight on him, some of his face was still in shadow.

"You're not going to answer me, are you?" I asked.

He wiped his hands on a rag then closed the hood. "Nope."

"Didn't think so."

I watched him rub the rag against the hood to clean it. I hadn't washed the car in at least two weeks and the clean spot he created made it look all the worse.

He crossed his arms over his chest, mimicking my stance. "Nice move downtown today. Are you going to tell me what you found out?"

"Nope." I figured one good nope deserved another.

Now I knew he was grinning because I could see him.

"Well, all right then," he said, sticking the rag into his back jeans pocket, then hefting a toolbox from the curb. "I guess I'll be going then."

It was all I could do not to stomp my foot against the cement. Both because he wasn't providing any help at all in this blasted case of mine . . . and because he didn't appear interested in staying only for me.

It seemed the only Sheila he was interested in tinkering with was my car.

Not that I wanted to be tinkered with.

Okay, maybe I did.

"Can I get you a beer?" I asked, surprised to hear the words come from my mouth.

The guy had just said he was leaving. The invitation was nothing if not desperate. And I usually made it a point not to appear desperate even if, in fact, I was. Especially if I was.

He came to stand in front of me, smelling like warm cotton, oil, and one hundred percent hunk. It was all I could do to keep drool from running from the corner of my mouth.

"Mmm. Next time maybe."

He chucked me under the chin and moved around me.

I looked over my shoulder. "Are you married?"

His quiet chuckle made my toes curl in my Skechers. "No, luv, that's one thing I'm not."

I was relieved by his answer, but only slightly.

I stood for long moments, considering what he'd done. Not a kiss. Not even a hint that he'd wanted to kiss me. Instead he'd done something my grandfather might have done. And there wasn't the excuse of marriage to explain away his actions.

I was appalled. And more than a little disappointed.

I turned to find out what car he drove, hoping to get the plate number. With a plate number I could find something on him.

He was already gone.

Yeesh.

I opened the car door, collected my keys, and locked Lucille, then made my way toward my apartment. If not for the inspired moves downtown today, I'd probably have felt like a complete loser. And that Porter knew what I'd done and had gotten a kick out of it provided a little thrill . . . even if he didn't want to kiss me.

Probably he'd wanted to, but he'd felt too dirty.

Oh, but that was lame. I usually wasn't into self-delusion.

Who was I kidding? Lately it seemed as if my entire life was a delusion.

An apartment owner who couldn't collect the rent.

A PI who couldn't solve a case.

A woman who couldn't get a guy to kiss her.

A daughter who couldn't make her parents happy.

I climbed the steps to my third-floor apartment, each move heavier than the one before. I'd reached the top floor when I heard Mrs. Nebitz unlock the three deadbolts on her door, which usually meant she wanted to talk to me. The time it took her to open the door gave me the choice of either ducking into my apartment and avoiding her, or waiting.

I waited.

I don't think I'd ever avoided Mrs. Nebitz. She was my only paying tenant.

Besides, she never blinked after I attacked a few of the more interesting-looking wedding gifts stacked in my bedroom and gave her the stranger ones, like the small kitchen appliances that weren't toasters but might as well have been. I suspected she had them stuffed in her closet for regifting, probably at Chanukah.

"Good. I was afraid I wouldn't catch you," Mrs. Nebitz said as she opened her door.

I don't know what it is about her that makes me think of Yoda, but I've always thought Mrs. Nebitz cute. The type of grandmother you could imagine baking you chocolate chip cookies and asking about your day (my own paternal grandmother didn't know what a chocolate chip cookie was and was partial to Castor oil and raw honey, sometimes together, for whatever ailed you).

"Good evening, Mrs. Nebitz. How are you?"

She waved a blue-veined hand. "The same. Which is just fine with me. I made some kugel today and thought you might enjoy a piece. I've noticed you haven't been home much lately."

For some reason that felt good. That someone had noticed I hadn't been home. Not because she needed something but because she was worried about me.

She handed me a plate covered in plastic wrap. I couldn't make out the contents but my stomach growled in response anyway.

"That nice young man who was working on your car . . . he wouldn't happen to be Jewish, would he?"

I smiled. "I don't know, Mrs. Nebitz. But I don't think so. He's Australian."

Exactly why an Australian couldn't be Jewish didn't make much sense to me, but there you had it.

"Shame. He looked a lot like my sister's nephew Samuel."

Of course, Jake Porter didn't look Greek either. But why that mattered was beyond me at the moment. All I could think about was dragging myself inside my apartment, picking over whatever was edible on the plate I held, and zoning out in front of a rerun of *Friends*.

"Thank you for thinking of me, Mrs. Nebitz." Did she even have a first name? I tried to think if I'd noticed one on her checks. It struck me as funny that she might endorse her checks "Mrs. Nebitz." "I'll bring the plate back in the morning."

I hesitated before I put my key in my lock. "You wouldn't happen to have gotten a look at the car he was driving, would you?"

"Of course. Only it wasn't a car. It was a truck."

It made sense that Jake would drive a truck.

"One of those newfangled things. Black."

I opened my mouth to ask if she'd gotten the plate number, scanned her thick glasses, then closed my mouth again.

"Oh, one more thing." She shuffled her orthopedic shoes back into her apartment and picked something up off the foyer table. Her apartment smelled like my grandmother's room at my parents'. A cross between lilac talcum powder and fish. "I know you've been busy, so I took it upon myself to accept this month's rent from a few of my fellow tenants."

I stared at her as if she'd just told me the main water pipe had burst.

The image of Mrs. Nebitz making the rounds in the building, banging on doors and demanding rent made my eyes water for some reason.

Mrs. Nebitz, debt collector.

I wanted to hug her.

Instead I accepted the checks she offered, said goodnight, and let myself into my apartment and closed the door behind me, standing in the dark for a long moment pondering the old woman across the hall.

Hands full, I stepped toward the kitchen, tripping over Thomas-the-Toad's recliner in the dark.

Damn.

I'd completely forgotten about the Barcalounger.

Putting the plate down on the sofa, I reached to turn on the light, then stood staring at the cursed chair while rubbing my shin. I'd meant to ask one of the guys in 2B if they wanted the stupid thing, but had forgotten. I shuffled through the checks I still held. Sure enough, there it was. A check from Don Meyers for the full amount, not a partial payment. I scratched the back of my neck. That was a first. Wonder what Mrs. Nebitz threatened him with.

Or maybe Mrs. Nebitz reminded Don of his own grandmother, inspiring the same kind of old-person awe in him that she inspired in me.

Nah. More than likely she'd shaken her cane at him. I'd seen her do this on the street to some of the nastiest-looking guys the neighborhood had to offer and they always moved out of her way, hands up in the air.

My apartment felt like the inside of an oven whose broiler had been left on. I put the checks down on the foyer table, put the plate Mrs. Nebitz had given me in the kitchen, then walked around throwing open windows and putting in two box fans, switching them on high.

Just like that, I was drenched in sweat. Which wouldn't have been so bad had my getting that way had to do with a man, more specifically Jake Porter. But it didn't, so it sucked.

I went into my dark bedroom, peeled off my clothes, grabbed the trusty old Amazin' Mets T-shirt I'd swiped from my brother, two sizes too big and with holes under the arms, then collected my plate, added to it from the refrigerator, and plopped onto the couch in front of the TV. Good. There was actually something on that I wanted to watch. While it wasn't *Friends*, it was one of my favorite *Sex and the City* episodes. The one where Carrie leaves her toothbrush at Big's place.

I spotted something black on my arm and flicked it off even as I dug into the kugel. You had to be a New Yorker or probably Jewish to appreciate the difference between a stale apple noodle kugel and a fresh one. And this was definitely fresh. And delicious.

I looked down to find a tiny black spot on my other arm. Had Jake gotten oil on me? I leaned my head closer and stared at the speck. And screeched when it jumped straight onto my nose. Which prompted me to jump from the couch, toppling my perfectly good kugel right onto my new rug. The bug disappeared from my nose in the process.

I picked up the food, put the plate back in the kitchen, then sat back down on the couch, very stiff and alert, my mind not on the television but rather on my person.

Another one.

I swatted at it, instantly flattening the bug against my skin (my bug-killing abilities came from years spent killing flies at my family's restaurants).

I slowly lifted my hand and turned it palm up to peer at the carcass.

Fleas. It had to be fleas.

I shook my hand to rid it of the offensive blood-sucking insect, then jumped up off the couch again.

Correct me if I'm wrong, but didn't fleas normally accompany animals? I looked around my living room. Everything was brand-spanking-new, as it should be in a prospective bride's apartment . . .

Except for the rug.

Eeew.

I began moving furniture away from it like a woman gone mad, ignoring the noise I was making or the sight I made in my T-shirt and purple panties. Finally I had the rug rolled up and managed to stuff it, while busily huffing and puffing, through the open window and out onto the fire escape. Just to make doubly sure none of the repulsive pests could make it back in, I slammed the window shut.

Great. The kind of pests I wanted to keep around—namely over-six-foot Australian ones in hot jeans—I couldn't tempt with edible panties, while the kind I didn't want had taken over my apartment.

I went into the kitchen to find my kugel covered with carpet fibers and a single solitary flea. I dumped the plate's contents into the sink, ran the water, then flipped the garbage disposal switch. Much ear-splitting grinding ensued. The kind that told me either the disposal was busted—which didn't make sense because it was new, the entire building having been renovated before my parents bought it—or that a piece of silverware was stuck in there.

Not in the mood to find out which, I instead shuddered and ran to change out of my favorite T-shirt lest any of the ugly critters remained, all the time wondering just when my life was due a much-needed upturn . . .

LATE THE FOLLOWING DAY I sat at my office computer, not about to give up on what had so far been a fruitless day.

Nothing on Muffy (okay, I hadn't had a chance to go to the animal shelter no matter my promise to visit yesterday. Hey, I figured they kept new dogs around for at least a week before destroying them, so I had time, no matter how often Mrs. K and my mother called).

Nothing on Harry Brooks, the missing dead guy.

No fewer than five calls from my client Bud Suleski demanding I find his wife, dead or alive, which gave me the willies.

And this morning I'd come in to find my cousin Pete tinkering around in my uncle's office doing Lord only knew what, but whatever it was had nothing to do with the agency and everything to do with what might be stashed in my uncle's filing cabinets.

All this and the guy who could probably solve all of my problems—well, my cousin Pete aside, who, I'm afraid, will always be a problem for my uncle Spyros—and all I could think of to do the night before was offer Porter a beer. A beer he'd wasted no time in turning down.

I made a face and typed harder than I had to as I finished up a client report on a power company employee I'd done some checking into for a couple days last week.

Something did, however, pop up on my grandfather's missing medal case. Namely an obituary dated six months ago noting my grandfather's friend's death. I'd called the Cosmopolitan Café and left a message but my grandfather had yet to get back to me.

My only triumph all day and I wasn't able to gloat about it.

Rosie had come in late that morning, so she was staying late, her fingers busily clacking away doing invoicing and some of the routine background checks on behalf of the businesses that kept us on retainer. Seeing as she'd spent the first couple hours sharing every detail about Lamaze and her sister's burgeoning stomach, she was more than making up for it by doing in one hour what it would take five people to do all day.

"What?"

Just like that she'd stopped and was staring at me, her mouth frozen mid-pop.

"*What* what?" I asked. "I didn't say anything."

"Yeah, but you was thinking something."

"Mmm." That I was. But I wasn't about to share it.

She stabbed her talon-ended index finger in my direction. "You know, you still haven't looked into that vampire thing like you said you would."

"I never said I'd look into it."

"Uh-huh, you did, too. I remember you did."

I sighed. "No, I didn't."

She gave an eye roll that reminded me why she was the queen of them, grabbed her purse out of her bottom desk drawer, and got up. "Come on."

I blinked. "Come on where?"

"Well, since you're such a wuss and all, I guess I'm just going to have to go over there with you."

"I thought you had this . . . thing about vampires."

"I do. But it's still daylight, so probably it should be okay."

I thought of the Greek eye my mom had given me to ward off evil and wondered where I'd put it.

Not that I bought into any of the vampire stuff. Yes, Mr. Romanoff was strange. Yes, you only saw him at night and he was pastier than my mom's raw phyllo dough sheets. But that didn't a vampire make. In order for one to be a vampire, you had to have victims.

I told Rosie this.

"Uh-uh. Not anymore you don't. I mean, they got the blood bank, or whatever, now. They don't have to kill nobody to get their blood. They just got to buy it."

I gave her my best eye roll, which didn't impress her. "You can't just go in and buy blood."

"Yes, you can. I checked. Mr. Romanoff has worked at Mount Sinai for the past twenty years. And guess what department he works in? The blood bank."

"Collecting blood for himself and his fellow vampires?"

"Bingo." Rosie was warming to her subject, her dimples popping, her hands gesturing like mad. "You see, he works the night shift and transports the plasma, that's what it's called, not blood, to area hospitals every night." She shrugged. "Who's to argue if a few packages come up missing?"

"His boss?"

"Oh, but what if his boss is in on it? What if they use the business to collect blood, then use hospitals as a front to distribute it to their pale buddies? I mean, sure they deliver some of the stock to the hospitals, but the bulk of it they keep for themselves. Oh my God. That explains the city's chronic blood shortage. They're always calling me to come in and donate."

"How do you think up this stuff?" I asked.

She shrugged. "My brother works for a wiseguy."

I raised my brows. I didn't know how this explained her newly acquired theories on vampire blood distribution, but I bit anyway. "Ricky works for the mob?"

"Nah. He just works for the main mobster. Doing his nails or something." She wrinkled her nose. "My mother hates it. Actually she hates that he's gay more, and what he does only emphasizes that she's not going to be getting any grandchildren from him, and since I'm not about to get pregnant anytime soon, my sister's her only hope."

I felt dizzy from the roundabout explanation.

What had we been talking about?

Oh, the neighborhood vampire.

"So are we going or what?" Rosie asked.

I wanted to say definitely not. But since I already had my own purse, and since I had nothing more to do with my night than delouse my rug and get rid of a recliner and wait for the FBI to catch up with me, I decided it wouldn't hurt to do a little snooping on behalf of the neighborhood.

For some reason I had the feeling I was going to eat those words . . .

Nine

OKAY, SO I'LL ADMIT, EVEN I felt a little freaked out about going to Mr. Romanoff's house. Why we'd had to wait until dusk was a mystery to me. But to even propose we wait till morning might give Rosie the idea that I was scared, and if I was scared then it meant I bought into all this vampire stuff. And I didn't.

I think.

At any rate, I was uneasy. I mean, there is the whole haunted manor factor going on here. Forget that the area immediately surrounding the house was dark. There was no streetlight in front. No safety lights shining from the house itself. And the security light on the right hand neighbor's house, aimed toward Mr. Romanoff's, somehow didn't reach the house in question. Rather, it seemed to end in a dead stop a good three feet from the structure itself.

And what was that mist? I sniffed. It would be just my luck for the cloud to be some sort of gas leak that would ignite the instant I opened the iron gate. But no, the yard smelled of all things growing.

Or rather, all things dead or dying.

Rotting vegetation and decay seemed to hang in the air like a bad case of BO.

"I don't like this," Rosie whispered next to me.

I looked to find her shivering, her arms wrapped tightly around herself as she stared wide-eyed at the second storey of the dark, Gothic-style house. The ridiculous picture she made was enough to snap me out of my own deepening psychosis.

"What?" she demanded of me again. "This place gives me the creeps." She lowered her voice and stepped closer. "When we was kids, we used to come here and egg the windows. I swear, one night we were chased all the way home by one of them bat things. You know, what vampires turn into when they're really mad and want to chase you?"

I didn't think that was the fictional reason behind vampires turning into bats, but I wasn't about to argue the point.

But I did sigh. "Oh, let's just get this over with already. The old guy's probably in there right now having a good laugh at our expense."

Rosie grabbed my arm. "There ain't nobody home. They ain't got no lights on."

I realized she was right.

The idea that someone might be lurking inside in the darkness watching us through the windows turned my blood to ice cubes. Was Mr. Romanoff in there even now trying to figure out which side of my neck was best to bite? I wished I had on something more substantial than a T-shirt, you know, something like one of those chain-link neck protectors I think I've seen in a movie or two.

I gave myself an eye roll. Oh, come on. The fact that there were no lights on indicated that no one was home, nothing more, nothing less. Which should make this easier yet. We'd knock, no one would answer, and we could both call it a night after a very long day.

"Come on, let's get this over with."

Rosie had a death grip on my arm and was wildly shaking her head. "I ain't going nowhere near that house. I mean, he could have Tupperware containers with our names all over them."

I stared at her.

"What? My cousin sells Tupperware and she says there's been a huge spike in sales lately. Probably Romanoff bought it all."

I pried her fingers from my arm one by one only to have her clamp them back on again when I was done.

"Rosie, would you stop? Nothing's going to happen. You stay right here. I'll be in plain sight the whole time."

She was staring at me in that bug-eyed way that made my lips twitch with the urge to smile. Her mouth was working a million miles a minute on her gum although the pops were quiet because she had her jaw clenched tight. "No. Don't."

"If, on the off chance, something should happen, I want you to run to my mother's house as fast as you can."

We both looked down at the familiar structure two blocks down. "What do I do then?"

"Tell my mother to come. No vampire would dare cross Thalia."

Rosie removed her hand and slapped my arm. "You're teasing."

"I'm teasing." I think.

I turned back toward Mr. Romanoff's house. The creak of my opening the gate made the fine hair at the back of my neck stand on end.

"I don't think I can do this." Rosie was full-out shivering now, her teeth rattling so that "this" came out as "dis."

Ten paces and I was climbing the old wooden steps, then knocking on the old wooden outer door that the screen had been pushed out of long ago. Mr. Romanoff really should look into a few repairs.

"See, no one's even home," I called over my shoulder.

"Good evening." A disembodied voice floated on the thick, foggy air.

I shrieked.

Behind me Rosie screamed and ran flat out in the opposite direction.

So much for backup . . .

OH, YEAH, IT'S ALL FUN and games until you come face-to-face with a real, honest-to-God vampire. I'd never met one before, but if I had, I was pretty sure this is what he would look like.

It seemed Mr. Romanoff's nephew had inherited the pale gene: Not only didn't he seem to have any color at all, he almost seemed to . . . glow.

"Um, yes. Hi," I said carefully. Had he really said 'good evening' in that low, drawn-out way I'd seen in the original Dracula movie when I was six and wasn't supposed to be watching TV? Christopher Lee had nothing on this guy. "I'm sorry to, um, bother you, but I'm Sofie Metropolis. My family lives down the street?"

He stared at me with all the interest a spider gives to a fly.

I swallowed hard. "I was wondering if I might speak to Mr. Romanoff?"

He didn't say anything, just continued looking at me in that peculiar way, as if trying to put me into some kind of trance. In my pocket I squeezed my fingers around the Greek eye I'd found mixed in with some spare change in my car ashtray. I told myself I'd been raised with far more dangerous myths than vampires. After all, Medusa could turn you into stone with one look.

Yeah, but that was quick and easy. One bite from a vampire and you spent an eternity wishing you were stone.

"I am Mr. Romanoff," the man finally said.

An accent. He definitely spoke with an accent. And not the cute, Australian kind either where he might call me mate or luv or ask to tinker around with my Sheila.

Although even as I stood staring into his dark, dark eyes I had to admit I was oddly fascinated by his appearance. Or maybe it wasn't so much his appearance as his confidence. Or a strange combination of both.

I was pretty sure he had yet to blink while I was having trouble getting a swallow down.

"I see," I said. "But I'd like to talk to Mr. Ivan Romanoff. The owner of the residence."

This had to be the nephew everyone was whispering about. The same one who had mysteriously appeared at the same time his uncle had disappeared.

I gave a mental cringe, reminding myself that people didn't just disappear.

I also braced myself for the possibility that the nephew might, himself, be an Ivan. Like the Greeks, many of the Europeans held the tradition of keeping names in the family. I couldn't count how many Kosmoses there were in the family tree. Or Sofias for that matter.

I realized I was doing the equivalent of mental babbling so I shut up and returned Romanoff's stare. I'd played this game many a time before, beginning with my brother and including and not limited to stand-offs with my mother every now and again when she refused to budge on a ludicrous idea. You couldn't be Greek and not master The Stare.

"My most humblest of apologies, Miss Metropolis. I am Vladimir Romanoff. My uncle is ill and is not up to entertaining guests."

"Ms.," I corrected without knowing why. What did my title matter? Well, aside from the fact that if I had been married it would be to Thomas-the-Toad and the mere suggestion made my teeth ache.

The nephew smiled at me in a way that made my skin itch at the same time as I shuddered with dread. "Perhaps you could return tomorrow?"

"Ill?" I repeated.

"Mmm. Yes, very much so. It is his physical state that prompted my sudden, how do you say? Visit."

My brows shot up. How many different ways could you say "visit"? Or did "visit" mean something else entirely?

I tried to look past him into the house. But even if it had been light enough to see anything, I wouldn't have been able to say if anything was out of place because, well, I'd never been inside Mr. Romanoff's house before.

I imagined Rosie and my mother bugging me to no end if I left without doing what I'd come to do. And that was to verify that Mr. Ivan Romanoff was still very much alive and not stuffed into Tupperware containers in the basement.

Although that was no longer my fear. Oh, I was afraid he was in the basement all right. But lying in a coffin as his nephew fed him fresh blood from a few errant rats.

"Really, I'll only be a moment. I could see if there's anything he needs . . ."

I tried to push past him but without moving he prevented my progress. He didn't even stumble, as if he'd expected the move.

I immediately backed up.

"I must insist you come back tomorrow, Miss Metropolis. Say at about ten or so."

I released a long breath of relief. While I hated the idea of coming back, the thought of returning in the light of day was much preferable to this. "In the morning?"

He smiled again. "No, in the evening."

Above me the skies lightened and a moment later thunder shook the ground.

I began backing away. Damn storms.

The nephew touched my right arm and I nearly jumped out of my skin.

"It was a pleasure making your acquaintance, Sofie Metropolis." He tried lifting my hand to his mouth and I fought him. When his cold lips lay against my skin I thought I heard him sniffing, as I might sniff a glass of wine for its bouquet. "Good evening."

Another burst of lightning and thunder and I was bolting through the gate and tracing Rosie's rapid steps, icked out to the core.

THE LAST PERSON I EXPECTED to see outside my apartment building was Pimply Pino. Rosie, maybe, and perhaps even Mrs. Nebitz, who might have heard my scream, but never Pimply Pino.

Then again, perhaps that's exactly who I should have expected to see given my activities in the city.

Adrenaline still pumping past my ears, I considered the likelihood of getting away from him for the second time in as many days and ruled it unlikely. Besides, I didn't know if I could handle another run. While I thought I was in pretty good shape, even I had my limits. And climbing eighteen flights of stairs yesterday and running from a vampire tonight was it.

I slowed my step and tried to regulate my breathing. Considering that a rolled-up rug had brought me under suspicion of murder, I could imagine what thoughts my facing Pino sweaty and out of breath would inspire in him. He'd probably arrest me just to find out.

By the time I drew even with his squad car, I was pretty much breathing normally again, although there was really nothing I could do about the sweat.

"I'm beginning to think you don't take any time off," I said, startling him so that his head nearly hit the roof.

Damn. I could have easily escaped the other way.

The cause of his distraction was evident on a clipboard against the steering wheel. He put it aside before I could see what he was writing. "If it isn't Sofie-the-Bug-Shake-Drinker Metropolis."

"What do you want, Pino?"

He squinted at my appearance. "You don't look so good."

I looked over my shoulder to see if any lights had gone on at the Romanoff place. Nothing but eerie darkness. "Just, um, out for a run."

He looked at my slip-on Skechers and jeans. "You really should get the proper gear. You can injure yourself without the proper gear."

"Proper gear . . . yeah." I pushed my damp hair away from my face.

He pointed toward the fire escape of my building. "That the same rug from the other day?"

I blinked at it, not having decided yet if I wanted to delouse it or pitch it altogether. "Mmm. Couldn't get the bloodstains out," I said.

"Oh, you're funny, Metro. Unfortunately you always were the only one who thought so."

Ouch.

"Is there a particular reason you're sitting outside my house or should I call in a stalking complaint?"

"Oh, there's a reason all right." He picked up the clipboard and flicked through some pages. "A six-foot-two-inch reason that's lying in the Queens morgue right now."

My adrenaline level spiked again. I eyed the bag of donuts on his passenger seat. "My dead body popped up?"

"Why did you use the word 'popped'?"

"Can I have one of those donuts? I think my blood sugar is low after, you know, all that running."

He tossed me the bag.

"I repeat, why did you use the word 'popped'?"

I was a good ways into a donut bearing pink sprinkles when I caught on to what he was asking. "Don't tell me. He's a floater."

I pride myself on keeping up on all the latest lingo, not by actually doing any police work but by watching television shows that focus on the same. "Floater" meant he'd been found floating on a body of water.

"East River, under the Hellgate Bridge. Discovered by a group of teens who'd gone there to knock back an illegal six-pack."

I wondered if that meant the dead guy had been denied entrance to hell or if he'd made it through and Satan had spat his body back out.

"That'll teach them to indulge in underage drinking."

Pino didn't find me or my comment amusing.

"Get in. I'll drive you over so you can ID the body."

I stared at the half-eaten donut, then put it back in the bag and handed it back to him. I didn't think it was a good idea to have a full stomach if I was going to be looking at dead bodies. Especially bloated ones fished from the East River.

I rounded the car and climbed into the passenger's seat, wondering if what had begun as a slow and uneventful day and turned into something just shy of my excitement capacity level had any more interesting surprises in store for me . . .

Ten

NOTE TO SELF: IF SCHEDULED to view dead bodies, don't eat donuts with pink sprinkles for up to five days beforehand.

As I puked up everything that had been hiding in my intestines for the past ten years outside the Queens morgue, Pino stood back and watched, merely increasing my humiliation.

It wasn't so much the sight of the dead body that had gotten to me. After all, I'd gone through the same dead man's pockets while his body was still warm and lifted his hotel room key. And I had worked for my mortician aunt. But nothing had prepared me for seeing a body that had been floating in the river for some three days. It had been all I could do to make a positive ID. The tattoo on his right hand had been all that separated a big question mark from a ninety-percent-positive ID. That and the *Men in Black* suit he had on.

I remembered the other men in black I'd run across at said dead man's hotel room . . .

"You done?"

I'd almost forgotten Pino was still there. I snatched the handkerchief out of his hand and made extra sure to give a loud blow of my nose to rid it of the smell of camphor before trying to hand it back to him. He made a face.

"*Stee hara sou eisai tora, etsi?*" I said to him in Greek.

For some reason whenever I was very upset or needed to get out of a jam, my parents' native language came back to me like second nature. Essentially what I'd said is that he must be getting a royal kick out of seeing me like this.

I tried to hand him back his hanky. He stared at me. "No, I'm not in my *hara* watching you upchuck." He hiked up his pants in that way that made me wince. "If anything, it makes me remember when I saw my first floater."

"Bad?" I asked.

He cleared his throat and looked around as if to check to make sure no one could hear him. "Let's just say that at least you made it outside."

I envisioned him hurling all over the front of the coroner's jacket and felt marginally better. Especially since I'd almost done the same.

I folded the handkerchief and stuffed it into my back pocket. "I'll wash this and get it back to you."

"With starch."

I made a face. "With starch."

I turned around and swallowed deeply, trying to rid myself of vomit breath. He held out a mint.

"So that's your missing dead body then?"

I nodded. "That's him."

"I thought you told me he was shot."

I nodded again.

"The coroner says this guy's cause of death was a knife wound."

A knife wound? There had been knives flying around along with bullets that night at the motel?

I shuddered. "Any idea who he is?" I asked.

"The owner of the car I called you about."

"Harry Brooks?"

"That would be him."

I nodded again, feeling ridiculously like one of those bobble-head dolls. I'd had one of the Mets' Mike Piazza on my dash for a few years until the head had bobbled right off.

I could relate.

It might have been a result of the vampire run-in (oh, stop it, there's no such thing as vampires), or the general uselessness of the day, but I felt tired to the bone and overwhelmed by everything that had happened.

When Pino finally pulled onto my street, looking all quiet and calm this late on a Tuesday night, I thought I spotted a black truck like the one Mrs. Nebitz had described. I tried to see through the tinted windows. I saw the flash of a lighter, then watched as cigarette smoke curled through the crack in the driver's side window.

Porter?

But why would Porter be parked on my street? Had he grown so attached to Lucille he'd come over for one last look and a goodnight?

Or were the answers he refused to provide darker than my practical mind could conjure up?

"How did you end up on that reality show, anyway?"

I blinked at Pino next to me as he pulled to a stop in front of my building. "What?"

"There's a whole application and interview process you have to go through to get on one of those things."

I didn't ask how he knew that. Probably he'd tried to get on and had been refused because of his complexion and bad attitude. "One of my second cousins is an assistant producer on the show. I met up with her while on . . ." I realized I'd nearly said "my honeymoon." ". . . in L.A. for vacation and she thought it would take my mind off things back here. So she bumped someone else off and put me on in her place."

"Things back here being Thomas Chalikis."

I coughed. "Yeah." I reached for the door handle.

"Do me a favor and stay out of trouble. The less I see of you, the better."

"The feeling's mutual, trust me."

He cleared his throat. "Oh, and tonight, don't watch any horror movies or detective shows."

"Huh?"

He stared through the windshield. "Try watching an infomercial instead. Those things are enough to clear everything out of your mind but boredom."

As I climbed out of the car, I thought that boredom sounded really good right about now . . .

NOT SURPRISINGLY, I DIDN'T GET much sleep that night. Instead of exorcising the images of Harry's bloated body from my mind, the infomercials I'd seen merely gave them a bizarre slant. In one dream, a reanimated Harry was demonstrating the advantages of having a food processor that—oops!—rotting flesh kept falling into. In another, Harry demonstrated the many uses of an exercise machine, including weight reduction by amputation of swollen, green body parts.

And in every dream Vladimir Romanoff stood in the background, his eyes glowing an eerie red as he watched me.

So I got up earlier than usual, and rather than going to an office that would be empty for the next hour, I decided to drive to Brooklyn so I could be at the animal shelter the minute they opened the doors.

I'd wanted to be a vet once. For all of two minutes when I was eleven. While some of the Greek families we knew had dogs—usually cute little ones that visited the doggie spa once a week and came back with little satin bows in their freshly washed fur—mostly they didn't own pets that couldn't later be eaten (like a chicken, a goat, or a lamb). So when my class adopted a guinea pig, I became fascinated with animals, wanted to learn more about them, wanted to have one of my own. Until my weekend came to actually take Oscar home with me, when that cute bit of fur turned into a screaming rat from hell. No one in the house had gotten any sleep that weekend, and when I took him back to school the following Monday morning, I'd also brought a note from my mother explaining that I was not to bring Oscar home again due to fear of disease and my grandmother's skill with a butcher knife.

So as I followed a girl named Heather and her neat white coat back to the holding pens at the shelter, I remembered all of this and wondered if Heather sometimes woke up in the middle of the night after having dreamed of a Great Dane extolling the many virtues of making your own dog food with the latest food processor.

"Let me see if I can remember where we put her."

She pushed open swinging double doors and I followed. "Her? I was told the dog was a male."

Heather gave me a wary look. "No. I told you she was a female."

"The terrier brought in last week was a female, but I very definitely remember you saying the one brought in a couple days ago was a male."

Heather gave a sigh that was usually given by women twice her age. I looked around at the myriad animals penned in cages: dogs barking, cats meowing, and one huge black pig I was not going to tell my grandmother about in case she came down and claimed it so it could decorate our table for Sunday dinner.

I decided Heather was allowed the sigh. I couldn't imagine being around so many orphaned animals, most of which would end up victims of euthanasia when they weren't claimed.

Bob Barker was suddenly my hero.

"She's . . . he's back here."

I narrowed my eyes at Heather, hoping she didn't think she was fooling me. I hadn't told her why I was interested in the Jack Russell terrier, but maybe she thought even if this dog wasn't the one I was looking for, I'd take her home anyway on account of her looking so much like mine.

I chewed on that. Seeing as Mrs. K's glasses were forty years out of date, maybe I could fool her into thinking a more docile version of Muffy the Mutt was actually her dog.

"Here she . . . he is."

We stopped in front of a cage in which the chain link reached to the ceiling even though the dogs within didn't even come to my knees. I stared at a dog that was close enough to Muffy to be his twin.

I crouched down. "Here Muffy, Muffy, Muffy," I said, even though the dog had never come when called in his life.

The scroungy animal stared at me, tongue lolling out of the side of its mouth, in dire need of a visit to his own personal doggie spa.

I stuck my hand through the fence. "Come here, boy . . ."

"I wouldn't do that if I were you—"

Heather's words came a dog bite too late. No sooner had I gotten my hand in to the wrist than the Muffy look-alike growled and fastened its sharp little teeth to the fleshy part of my hand.

"Yeow!" I pulled my hand free and shook it.

"That's going to leave a mark."

I wished a stain on Heather's neat coat even as she referred to the clipboard she held. "Yep. Like I said. A female."

I got to my feet. "You mean I got bit for nothing?"

Heather's expression looked a tad too amused and I pondered what it would take to shove her into one of the pens, leaving her to the mercy of the hungry animals.

"You'll need to get to a doctor and get a tetanus shot."

"No need. I got a shot when Muffy bit me three months ago."

The day before my wedding, right on the ankle. I should have taken it as a sign and canceled the wedding then.

"Sounds like the dogs have the same temperament. Want to take this one home?"

If I was going to try to foist a Muffy-like dog on Mrs. K it would be one that would roll over and whine when I gave it a dirty look.

Besides, I didn't think I could convince her Muffy had had a sex-change operation. "Better luck next time." I considered the damage to my hand. "Got a Band-Aid?"

I wasn't surprised when she took an array of Band-Aids from her right coat pocket.

"THANK GOD YOU'RE ALL RIGHT!"

As far as welcomes went, Rosie's ranked right up there with the best of them when I walked into the office an hour later.

Of course, it probably would have helped had she stuck around last night to make sure Romanoff's nephew hadn't had his vampire way with me, but hey, after the dog bite incident, I wasn't complaining.

Rosie looked a breath away from hugging me for all she was worth. Until she caught sight of the bandage on my hand.

"Oh my God, he bit you!" She backed away, her hands flattened against her chest. "Do you feel anything yet? Does the sun hurt? Do you have this incredible craving for blood?"

"No, but I do have an unusual craving for dog chow." I plopped down in my chair, thinking it was bad enough I had woken up this morning and run to the mirror to check my neck for any suspicious puncture marks. "I went to the shelter to look for the Hound from Hell and got bit by his evil twin sister."

"So that's a dog bite, then?" Rosie appeared unconvinced. And I couldn't blame her. Did vampire victims ever fess up to being bitten?

"Uh-huh. Seems the taste for Sofie flesh runs in the breed or something. Remind me never to own a terrier." I looked through the messages on my desk. "So what's going on?"

Rosie still looked dubious and I felt like sticking my fingers in my eyes until she went away. "The usual. Sent the servers out. Doing background checks."

"No new clients?"

"No. Why? You can't handle the ones we got." Rosie finally went back to her desk and I stuck my tongue out at her turned back.

"I saw that," she said.

"Saw what?"

"Whatever you did behind my back."

"So you didn't see it, then."

"But I know you did it and that's all that matters." She clacked away at her computer and popped her gum (I wondered if I should invest in a gum company). "By the way, I have to take off early. Lupe and I are going shopping for maternity clothes. She's already grown out of everything she has. You want I should make up a missing dog poster before I go?"

I stared at my own desk, feeling a little out of sorts. "Yeah. You still got the picture?"

"Yeah, I still got it. But I don't know how it'll come out in black and white."

"Can we do it in color?"

She gave me a long look. "Do you know how much color ink cartridges cost?"

"Do you know what my mother will do to me if I don't find this damn dog?"

Her mouth paused mid-chew. "Good point." She turned back to her screen. "By the way, my guy at the photo shop was able to salvage some of those shots from Kosmos' demolished camera."

I'd forgotten about the camera. "Was he able to fix it?"

She merely stared at me.

"Right."

I sifted through the items littering my desk. Some invoices to sign off on. A follow-up on a delinquent payment. Ah, yes, there they were. The pictures.

I picked them up and leafed through them. Considering what had happened, the shots were pretty clear.

What was also pretty clear was that the guy who had let Mrs. Suleski in and the guy in the morgue were two different people.

I looked through the photos again, trying to make out the ones I'd shot through the curtains before someone decided to shoot me back (okay, so I was pretty sure they hadn't been aiming at me, but that's my story and I'm sticking to it). The one of the door opening to let Mrs. Suleski in showed only a blond guy in a white shirt and khaki pants. His head was down, leaving his features in shadow.

I got up from my desk.

"Where you going?" Rosie asked without looking up.

"I think it's long past time I paid a visit to my client."

"Spyros is due to call at around one."

My uncle, the owner of the agency.

"Pull me in on conference."

"We tried that last time, remember? Didn't work on your cell."

"Okay, I'll make sure I'm back at one, then."

Rosie looked doubtful. I made a face and walked through the door, pictures tucked into my purse.

Eleven

BUD SULESKI'S AUTO SHOP RESEMBLED every other auto shop in the Queens area. Tucked between a gas station and a delicatessen, blink and you'd miss it if not for the cars parked out front . . . and the large FOR SALE sign blocking the Suleski part of SULESKI'S AUTO REPAIR.

I sat in my Mustang with the top down taking in the sign and the two open bays that showed some activity. The sun disappeared behind a mammoth gray cloud and I eyed the sky. It wouldn't dare rain on me again after all that I'd been through.

Would it?

I parked Lucille and put the top up. No sense taking chances, as my mother is fond of saying.

God, when had I taken to reciting my mother's sayings? Maybe it had something to do with my not hearing her say them twenty times a day now that I no longer lived at home. I didn't know. But it was for sure the first time I'd ever repeated anything Thalia Metropolis had said. And was more than a little cause for concern.

You see, growing up I wanted to be anyone but my mother. She was overbearing, nosy, and made my life a living hell in more ways than one. I'd always resolved that when I became a mother I would be more compassionate and trusting, and would encourage my children (the word made my eyes widen) to follow the path they wanted instead of the path I had mapped out for them.

The path my parents had mapped out for me the day I was born had been simple: work at the family restaurant until I got married, then have lots and lots of little Greek-American babies that would visit *Yiayia* and *Pappou*'s house often.

I found myself grinning. I liked that I'd not only jumped from that path, but that I was putting it farther behind me with every day that passed.

Now if I could only get my mother to stop trying to find me another groom, my life would be just about perfect.

Well, except for the missing, now found, dead guy and my client's missing wife.

Oh, and Muffy the Mutt.

Then there was the neighborhood vampire and his icky nephew.

And in case all that wasn't enough, I could swear I woke up this morning to the sound of my body humming. Humming. You know, like some kind of internal alarm clock had gone off denoting how many weeks had passed since I'd last had sex.

It hadn't helped when I'd figured out I'd been lying on my vibrating cell phone and that the caller was a wrong number.

I figured that at this point I was lucky not to have lost my mind, although even that might be up for debate.

I looked through the grimy shop window of the door marked OFFICE before opening it. The smell of oil and gasoline assaulted my nose. It reminded me of Porter. Then again, everything lately seemed to remind me of Porter.

"Hello? Anyone here?"

Nothing.

I looked around the dim waiting area. Six cracked pleather chairs sat against the wall, a dusty pre-remote television was in the corner, and magazines that looked like they were older than me sat on a low plastic crate. There was a rectangle cut into the right wall leading to the garage bays, and along the back wall was a glassed-in office I guessed would be Bud's. I went to it but found the door locked. I cupped my hands against the glass and looked inside. Nothing out of the ordinary. Just a desk, a few filing cabinets and different colored invoices strewn about.

"Hey, what do you want?"

The voice came from behind me and normally I probably would have jumped. But in the past few days I'd faced things far more in-timidating. A suspected vampire came to mind.

I turned to face what had to be a mechanic. He was wiping oil-covered hands on an equally oil-covered cloth.

"Sofie? Is that you?"

I blinked, trying to see the man underneath the oil.

"I'll be damned, it is you."

Even teeth that appeared whiter because of the darkness of his skin flashed at me.

"Jesus, I haven't seen you since my sister went off to that rinky-dink college in New Hampshire. And certainly not since you were on that stupid show drinking bug shakes."

I made a face, finally placing the guy. Joey DeMarco. I was friends with his sister Chris during high school. I used to go over to her house and sit at their kitchen island sighing over him, wondering what it would feel like to run my fingers through his perfectly feathered black hair, which is about all I used to see of him because he always seemed to have his back turned to me. I'd been infatuated with him for all of two seconds. Essentially the amount of time it took for me to walk by him while he had his head stuck in the refrigerator and get the stinging swat to the rear he'd obviously thought was sexy.

Judging by the way he was eyeing my breasts now, I guessed things hadn't changed much in the past nine years.

"Hey, Joey. How's Chris?"

He shrugged. "Okay. Married. One kid, another in the oven, if you know what I mean."

I did, and I didn't want to further pursue the issue, should the conversation circle back to my own disastrous wedding day. "Your boss around?"

"Bud? Nah. He hasn't been around for the past few days."

"Is that the norm?"

"Nope. But nothing has been normal around here for the past few days."

Ah, yes. Another thing I'd forgotten about Joey DeMarco was that he liked to gossip, if only because he thought it made him look knowledgeable.

Those who know less, speak more . . . and usually at length.

The saying my father muttered at the dinner table when we were younger came back to haunt me.

First sayings from my mother, now from my father.

Correction: I *have* officially lost my mind, along with everything and everyone else.

"Do tell," I said, crossing my arms to push up my breasts even further and smiling.

"Why you wanna know?"

Okay, maybe some things had changed.

I shrugged, making sure the move jiggled my breasts. Okay, so they weren't much, but even I could make the best out of a bad situation. "Let's just say Mrs. Suleski's a friend of mine."

Joey nodded his head even as his gaze stayed glued to my breasts.

I would have turned and offered him a view of my backside, but figured that would be too obvious, not to mention encouraging.

"Yeah, I could see where Mrs. S would be real upset right now. She about blew a gasket when she found out how much Bud owes the mob."

My brows shot up.

Things had to get better at some point, didn't they?

"The mob?"

Joey's smile widened. "Yep. You see, Bud's got a little prob with the cards, if you know what I mean."

Gambling.

"From what I've heard, not only is he in it for the shop, but the house is under, too."

Bud Suleski was due to lose his shop and his house and had hired me to follow his cheating wife around. A cheating wife who was now missing.

Interesting.

I jabbed a thumb over my shoulder at the locked office. "Any way I can get in there?"

"Depends."

"On what?"

"On what you're going to give me."

I always carried around a couple of crisp bills for just this occasion. I pulled out a twenty.

"I'm not talking about money."

Oh.

I twisted my lips. The problem with men like Joey isn't just that they don't get it, it's the way they go about getting it wrong. I mean, the guy could have had just about any girl he wanted if he went about it the right way. But no. He had to get down and dirty and ask me to flash my breasts at him or something.

A definite waste of good looks.

"Thanks, but no," I said, pocketing my twenty.

My palms itched with the need to get inside that office, but there had to be another, cleaner way. I discreetly eyed the door lock. Nothing more complicated than the lock that had been on the bathroom door growing up. And I'd learned how to pick that one when I was four. Of course, I'd only picked it once, got a full frontal of my grandmother as she was coming out of the shower, and never messed with the lock again.

I smiled at Joey. "I think I'll just wait around. You know, see if Bud stops by."

"He won't."

"You can't know that."

"Yes, I can 'cause he called this morning and said he wouldn't be in today."

"Yeah, well, people have been known to change their minds. I'll wait for a few minutes and see if he doesn't show anyway."

Joey planted his feet as if he had nothing more interesting to do than to stand there thinking of other ways he might get me to flash my breasts.

Whoever had made those *Girls Gone Wild* videos ought to be taken out back and shot.

"Tell me why you really want to see Bud," Joey said. He made a pumping motion with his closed fist and winked. "You getting a piece of the ole sausage?"

I made a face that left little doubt as to what I thought of the mere suggestion.

"On the other hand, maybe I should stop by the house, you know, see if he's there."

Another wink. "Better yet. There's a bed there and everything."

The mere suggestion that I would even consider having sex with Bud Suleski made me want to toss my cookies, preferably all over

Joey. Not that he'd notice, seeing how dirty he already was. He'd probably just wipe off the bigger chunks and go back to work.

I couldn't have moved out of there any faster.

Rosie. If anyone could distract Joey, it would be Rosie and her much more satisfying breasts. I could call and have her come over. Then again, no. Probably she'd knee Joey in the gonads and I'd be back right back where I'd started.

Vampires scared her, but very little else. Why Spyros didn't make her a full investigator stumped me.

Me, on the other hand . . . well, I guessed I should thank my lucky stars that I was related to Spyros or else I'd probably be back serving tables over at my dad's Metropolitan Restaurant in no time flat.

I SPENT AN HOUR THAT afternoon hanging posters of Muffy the Mutt on business windows up and down Broadway and 31st all the way up to Ditmars, hoping against hope that someone would contact the office posthaste. My mother was driving me insane, and I could virtually feel Mrs. K's scathing gaze on me every time I left my apartment building or went to my mother's. Probably she thought I was not finding her dog on purpose. Which wouldn't be too far from the truth except that I had a bite on my hand to prove that I'd done a few things. The poster bit would probably earn me some points, but not many. Like with missing persons, the more time that passed, the more unlikely it was that the person or pet would be found. Alive and recognizable, anyway.

During our last call my mother even had hinted that Mrs. K thought I might be responsible for the Hound from Hell's disappearance. Well, okay, she hadn't hinted, she'd come out and said it. It seems Mrs. K had spent the morning over at the house and the two women had brainstormed what could have happened and, my mom said, my name had come up just like that.

Okay, while I may have somewhat of a rep for getting into trouble now and again, never did the stories that evolved as a result include children or small animals. I prided myself on that, at least.

And now it looked like even that was going to be taken from me.

I spied a black pickup truck driving slowly by on 31st and openly watched it although it was a good block away. Ever since the day Porter had worked on Lucille I'd thought I'd spotted the same black truck nearly every time I went out. Of course, black trucks weren't exactly rare in the city, but knowing that Porter owned one made me a little more aware of how many there actually were.

At any rate, my visit to Suleski's house earlier hadn't been any more successful than my visit to his shop. There had been a Realtor's sign out front with an added PRICE REDUCED sign tagged on top of that one, but no one had answered when I knocked. So I backtracked to the office, picked up the posters, then went out to staple signs to poles and tape them inside the windows of cooperative businesses, usually Greek.

Of course, I missed my Uncle Spyros' phone call. I didn't much go in for pop psychology, but even I had to admit that I'd been reluctant to talk to my uncle. I mean, what did I have to tell him, anyway? That I had landed a cheating-spouse case that included vanishing and reappearing dead bodies, missing wives, the FBI, and the mob? If our roles were reversed, I'd have fired myself before the second comma was out.

Through luck or another swerve of chance I found myself just up the block from my grandfather's Cosmopolitan Café on Broadway (ignoring my father's Metropolitan Restaurant on the opposite corner). I thought I could get a fresh frappé and hang a couple of posters in his window, then give him the obit I'd come across on the old army buddy who'd stolen his medal.

There was a crack of thunder and I squinted at the sky. The meteorologists were calling this the stormiest June on record and I had to agree. I couldn't remember when we'd received so much rain in such a short period of time. Basements were flooding, storm drains were overflowing, and everyone seemed to be in a generally bad state of mind.

The threat of more rain along with the searing heat had chased the Cosmopolitan Café's customers from the outside tables to the inside. From what I could see, business was going like gangbusters. I opened the door and no sooner had it closed behind me than my grandfather was handing me an apron and an order pad and shoving me toward the tables.

"The new waitress called in sick. Fill in for her, will you, *koukla mou?*"

And just like that the past three months disappeared and I was again a waitress in a restaurant . . .

Twelve

"HEY, SOFIE, I'LL BE YOUR *groom.*"

"Hey, Sof, you aren't adding those worm shakes to the menu, are you?"

"Hey, Sofie, is it true you coldcocked the priest when he tried to talk you into going through with the wedding anyway?"

Within ten minutes of rushing around in my old waitress shoes, I realized that while I'd moved on, nobody else had. Probably because this was the first time I'd seen any of them since Thomas-the-Toad screwed more than my maid of honor and I'd spent my honeymoon trying to prove Lord only knows what.

From my grandfather's oldest friends who, without fail, occupied the three tables in the corner (when they weren't outside harassing innocent passersby in Greek), to the newer customers with whom I'd become acquainted in the months leading up to my wedding, I heard something from everyone, up to and including the staff.

I carried a tray full of coffee and water to a table, thinking that I'd done this to myself. Whatever sympathy I might have gained as a result of Thomas' pre-wedding chapel nookie I'd cashed in with my stupid stint on that reality show. Where I should have been re-ceiving sad headshakes and "that no good pig doesn't deserve you," instead I got "how could you drink that slime?"

I'd only been at the café for an hour and already my feet were be-ginning to ache.

Don't get me wrong. Waitressing is a good, solid job if you know how to do it right. If you smile and don't interrupt and spend more time attending to your customers than gossiping in the kitchen, you can pull in some pretty good tips. I'd just figured out I didn't want to make a career out of it. Sometimes I caught myself watching Ingrid, who was as old as dry dirt and just as cracked, and saw myself thirty years from now, still waiting tables for my grandfather or father.

I shuddered so hard I nearly spilled the coffee I was putting in front of one of my grandfather's oldest friends.

"Out of practice already, Sof?" Aggelos asked, using his napkin to soak up the overage that had dripped into his saucer.

I smiled. "I guess so. Sorry. Here, let me get you a fresh coffee."

He immediately put his hand over his cup. "Don't mess with my karma."

Greeks had strange beliefs. One of the thousands of them was that if a beverage meant for you spilled over while being served, money was coming your way. Of course, it didn't matter that the guy in question owned a string of convenience stores and had cold, hard cash rolling in in waves. I'd probably just made his entire day because I'd nearly spilled his coffee.

A Greek restaurant was probably the only place you could almost spill coffee on someone and be rewarded for it.

A short while later the afternoon crowd finally thinned out. I was writing out the check for my last table when Grandpa Kosmos motioned for me to join him at the end of the main bar. I slid the check onto the table under a coffee cup and wished my customers a good day before taking the stool next to my grandfather.

"You do know I have a real job, don't you?" I asked.

"Bah." He grinned at me, then patted my arm. "Real. What can be more real than feeding people?"

"Feeding myself?"

He looked affronted. "What? You don't make enough here to feed yourself? You probably make more here than at Spyros' poor excuse for a business."

My uncle Spyros had broken some unwritten Greek rule by not going into the restaurant/café/club/travel-agency business. While there were a few others who had done so, and successfully at that—my Aunt Sotiria, Kosmos' daughter, came to mind—Uncle Spyros was looked upon as the black sheep of the family because of his two marriages to and then divorces from two American women.

Of course, my father's owning a restaurant didn't earn him any points with my grandfather, but that was another story altogether.

"Uncle Spyros does very good business."

My grandfather dismissed this with a familiar wave of his hand. "Taking pictures of people through windows is no way to make a living."

"It is if the people are doing wrong."

"What are you, *o Theos*?"

I grinned at his asking if I was God.

"Oh. I forgot." He waggled his thick index finger at me. "You know, you've got to get over that. After all, men will be men."

I was filled with the incredible urge to smack my forehead against the bar, if for no other reason than to remind myself that my grandfather had no idea what it meant for a woman to be a woman.

"Anyway, I didn't come here to defend my job, or Uncle Spyros, or even to wait tables." I put my tips in that tip jar, removed the apron, then folded it and put it on the bar. "I came to give you this."

I put a copy of the obit on the counter. He picked it up.

"Do you want me to contact the widow?"

"Let me think on it and I'll let you know." He wasn't meeting my gaze and I knew whenever any of my family members didn't meet my gaze, it meant they knew something they weren't sharing. Like my groom's extracurricular activities before my wedding day.

He pocketed the obit.

"You know that guy down there?" he asked me.

"Don't try to distract me."

"I'm not trying to distract you. I'm thinking to kick him out if you don't know him. He's been watching you for the past half hour."

I rolled my eyes and looked down the bar, expecting to find my grandfather gone by the time I turned back. Instead I did a double take. Not only did I know the guy at the end of the bar, but I wished he was on my own personal menu.

Jake Porter.

TEN MINUTES LATER I WAS still in the ladies' room staring at my pitiful reflection and wishing I at least had some eyeliner with me. But, stupid me, I hadn't thought to take my purse when I left the office, since all I was going to be doing was hanging Muffy the Mutt posters.

I considered asking Ingrid if I could borrow some of her makeup, then remembered hearing somewhere that you could get Hepatitis B from using someone's lipstick and decided against it.

Reconciling myself to the fact that I could do no more to improve my appearance, I sighed and pulled open the bathroom door. There Porter was, still at the end of the bar. Only he was no longer alone. My grandfather flanked one side of him while the biggest gossip alive, Takis Voskopoulos, sat on his other side, his mouth moving a million miles a minute.

Oh, shit.

In ten minutes flat Takis could have told Porter my entire life story, up to and including the worm-shake incident.

I hurried across the room and made no attempt to hide my irritation. "Don't you two have anything better to do?" I asked Kosmos and Takis.

"Bah," Takis said, not missing a beat as he continued telling Porter God only knew what. "Then she—"

I forcibly swung his chair around. "I'd like a moment alone with Mr. Porter if you don't mind?"

Grandpa Kosmos raised his hands in surrender, a grin on his craggy face. "Just making a new customer feel welcome."

"Mmm."

I wasn't sure if my response came out as a hum or a growl, but it was too late to take it back. At least it made them move away.

How was it that Porter could grin at me with his eyes without cracking a smile?

I took the stool my grandfather had vacated.

"I like him. Your grandfather, I mean."

"What are you doing here?"

"Following you, of course."

I stared at him so hard I was surprised my eyes didn't fall straight out of my head. "Why would you, um, want to do that?"

"Because I'm worried about you."

Every last fantasy response pitched straight to the faux marble floor.

He couldn't have said something along the lines of "I've been thinking about you and decided I couldn't go one more minute without asking you out" could he? No. Instead he'd said . . .

He was worried about me?

Okay, on a scale from one to ten, that rated about a five. It wasn't "I can't wait to get you back to my place where I can lick you all over," but it wasn't chopped liver either.

All things considered, I wished he wanted to lick me.

"Why would you be worried about me?"

His eyes narrowed the slightest bit, although the smile didn't leave them. "Let's just say there are one or two people interested in your whereabouts right now."

"Why would anyone care where I am?"

Then I remembered the FBI and my throat closed. I cleared it.

What was the penalty for lying to a federal agent, then running? I wasn't sure, but I did know I had absolutely zero interest in personally finding out.

"Did you really drink worm shakes?"

I cringed and motioned for the barkeep to bring me a frappé. "And Takis wonders why the Greeks are no longer a major shipping power."

"I'm not following you, luv."

Luv. I shivered all over, the word standing in quite well for his tongue against my skin. "You know the saying: Loose lips sink ships? Well they don't come any looser than Takis'."

Porter laughed. A genuine sound that made my chest tighten and heat dive straight for my delicates.

I don't think I'd actually heard him laugh before. Chuckle, maybe. Definitely. But not laugh like he hadn't been able to help himself.

I looked at him through this new filter and saw that he looked even more appealing to me. Which wasn't good. I didn't want appealing, I merely wanted sexy. As in "my bed or yours?" I didn't want a relationship, and if Porter and I didn't end up in bed together posthaste, that's what I was afraid might develop. Well, maybe not so much a full-blown relationship as a one-sided relationship with me being the one building castles in the sky and scheduling our honeymoon to Sydney.

When it came to guys, one thing was guaranteed. If you slept with them early on, they immediately crossed you off their short-list. It was the mistake, I realized, I'd made with Thomas-the-Toad. I'd made him wait an entire month and seven dates before he even got to third base with me. I should have slept with him on the first date.

Of course, later I'd learned he'd hit grand-slam home runs with at least three other girls during that same time, so that stole some of the wind out of my sails.

Some? Hell, it sank my boat altogether.

But there you had it. The old double standard. The women you sleep with are not the women you marry. Or something like that.

Maybe my mother was right. Maybe I should have my hymen replaced.

I made a face. What was I talking about? I didn't want to marry anyone. I wanted to sleep with Porter.

Big difference.

Now I just had to convince him he wanted to sleep with me.

I smiled at him.

He narrowed his eyes at me.

"Now that's a look a guy doesn't see every day."

"I find that hard to believe of you."

He grinned. "It's a figure of speech."

"Ah. Meaning you don't get to see it as much as you like, then."

"Meaning I don't get it from women I want to get it from as often as I'd like."

Whatever expression I was wearing vanished as I tried to figure that one out. Was he saying he didn't want that look from me? Or that he'd wanted it and was only now getting it?

I pressed my palms against my temples, then rested my elbows against the bar. "It's been a long day."

"Let me take you home, then."

Oh, boy.

My aforementioned delicates were in full agreement with that suggestion.

And you couldn't have gotten me out of the café faster.

Black pickup.

I suppressed the desire to punch my fist in the air as I climbed into the familiar truck. He *had* been following me. And although his reasons inspired more than a bit of fear about who might also be on my heels, it also allowed me some fantasy wiggle room. I mean, who would know if I imagined sexy Jake Porter following me around because he wanted me so bad he couldn't help himself and he was using his concern as an excuse?

I settled back in the seat, pleased with myself.

Until he pulled up in front of my apartment building a couple blocks later.

He reached across my lap and opened the door.

"This is where I say goodnight."

I blinked at him. "Upstairs might be better." Tomorrow morning, maybe? But then it would be way past night and would be "good morning"—and I expected it would be very, very good.

"You don't want me to come up."

"I don't?"

"Uh-uh." He shook his head.

I swallowed hard, and the click was loud in the truck cab.

Okay, maybe I didn't. Maybe I was just convincing myself I wanted him to come up and I really didn't.

No. I wanted him to come up.

But I got the feeling that, short of throwing myself at him, I wasn't going to get my wish.

"All right then. Goodnight."

I was just about to turn from him when he grasped my chin in his large hand and held my head still. I watched as his pupils nearly took over the dark blue of his eyes, then he drew closer. I licked my lips in preparation . . . and he kissed my cheek.

My *brother* kissed me on the cheek.

He started to draw back, amusement clear on his face.

"I think we'd better try that again," I said.

Then I did what I promised myself I wouldn't: I threw myself at him.

Thirteen

JAKE PORTER TASTED LIKE COFFEE and cream and I couldn't seem to get enough of him.

I pressed my palms against his cheeks and held him still as I launched a no-holds-barred assault on his mouth. I flicked my tongue out and ran it across his lips then went in for a more thorough investigation.

A part of me wished there was something there I could criticize, but an even bigger part was glad that kissing him made my panties feel tight.

It had been a long, long time since a simple kiss had done it for me. But as I tilted my head and went in for more, I felt like I could kiss him for hours. Just kiss him.

When I heard my own breathing grow ragged, I pulled back and smacked my lips.

"That's much more like it," I said.

Then I bounced back over the seat and climbed out of the truck.

At the top of the stairs leading to my building I turned to find him staring after me, absently running his wrist against his chin. My adrenaline level shot up another notch. But despite how tempting it was to crook my finger at him and invite him up to my place yet again, I forced myself to turn and enter my building without another glance.

I was desperate, but I had no intention of looking any more desperate than I already did.

TWO FLIGHTS OF STAIRS LATER I closed my apartment door and leaned against it, listening to the uneven beat of my heart. I'd always had a reputation for taking what I wanted, when I wanted it when it came to men, but at some point over the past three months I'd lost that edge, my no-fear-and-no-regrets motto melting away at the sight of my groom taking conjugal privileges with my maid of honor. I'd retreated into some sort of emotional cave, daring only to peek out when an extraordinarily sexy pair of buns presented themselves for inspection. But rather than giving in to the itching-palm urge to touch those buns, I had instead retreated back into my cave, finding the place dark and confining but safe.

Now, with one simple kiss, I'd not only popped out from that cave but was so far away from it I wasn't sure I could find my way back. Which was a good thing, no? I mean, caves weren't healthy places for anyone to hang out. And I sure wasn't used to the dark, fearful depths. When there's no light, every sound is cause for alarm.

Speaking of light, enough still streamed through the window—however gray—for me to see. I glanced at my watch, fully expecting the day to have passed. It hadn't. Not yet. It was only eight o'clock. The most difficult hours still lay ahead of me.

I opened the door and stepped across the hall and knocked on Mrs. Nebitz's door. I wasn't sure what I wanted besides company, to verify I was awake and by extension that what had happened had.

No answer.

I frowned and pressed my ear against the wood. No usual sound of the television.

The door opened and I looked to find her smiling up at me, the scent of lilac powder overpowering.

"Oh! It's you, Sofie. I thought it might be my grandson Seth. He's taking me out tonight to Fine and Schapiro."

Mrs. Nebitz had a date. Granted, it was with her grandson, but she was going out.

"That's nice," I said. "I just stopped to thank you again for the *kugel.*"

It probably would have been a good idea if I had had her plate, but it still sat inside my sink waiting to be washed.

She took me in. "Would you like to come with us?"

"No. No thank you. I have a date with the bathtub and a book tonight."

Her expression of . . . was that pity? Yes, that was definitely pity. Anyway, it was a little much for me to take just then.

It bothered me to realize that even Mrs. Nebitz, as cut off as she appeared to be from the rest of the world, not only knew my past, but what I did with my present.

"You have a nice time," I told her, then slinked back through my door and closed it.

Great. Mrs. Nebitz pitied me. Me. Sofie Metropolis, worm-shake drinker.

Ugh.

I fished my cell phone out of my pocket. My mother had called no fewer than five times while I was helping out at Grandpa Kosmos'. I hit the return call button and listened as the phone rang and rang. I stared at the display. The right number. But it couldn't be. My mom was always home. And if she wasn't my grandmother was.

I hit redial and got the same results.

I called my sister Efi's cell.

"Hey," she said four rings later.

"Where is everybody?"

"Define everybody."

"Mom, Grandma . . ."

"It's Calliope's name day. They went over for a visit."

Ah, yes. The Greeks and their name days.

While birthdays were celebrated to some degree, among the Greeks who had come directly from Greece—such as my parents—name days still ruled. Essentially all Greek names could be traced back to a Greek Orthodox saint's name (we have a lot of saints). So when the day of the saint you were named after rolled around, you celebrated with at the very least sweets and often times with dinner and drink. So that meant everyone with the name Yianni, aka John, celebrated on the same day. Knew someone named Yianni, even distantly? If you saw them on their name day you wished them *Chronia Polla*, which literally means "many years" but is pretty much the Greek catch-all for all occasions, said on Christmas and New Year's and Easter as well.

Birthdays were celebrated by the immediate family.

Name days were celebrated by everyone.

One of my non-Greek friends once joked that the Greeks seemed to be constantly celebrating something. I remember telling her that yeah, we celebrated life.

Right now I wasn't feeling in a very celebratory mood, however.

"Where are you?" I asked Efi.

"Working."

Which meant waitressing at my father's restaurant.

"After, I'm heading over to Calliope's."

Of course.

"You should go."

Actually I was a little put out that my mother hadn't bothered me about going. Hadn't started from last week talking about the family visit and pestering me about what I should wear.

Had she said anything? I was pretty sure she hadn't. Which left me scratching my head.

"Naw. Actually, I have other plans."

I could virtually hear Efi's skepticism, although she said nothing.

"Talk to you later."

"Bye."

I closed my cell and tossed it to the couch, deciding to go ahead and have that bath and read that book.

I thumbed through my collection of hardcovers and settled on one of Janet Evanovich's earlier Plum novels, one of my all-time faves, and headed for the bathroom.

THE ADVANTAGE OF LIVING ALONE is that you don't have anyone around to bother you. The problem with living alone is, well, that you don't have anyone around to bother you.

An hour later I was squeaky clean and smelled of peaches . . . and I was ready to jump out of my skin. Nothing was on television but reruns and I didn't know if I felt all that good knowing that I'd already seen all the shows on their first run, and in a few cases second and third as well. I'd demolished most of the contents of the fridge except for a leftover knish Mrs. Nebitz had given me last week that was going untouched because, well, she'd given it to me last week. Instead of cleaning my new rug myself, I'd taken it into Pappas' Dry Cleaners to have it deloused, and it now sat back in the living room looking much the worse for wear. I spotted something on the corner and moved closer. What was that? A round mark about an inch in diameter stared back up at me. I bent over, rubbed it, and looked at my hand to find it had transferred to my skin.

Great. The dyes were running.

I rinsed my hand off and glanced out the window at where the last of the dim day was fading away. Nine o'clock and all was not well.

I headed toward the door. Sometimes a long ride in Lucille helped relax me. But not even that appealed to me now. Instead I headed up the stairs to the roof.

I stepped to the edge and took a deep breath of the pregnant air. New York rooftops are the most overlooked attraction in the city, in my humble opinion. Long slabs of undeveloped blacktop that get noticed only when repairs are necessary or if satellite dishes need to be repositioned. But as for me . . . this was my favorite spot in the whole building, up here on the roof. I glanced in the direction of my parents' house. The roof had been too slanty to go up on, but I had tried once when I was ten, and had snapped my ulna in two as a result of my efforts.

But here . . .

I squinted around in the waning light. Small puddles from the rain earlier had collected, but the spot I stood in was dry.

The first time I'd come up was the day of my wedding—when I should have been in the honeymoon suite in the famous Waldorf-Astoria—and the view had managed to soothe me in a way no words from anyone could have. I'd watched as one after another of the members of my well-intentioned family had come over, and I'd sat up here and watched each of them go without knowing where I was. I'd justified my isolation with the thought that I wasn't really home, since I wasn't in my apartment.

And there I had sat in the chilly March air, in my wedding dress, my winter coat and a blanket, not caring that the wind chafed my cheeks and whipped at my hair. Not caring that I'd lost feeling in my hands after the first hour. I just sat there and sat there. Until the next-door neighbor had climbed up to his roof and asked if I was all right.

I looked over. Sloane's chair was empty. Probably even he had plans tonight.

Somehow the city looked both bigger and smaller from up here. Small enough to make you wonder how so many people lived together in such a small place without killing each other. Big enough to force you outside your everyday box and consider the forest instead of just the trees.

A raindrop landed on my forehead. I wiped it away, and while I was there, wiped away another one that landed on my ear. I stared up at the angry dark clouds, exasperated that even this little respite was going to be taken away from me. I sighed, thinking that maybe I could use the time to put together some things to bring up here from my apartment when the storms finally passed and summer officially set in. Something to sit on, maybe. A small table where I could put my frappé. A portable radio.

The raindrops were coming down faster now and in the distance lightning flashed brightly enough to finally chase me down from the roof and back into my apartment. The instant I was inside I heard something thump to the floor and realized it was my vibrating cell phone.

I picked it up and stared at the display. *The Toad* was written across the screen.

Why I'd even kept his number in my address book was a bit of a mystery. By all rights, I should have deleted it just as I had deleted him from my life. But I rationalized that it would help to know if it was him should he ever call.

And he was calling.

I reached to put the phone down, then swallowed and answered it, at this point desperate enough to somewhat welcome even a phone call from my maggot of an ex.

"Sof? Is that you?" he said in a low, familiar voice.

"What, did you dial the wrong number?" I was mildly surprised he still had me in his phone book, considering the well-placed kick I'd given him after he'd put his pants back on at the church. Let's just say his future bride should be worried about his ability to have kids.

He chuckled softly. "No. I meant to call you."

I rounded the couch and sat down on the arm, switching the phone to the other ear.

It was strange, somehow, talking to Thomas. The day of our wedding seemed like eons ago, yet just like yesterday.

"So . . . how are you doing?" he asked.

I made a face. "Fine. You?"

"Fine."

Well, that was nice. I'd hoped he was going to say something along the lines of he'd caught a raging case of syphilis and had to have his member amputated.

Okay, maybe that wasn't entirely fair.

Or maybe it was.

Considering my current mood, I couldn't decide.

"Look, I've been meaning to call you . . ."

I squinted at nothing in particular. "Oh?"

"Yeah. There are a few things I need to say."

Was he calling to apologize?

I rolled the possibility around in my mind, trying to decide where to put it. I wasn't sure I was ready to forgive him yet. My feelings were too raw, too close to the surface.

Besides, I was using the anger the memory still generated to motivate many of my actions. Like that of being a PI.

"I wonder when we might arrange a meeting."

I squinted to the point where I couldn't see. "A meeting?"

He cleared his throat. "Yes. So you can give me back my ring."

Fourteen

GIVE . . . HIM . . . BACK . . . HIS . . . RING.

And here I'd thought he'd called to apologize.

Ha.

I wasn't sure who was the bigger fool, he or I.

Then it occurred to me that the reason my garbage disposal didn't work was that the ring in question was probably jammed in the mechanism. With my luck, it would probably be minus the two-carat marquise-cut diamond.

"My attorney says that since you broke off the engagement, I'm entitled to get it back."

I did an impression of a wide-mouth bass caught out of water. "I broke the engagement because you were doing more than showing Little Thomas to my maid of honor. Five minutes before we were supposed to get married. In the *church*."

"My attorney says that doesn't matter."

"Then your attorney needs to go get his head examined."

"It's my cousin Nino."

"All the more reason for him to seek professional help. The sooner the better."

"He thinks we have a strong case if I decide to sue."

I slid down from the sofa arm to the sofa proper, mulling over words I'd always wanted to say without sounding like a cliché. "So sue me."

I stared at the display and took a certain satisfaction in depressing the disconnect button. Then I turned off the phone and tossed it to the love seat across the way.

What was this? Pick on Sofie Metropolis Year? They should have had signs made up. And have thrown a parade. No celebration is complete without a parade. You know, in case someone out there was holding a grudge and wanted to get a kick or two of their own in.

I sat staring at nothing and thinking about everything for a long time. How long, I couldn't be sure. But I started coming to from my shock-induced conscious coma to hear the strains of someone's stereo in the building. Was that the big-butt song? "Baby's Got Back"? I sank farther into the cushions and groaned. Must be the DeVry students. I peeled myself off the couch and stepped to my own stereo, sifting through my CDs until I came across a Greek one I hadn't listened to in a while by an artist named Antonis Remos. I slid it in, caught the opening notes of a love song, then quickly hit the EJECT button. I exchanged the CD for vintage Heart, then adjusted the volume so it was high enough to drown out the other stereo, but not high enough for anyone to complain (although I figured that as owner of the building, I should be entitled to a few liberties every now and again).

I threw open the refrigerator door so that it slammed against the wall, then stood staring at the contents even though I'd officially eaten everything in it an hour or two earlier. Everything but the knish still on Mrs. Nebitz's plate on the top shelf.

It wasn't long ago that I would have dressed to the nines and gone out to the Zodiac or Caprice on a night like this. The walls of the Greek clubs would be thumping with the sounds of bouzouki guitars and drums, the dance floor teeming with both people I knew and didn't know doing sexy Greek dances and drinking ouzo and apple martinis. Offering me a temporary, happy escape from the stresses of the day.

But strangely enough, now that I had real problems to deal with, the clubs didn't interest me.

Either that or I was afraid of running into Thomas and his friends there. Which was probably more the case, but I didn't want to think about that right now.

Instead, I spotted a bottle of champagne that had been intended for my wedding reception. I'd put it in to chill a week or so ago and had forgotten about it. Hauling it out, it took me a good ten minutes, a kitchen knife, and a towel to get it open—I'd always been clumsy with this sort of thing. I held the bottle over the sink, watching as bubbles boiled over and down the drain where I suspected my engagement ring was stuck. The same engagement ring Thomas was threatening to sue me for.

I took long, deep gulps from the bottle, immediately regretting the move when bubbles filled my nose and champagne head kicked in. I'd never been much of a drinker outside of the retsina wine Mom served with dinner every Sunday. The mere smell of alcohol made me high. A beer here and there, with a long time between the here and the there, was about as far as I ever went. When I was a teen and all my friends were drinking to the point of alcohol poisoning, I think I was too afraid of what my parents might do if I got caught—and I always got caught. Probably they would have locked me in my bedroom until I turned eighteen, or worse, sent me to Greece and married me off to the hairiest, oldest Greek bachelor goat herder available, probably a fifth cousin three times removed so the chance of our kids coming out normal would be pretty good.

I toasted the bizarre twists and turns of my life and took another deep gulp.

There were other things I could do instead of getting stinking drunk. I thought about going into the office where I might be able to follow up on a few things, even considered stopping by Suleski's house to see if I couldn't find out what was going on, but in the end I stood in the doorway to my bedroom and forced myself to look at what I spent much of my time ignoring, champagne bottle tightly in hand.

Oh sure, I slept in my bedroom every night. In the handsome king-size sleigh bed that had been a wedding gift from Aunt Sotiria. But I usually relied on the hall light to light my way rather than switch on the lamps in the room, because to do that would show more than the bed.

I'd offered Aunt Sotiria the bed back but she'd refused, saying she couldn't do anything with it since it was special ordered (rumor was she had had one of her casket suppliers make it). But the still-wrapped gifts that were piled up in the opposite corner of the room from floor to ceiling I had no intention of returning. Mainly because they'd come from Thomas-the-Toad's side of the family, and right now I didn't like any of them very much. Forget that his parents had threatened to sue my parents for half the value of the building I stood in and even now held me responsible for the interruption of the wedding. (I flashed on an image of me dragging my groom to the altar while he was still zipping up his pants and my maid of honor was pushing up her breasts in her wrinkled dress.) I'd gotten nasty letters and phone calls and even one death threat from Thomas' favorite aunt, who could probably do some real damage with her forty-year-old Olds if I ever came across her on the road.

So I kept their gifts. And every now and again I opened one or two that looked interesting.

I took another slug from the bottle, put it down on the dresser, then took an old T-shirt out of a drawer and put it under the bottle so there wouldn't be a moisture ring on the gleaming cherry wood.

I stood in front of the tower of gifts and tapped my finger against my lips. I gave a disgusting hiccup and wondered if maybe I hadn't stacked the boxes right, because they appeared ready to drop on me. Probably the champagne. I swayed. Very definitely the champagne. Maybe I'd been missing out on something all these years of not drinking. I no longer felt alone or lonely or unwanted or betrayed. I merely felt . . . happy. Okay, maybe not happy. Happily fuzzy was closer to the mark.

I chose one of the larger gifts near the bottom of the pile, wrapped in silver paper with wedding bells all over it, and started shifting it out from under the rest. This time I was pretty sure the tower was actually swaying, and I put a hand up to steady the rest as I worked out the one I wanted. Finally I accomplished my goal and hoisted the sucker to the middle of the bed. The white bow was smashed and the paper torn in a couple of spots. I turned back toward the tower. Two. I'd open two tonight. If I didn't like them, I could give them to Mrs. Nebitz, whose collection should be coming along quite nicely, or maybe Rosie this time. I chose a smaller box about the size of a large shoebox, covered in shiny red paper with a gold ribbon. I put it next to the other, mammoth one, then climbed onto the bed. I set the champagne within reach on the nightstand and slowly began opening the ribbon on the larger gift.

I think all little girls dream of their wedding, that one day when for a few hours they'll get to be a princess marrying a prince. Even though I'd always been pretty much a tomboy, even I had allowed myself that dream. I'd spent long hours with my friends when I was thirteen snipping pictures out of bridal magazines and planning what the DJ would play at the reception. I'd cut out snapshots of dark-haired grooms and snipped out their features, the image of my dream groom yet to be fulfilled.

Just thinking about all that made me feel sick to my stomach. In my humble opinion, every last Cinderella story and bridal magazine should be gathered together and burned in the town square. What b.s. it all was.

I tugged harder on the ribbon but it refused to fall away. I realized it was because someone had knotted it. I opened the small card attached. From Thomas' brother and his wife. Figures. I could see George and Eva taking great joy in making the gift as hard to open as possible.

I considered trying to untangle the knot, then instead retrieved the same kitchen knife I'd used to open the champagne bottle. I cut the ribbon, tore the paper away from the plain cardboard box, and found I needed the knife again to cut through the layers of box tape. Geez. Whatever was in here had better be worth the trouble.

Finally I tore open the flaps and stared down into a snowbank of peanuts. I debated the wisdom of blindly putting my hand in there and feeling around. It was said that Thomas' sister-in-law was an amateur witch, and she'd once read my coffee (a modern take on reading tea leaves). I wouldn't have been surprised if Eva had known what was going to happen on my wedding day and had chosen her gift accordingly. Of course, it didn't take a psychic to know that given the extent of Thomas' extracurricular activities, odds were pretty good I might find out before the ceremony. Only I don't think many would have guessed I'd find out five minutes before.

Taking another gulp of champagne, I stuck my hand into the

bits of Styrofoam, having to do some considerable fishing around until I finally found something that wasn't shaped like a peanut. I put my fingers around it and tugged, littering the bed with snow. I stared at the item in my hand. A pair of oven mitts and matching kitchen towels.

Oven mitts and fucking towels.

I wished Eva or George, or even Thomas himself, were there, so I could bat them about the ears with the cheap gift.

I sighed. I couldn't even give these to Rosie, 'cause she'd likely bat me about the ears with them.

I tossed the items back into the box and kicked it until the box dropped over the side and onto the floor. That was one I could happily send back.

Well, that was anticlimactic, wasn't it? Much like my entire wedding experience itself.

I picked up the other, smaller box and shook it close to my ear. I was fairly certain it didn't hold oven mitts. It was heavier than that. I checked the card. It was from Thomas' sister Roula.

I knew a moment of sobriety.

I'd liked Roula. Out of all of them, Thomas included, Roula was the one I would miss most from the Chalikis family. She and I shared more than our ages. We'd seemed to see eye to eye on almost everything.

She'd been the only one to curse her own brother when she'd hugged me goodbye. Including my own family.

I took special care in opening this gift. I knew it was meant for both me and Thomas, but Roula deserved at least that much consideration if only because she would have given me the same.

I thought I heard a sound in the other room. I craned my neck and listened. Probably the storm, blowing the curtains against the window.

I returned my attention to the box. Cradled in a nest of tissue paper was a heart-shaped pillow in pink and white satin. Embroidered on the cover was *Now we're really sisters*.

I stared at the neatly sewn words so hard they grew blurry. Either that or I was crying.

I knew Roula had made the pillow and that made the gift that much more thoughtful. Through what I now knew were tears, I caught sight of something else. I reached into the box and took out a hot red teddy. "For heating up cool nights," a tag read. Under that was a neatly handwritten card: "For even cooler nights when only the warmth of friendship will do"—and her phone number.

I pressed the pillow against my chest and allowed myself the brief luxury of a cry even though I was mildly surprised I had any tears left.

I should have made Roula my maid of honor. If I had, maybe none of this would have happened. Maybe Thomas would have kept his pants on, we'd even now be married, and maybe like my grandfather claimed Thomas would have changed his ways the instant we became man and wife.

What a woman was willing to sacrifice for a good sister-in-law.

I carefully placed the heart-shaped pillow against my bed pillows, even though the pink clashed with the green jacquard shams. It was only ten-thirty. I could call Roula. See if we couldn't keep what we'd had even though her brother and me were no more.

I looked around for my cell phone, then remembered I'd left it out in the living room.

I pushed up from the gigantic bed made for five. Yes, I'd call Roula. Thank her for the gift. Arrange maybe to go out to lunch or something.

I padded into the hall, realizing as I went that where usually the lights in the rest of the apartment were on and the bedroom lamps off, now it was the opposite.

Funny, I didn't remember shutting off the lights . . .

I reached for the switch and flicked it up and down with no re-
sults. Had the storm knocked out the power? I looked behind me.
The bedroom lights still shone brightly and the CD was still playing.
Strange . . .

I wondered how quickly I could get to the front hall, to my purse
and the can of professional-grade mace it held. But no sooner had
I taken two steps than I found myself mouth to carpet with my
new area rug. Another hit to the back of the head and I was aware
of nothing at all . . .

Fifteen

WHAT TIME WAS IT? AND what the hell was all that banging? They couldn't possibly be doing roadwork at this ungodly hour of the morning.

The problem was that the jackhammer wasn't on the street outside but instead felt like it was trying to crack my skull in two.

I blinked. What was that? Why did it look like I was lying on my new rug instead of in my perfectly good bed?

Then it hit me. Or rather, the fact that someone had hit me, hit me.

I tried to scramble to my feet but the floor pitched under me, sending me headfirst into the Barcalounger. Ow. I put my hand to my head, trying to hold in the gray matter that felt like it was about to explode all over my rug at any second. I'd never really had a hangover. Was this what one felt like? Of course, the hits I'd taken probably weren't helping matters either.

Pounding. And this time I was sure it was coming from outside my head instead of inside.

I stumbled to the door and opened it.

"Jesus, Joseph, and Mary, girl, where have you been?" Rosie burst in and slammed the door behind her. "I've been calling you all morning." She took in my appearance and the way I held my head. "You look like shit."

"Thanks." I stumbled into the kitchen, filled a dishcloth with ice, and held it to my forehead.

"Are you bleeding? Holy shit, you're bleeding."

I stepped to a nearby mirror and stared at my right cheek. I rubbed it with my free hand. Dye. My new rug had run on me.

"Settle down. It's not blood," I told Rosie, flinching with every word I said.

"God, girl, you look like you got run over by the train."

Funny, that's exactly the way I felt.

"You'd better sit down before you fall down."

I agreed and slowly, ever so slowly, to keep from jarring my brain any farther, sank into the couch.

"You need to take some aspirins or something."

I'd always thought "aspirin" was both singular and plural. But hey, I'd been wrong about a lot of things lately. Like last night, thinking the sound I'd heard had been the storm, when it had been somebody in my apartment.

Keeping the ice to my head, I looked around without moving anything more than my eyes. Nothing was out of place. And despite the way it felt, my head had not been hit by one of my lamps. Everything was still in its place, unbroken.

I shakily got back up and looked around. Nothing gone from my drawers, although they'd obviously been gone through. Strange. Who would go to the trouble to break in and then not take anything? I opened the refrigerator door. Mrs. Nebitz's knish was gone, the empty plate still sitting there.

"I didn't find any aspirins, but these should do. I got some stuff with codeine at the office."

I didn't want to know where Rosie had gotten pills with codeine in them. "Did you eat the knish?"

She drew her head back like a duck. "What?"

I closed the refrigerator door. "Never mind."

"I think you need to sit down again."

"I think I do, too."

This time I sank into one of the kitchen chairs instead of walking all the way back to the living room. I switched hands holding the ice on account of my right one going numb, then accepted the pills Rosie offered along with a glass of water.

"Midol?"

Rosie grimaced, an action that shouldn't have made her dimples pop but did. "That's all I could find. You needa go shoppin' or something."

"You don't have anything in your purse?"

I reached for the object in question, a Gucci knockoff.

"No, I don't." She jerked away the bag while I was in the process of opening it and out popped at least ten bulbs of garlic.

I blinked, sure I was seeing things.

Rosie hurried to put the garlic back inside her purse.

"That's not . . ."

"Uh-huh, it is, too." She put the purse strap over her shoulder. "I know you don't believe in all this vampire stuff, but I'm telling you there were at least two of 'em flapping their bat wings outside my bedroom window last night. The only thing saved me was this garlic and"—she pulled what had to be ten crosses of different sizes, shapes, and metal contents out of the neck of her tight black shirt—"these."

I gave an eye roll that sent searing pain over my scalp. "Rosie, there are no such things as vampires."

"I knew you'd say that but I brought you this anyway."

She held out what looked like a small perfume bottle. I stared at the J.Lo emblem on the front. "How is perfume going to help me?"

"It's not perfume, it's holy water." This last part she had to bend toward me and whisper, but for the life of me I couldn't figure out why. Maybe anything that held the word "holy" in it had to be said with reverence no matter how ridiculous the sentence. "I had the priest bless it this morning." She shrugged. "He said it didn't matter what bottle it was in and said the sprayer might be more accurate anyway."

I didn't know whether to laugh or groan so I did both. The image of Rosie having a priest bless water in various perfume bottles was too much for me to bear at that moment.

"What are you doing here, anyway? Aside from feeding me Midol and giving me perfume?"

"Oh! God, I almost forgot. What did you do that the FBI is looking for you?"

That was it. I was throwing myself off the roof that very minute to keep my life from spiraling even farther down into hell . . .

AFTER A VISIT FROM THE local NYPD to report the break-in (I'd specifically requested that Pino not be sent, although I knew he'd find out and use the info against me), and a relatively quick visit to the hospital to make sure nothing had been permanently knocked loose (a mild concussion was the diagnosis, but after hearing the symptoms I figured I'd been suffering from one of those for the past three months), I thought it would be a pretty good idea if I avoided the office for a while. Like however long it took the FBI to forget I existed. Rosie agreed, but only on the condition that I carry the J.Lo bottle around with me at all times. And I had to agree, in principle, that there was enough going on just now that I didn't need to be taking any chances.

So in addition to the blessed perfume, Rosie gave me copies of everything she'd been able to pull together on the Suleski case, along with the original information sheet. I still wasn't sure how I felt about someone not only having been in my apartment last night, but having knocked me on the head. But since nothing was missing, and I'd called in a locksmith to change the deadbolt, the incident ranked low on my list of things to worry about. I figured I'd just move the Barcalounger in front of the door tonight and close all the windows.

My head felt like it was expanding with every heartbeat, despite the double dose of Midol. I really needed to throw out the leftover champagne. Either that or give it away. I was sure the DeVry students could put it to good use. One night and the remaining fifty bottles would all be gone.

Of course, it only stood to reason that since I had to be in my car pretty much all day, it was still raining. The carpet had yet to dry out completely from the other day, when I'd got caught with my top down, and the green smell wasn't helping my pounding head any.

I sat near Astoria Park overlooking the East River. I found it interesting that the spot I'd chosen was under Hellgate Bridge, where Harry Brooks' body had been found floating.

In the first file, I stared down at the original information sheet outlining Mrs. Suleski's friends and daily schedule. A Lynn Halsey in Corona topped the list. I noted the address, then put the file on the passenger seat. It wouldn't hurt to pay Ms. Halsey a visit and see if she knew where her best friend might be.

And while I was at it . . .

As I made my way to the Grand Central Parkway on-ramp I found a number I had yet to call in my cell address book and pressed dial.

"Morning, Sofie."

I squinted at the road ahead of me. How did Jake Porter know my cell number? "I don't suppose you're ready to tell me what was in that bedspread yet?"

"Mmm . . . I don't suppose I am."

"Then how about sharing how you know about the FBI and whether or not the dead guy was an agent?"

"You feel up to a bagel?"

The mention of food made me feel sick. "Where?"

He named my favorite bagel shop.

"See you there in an hour."

Fifteen minutes later I pulled up outside the address of Ms. Lynn Halsey's apartment and shut off my car engine. The flying saucers from the 1964 World's Fair were visible from Flushing Meadows and looked eerie through the fog of rain. Of course, the instant I wanted to get out of the car, it rained harder. I combined the contents of the two manila folders Rosie had given me and used one of them as a shield as I ran for the door of the duplex across the street. One of these days I would actually remember to put my umbrella in my car.

Once safe on the porch, I shook out the wilted folder and looked around the neighborhood. As with much of the city I was familiar with, I saw at least three curtains ruffle as neighbors peeked out to see who was on their street and who I was visiting. A few of the places had ground-level garages, but most people used street parking. There was an old Honda parked in front of my Mustang and a newer Cadillac behind it.

Ms. Halsey was a single mom of two and worked as a freelance editor for a New York women's magazine. Bud and Carol Suleski had two children I'd found out were staying with her parents.

Eyeing the two marked doorbells, I looked through the door's window into the hall before settling on the bell for the upper floor.

Almost immediately a young woman came down the stairs and opened the door to stare at me warily.

"Yeah?"

"Sorry, I must have rung the wrong bell," I said. "Is Ms. Halsey on the first floor?"

She blinked at me.

"Lynn Halsey?"

"Oh, Lynn. Yeah, she lives downstairs. Try the bell."

She closed the door on me and disappeared back up the stairs.

Damn.

Obviously age had nothing on a duplex dweller's familiarity with the ring-the-wrong-bell-in-order-to-gain-entry-to-the-hall trick.

I leaned back and eyed the front window of the downstairs apartment but couldn't tell if anyone was home or not. So I rang the bell.

I heard the bell ring and a dog barked, but otherwise, all was quiet.

I tried again at the same time I pulled my vibrating cell phone out of my pocket. My mother. I frowned and ignored the call. I didn't need the reminder that not only couldn't I get someone to answer their door, I was completely incapable of finding a measly mutt.

I rang the bell again even as I checked the info sheet and entered Ms. Halsey's phone number into my cell.

Two rings and she picked up.

"Yes, I have a delivery for Ms. Halsey," I said, and named the magazine she did the bulk of her work for.

Moments later the inner door opened, then the outer, and I was facing Lynn Halsey.

I'd briefly allowed myself to hope that Mrs. Suleski herself might be inside the apartment and be the one to answer the door, but I should have known better. Nothing in my life was that easy.

I flashed my ID. "Sofie Metropolis, PI," I said as she looked for the package I'd claimed to have. "I'd like to ask you a few questions about your friend Carol Suleski."

The woman stared at me. "I don't know where she is."

"I didn't say that you did." But her response told me that she knew Carol was missing and thus probably did know exactly where she was. "Do you mind if I come in for a few minutes? I'm getting drenched out here."

She stood so that gaining access was impossible without plowing her down. Which I considered for a whole two seconds before deciding that that wouldn't put her in a cooperative mood.

"Would you have any idea where I might find Carol?"

"I just told you, I don't know where she is."

"But you do know that she isn't home."

She stared at me.

I took a card out of my pocket and held it out. "Look, I'm not the enemy here. I'm concerned about her welfare, considering the last time I saw her, someone bought it, if you know what I mean."

"If you work for Bud, then you are so the enemy."

I lifted my brows. "Why would that be?"

"Because he's slime, that's why."

She didn't take the card so I worked it into the screen. "Mind sharing why you feel that way?"

"Where do you want me to start?"

"Okay, then. Would you happen to know the name of Mrs. Suleski's lover?"

She blinked at me. "I think I've said about all I'm going to say on the matter."

She slammed the door and my card fell from the screen. My throbbing brain felt like it was going to roll out of the top of my head as I bent over and worked the card back into the screen door window. Shielding myself once more with the manila folder, I dashed back to my car and sat for a long while hoping Lynn would retrieve the card. She didn't.

Not that I could blame her. I probably wouldn't come back for the card either, except maybe to tear it up and throw the pieces to the wind.

The fact was, I wasn't having a good feeling about all this. I mean, if Mrs. Carol Suleski was simply having an affair as her husband had suggested, why were there two men involved? And—I'm talking about a big "and" here—why would one of them show up dead by a knife wound when gunshots had taken out my brother's camera?

I looked at my watch and started the car. Time to meet Porter. Somehow, I didn't think I was going to get any more answers from him than I'd just gotten from Lynn Halsey.

Sixteen

IT WAS HARD TO BELIEVE it was only last night that I'd last seen Jake Porter. It seemed like weeks ago when viewed through the lens of my desire for him. And only minutes when I thought about how shamelessly I'd thrown myself at him.

I arrived on time at the Astoria bagel place, my own frappé in hand, but he wasn't there. I ordered a plain bagel with butter and sat at a stool near the window watching for him. Ten minutes later he walked through the door. I'd already polished off my bagel and was considering another. Strangely enough, the food had made me feel better. My stomach was no longer churning and the pressure on my brain had let up a little.

"Rough night?"

I was so busy considering what was going on inside me I'd completely forgotten about the outside. I probably looked like death warmed over. "You could say that. You wouldn't happen to know who was skulking around my place last night, would you?"

He didn't say anything, but given the way his jaw tensed and his blue eyes went from smiling to glitteringly dangerous, I guessed he didn't.

I waved my hand. "Never mind. That's not why I called. I need you to share some things with me or else I'm never going to solve this case."

"Did you call the cops?"

I blinked at him. "About last night?"

He nodded.

"Of course. About the bedspread—"

I felt my cell phone vibrate in my pocket. Either that or Porter was having some major impact on me. Both were possible.

I took the phone out. My mother. Again.

I ignored her and put the phone back in my pocket.

"Back to that bedspread . . ."

The smile was back in Porter's eyes.

"What?"

He shrugged and drank his coffee. "I didn't say anything."

"You usually don't have to say anything. Your face gives you away."

"I hope not, luv, or else I'd be in trouble."

"Job hazard?"

His mouth smiled along with his eyes. "Something like that."

What was it about this one man that no matter what was happening, who was missing, who was looking for me, or how hard it was raining, he made me feel . . . grounded somehow?

"What is your job, anyway?" I asked.

"I'd tell you, but then I'd have to kill you."

I laughed. I'd heard the saying often enough but hearing him say it with his Australian accent made my stomach bottom out. "No, seriously."

The smile disappeared from both his mouth and his eyes. "Who says I'm not being serious?"

Well, there was an answer for you.

"Are you a bounty hunter?'

"Sometimes."

"But that's not where you make the bulk of your money?"

"Let's just say that I don't do what I do for the money."

"So you're a vigilante then?"

"I get paid. I'm just not going to get rich. Not in this lifetime, anyway."

Government. Had to be.

But if he was an agent of some sort, wasn't it written somewhere that you had to be born in America?

Jake Porter was definitely not American.

Then again neither was my cousin Manoli, who'd immigrated from Kalymnos ten years ago. It was rumored he worked undercover for the NSA. Personally I thought he just lived in D.C. and worked for an insurance company or something. But what did I know?

"Are you going to tell me exactly what you do?"

"No."

"So essentially you're a Jake of all trades and a master of none."

He held up his finger. "A master of one."

Well, that helped.

"So . . ." I began, crossing my legs and moving discreetly closer to him. Only I must not have been too discreet, given the way he was eyeing my legs and me with a grin. "What exactly was in that bedspread anyway?"

I'D GOTTEN AS FAR AS I could with Porter, which was nowhere.

Back out in my car I gave my mother a call and nearly suffered hearing loss from the volume of her shouting.

It seemed the FBI had also been to the house.

Great. Not because I was afraid Thalia had given them my home address, but because she was more determined than ever to arm-twist me back into my waitress uniform.

I don't know why, but when a stranger approaches a Greek, any Greek, looking for information on a friend or a family member, they will argue to the death that they don't know the person even if they'd given birth to them. Probably it's a result of four hundred years of Turkish rule back in the homeland, I don't know. But I could just see the agents standing in front of the photo of me over the television while Thalia claimed she didn't know a Sofia Metropolis.

As I ended the call, I wondered how long it took for a building deed to show up on the books. It must be a while because the agents had been everywhere but to my place. Which meant it was safe for the time being.

Unless they talked to Mrs. Kapoor. Mrs. Kapoor would tell them exactly where they could find me. Especially considering she wasn't very happy with me at the moment.

Within five minutes I'd parked around the corner from the woman in question's house. I'd asked my mother to meet me there rather than chance going to my parents' house in case the FBI was watching. I knocked on Mrs. K's back door, wondering if it was ever going to stop raining, then stood staring at the petite Bangladeshi woman who had probably trained her dog to bite me.

A dog that was missing and in whose disappearance I was currently Prime Suspect Number One.

"You look awful," Mrs. K seemed to take joy in saying.

"Thanks."

I wiped my wet feet as best I could and moved into the kitchen where I got the same greeting from my mother, though without the joy.

"You're going to get sick running around wet like that." She handed me a kitchen towel that smelled like curry and cinnamon. I ran it over my face and my hair, glad there weren't any mirrors around because I probably looked as bad as I felt—and that was pretty bad, despite my minor rebound at the bagel shop (of course, I was beginning to wonder if it had been the food or Porter that was the cause of my feeling better).

We all sat down at the table. "Where's Barb?" I asked.

My mom waved her hand. "Sick. Tell us what's going on."

I shrugged. "Unfortunately, nothing. I checked with the shelter, I've posted posters, talked to the neighbors and no one's seen hide nor hair of Muffy."

My mother made a sound of disbelief. "He couldn't have just disappeared off the face of the earth."

I had the image of Muffy spontaneously combusting and had to squelch the smile that threatened. Especially when I got a look at Mrs. K's face.

Uh-oh.

It wasn't often that I had humane, compassionate thoughts about the older woman. After all, she had been the cause of so much trouble for so long that I preferred to think of her as a pain.

Proof that she was not only human, but missed what amounted to her only constant companion made me feel . . . well, sorry.

I was surprised to find I'd reached out and taken her hand. "Don't worry. If he's out there, we'll find him," I said quietly.

She seemed to search my face for some sort of hope. And resolve is what I gave her.

When I left a little while and half a *milopita*—apple cake—later, I did so with the renewed conviction that someone must have taken Muffy. Whether it was while he was out on one of his terror runs or right out of the yard, someone had taken the dog. I'd tried to rule that out early on because, well, I had assumed no one would want that sorry excuse for fur. But the truth was that while Muffy didn't like me or Mr. Newman, he got along well with everyone else. How many times had I seen Mrs. K sitting outside with the hound sprawled in her lap getting a belly rub? While I may never have experienced that kind of affection and trust from an animal, obviously others had. And while it didn't really matter one way or another to me, for someone like Mrs. K it probably meant the different between happiness and a gray, monotonous existence.

Considering that the FBI was still looking for me, I didn't go into the front of the office but rather gained access from the back, which took me through Uncle Spyros' office. Rosie about hit her head on the ceiling when I opened the door and *psssted* for her.

"Oh my God, scare the hell out of a body, why don't you?" she said, looking over her shoulder at the front window, then gathering papers and a bag together and coming into the office. Once she was inside, she slammed the door closed. "They're sitting out front."

"Who?" I felt compelled to ask since I was talking to Rosie and "they" could mean anyone from vampires to the meter maid.

She slowed her chewing then popped her gum, probably wondering if I was especially dense or if I was treating her like she was. "The FBI of course. I don't know who they think they're fooling with that SUV. Although they used to be easier to spot when they drove those Chevy Caprices. But they don't make them anymore."

I'd given up trying to follow Rosie's logic a long time ago, but it didn't pass my notice that she was familiar with the FBI.

"Anything going on?" I asked, hoping Bud Suleski, or preferably Lynn Halsey, had called on the cheating spouse case, or someone was looking to collect the reward for the return of Muffy the Mutt.

"Uh-uh," she shook her head. "Nobody." She shoved the bag at me. "But I got these for you."

Thinking it might be food, I opened the top of the bag and stared inside. A big cross, a little cross, and something that looked suspiciously like a wooden stake.

I closed the bag and shoved it at her. "I don't want this."

She shoved it back. "I won't rest until you take it."

I sighed and tucked the bag under my arm. I needed to end this vampire thing as quickly as possible. Find out what had happened to Mr. Romanoff, if only so I could get some peace.

"What did you do anyway?" Rosie eyed me. "Never mind. I don't want to know. They could get me for being an accomplice or something."

"Has Lenny been in?"

"Yeah. He picked up his mail a little while ago, then left again."

Figured. "Do you have his home address?"

She shook her head. "No."

How could she not have his address? Rosie had everyone's address.

"Where are you going?"

I turned. "I don't know, but I can't stay here."

She was nodding her head. "Okay. But call if you need any help."

I didn't know how, exactly, she expected to help me, but I agreed anyway, thinking that I had to figure this mess out before I got in any deeper.

Two hours later I was sitting outside Lynn Halsey's house, *souvlaki* in a bag on the passenger's seat. While I'd followed cheating spouses before, usually they led me directly to the motel and I didn't have to wait more than an hour for their extramarital activities to draw to a close. Most often, much less. About as much time as it took to get their groove on and to get back into their clothes so they could return to their regularly scheduled lives.

I snatched up the bag and picked at the cold pita bread. I really didn't get what all the fuss was about. If you were that dissatisfied with your life, why didn't you change the whole thing instead of stealing five minutes here and there with a person who had been with Lord only knew who before you? I mean, what did those five minutes really get you besides in deep trouble when you got found out? And if I was on the case, there was a one-hundred-percent guarantee that you would be found out.

I considered my first case. The one I'd been on when I'd first met Porter. That one hadn't been about five minutes of a cheap thrill. Instead, it appeared to be a genuine love thing. I'd felt . . . dirty somehow watching the couple as they met and strolled down the Coney Island pier hand in hand. Dirtier than I ever felt later, getting shots of couples going at it full coital.

I'd watched the guy kiss the girl and found myself longing to be kissed that way . . . then looked up to find Jake Porter grinning down at me for the first time.

I stopped picking and lifted the *souvlaki* to my mouth and took a hefty bite, chasing it with frappé. I don't know. Something had happened in that one instant. An exchange of energy. A shared knowing. A kind of "did you see that?"—"yes, I saw that" kind of moment.

I made a face and wiped a drop of *tsatsiki* from the corner of my mouth. Stupid, I know. I mean love—real love—didn't exist outside a hot book or a good movie. I had only to think of Thomas to be reminded of that. I'd never really witnessed my parents sharing any private moments. Or any other married couples that I knew of.

I caught a movement out of the corner of my eye, *souvlaki* inserted in my mouth. A car had pulled up across the street and parked. A woman got out and ran through the pounding rain toward Lynn Halsey's house.

Carol Suleski.

I stuffed the *souvlaki* back into the bag, spit the mouthful out into the street, then ran after her.

"Freeze!" I called.

Freeze? Where the hell had that come from? I wasn't some rookie cop chasing a suspect; I was a PI looking for a few answers.

Mrs. Suleski turned and stared at me before the door opened and she disappeared into the house.

My steps slowed as Lynn Halsey slammed the door shut, then stood on the other side, her arms crossed like it would take an act of God for me to get past her.

Shit, shit, shit.

I couldn't have waited until I'd gotten closer to Carol Suleski. No, I'd had to yell out like some kid playing cops and robbers and let her not only get away, but get a good look at me so that sneaking up on her wasn't ever going to be an option again.

I threw up my hands at Lynn indicating surrender, then back-tracked to my car and the *souvlaki* waiting inside.

Seventeen

SUNDAY MORNING AND ALL WAS still not well.

I lay staring at the ceiling of my bedroom, ignoring the wedding gifts against the wall, the heart pillow Roula had made for me— well, for her brother's bride—stuck to the side of my face. It had been a good long time since I'd slept in. Which struck me as odd, because it wasn't that long ago that you'd needed a crowbar to separate me from my bed when I lived with my parents. I ran my tongue around my mouth. Maybe that was because back then I knew there were others there to take care of the house.

Or maybe it was the thought of facing others so early that had kept me in bed.

At any rate, this was the first time since moving into my own apartment that I hadn't awakened before eight. And I wasn't sure how I felt about that.

Okay, so it was a Sunday, and certainly everyone had license to sleep in on Sunday. But somehow I felt as if I'd, well, wasted hours I could have better spent doing something . . . I don't know, constructive, maybe? Like figure out what was going on in the Suleski case. Find Muffy the Mutt. Confront the vampires down the block.

I rested against my elbows, my tangled hair drooping down in front of my face. I blew it out of the way as best I could and squinted at the clock. Ten-thirty. I didn't have to be at my parents for Sunday dinner until noonish, oneish at the latest. I could go to St. Constantine's, where my mother and grandmother and the female half of the Kalamaras/Metropolis family above age forty would be. Then again, no. Better not to go at all than to go late. I flopped back against my pillows, staring at the rain outside my window. Maybe I could just sleep until noon and pray that when I woke up again everything would have solved itself. The dead guy in the motel room would have been an intruder who'd deserved to be shot—I mean knifed—to death. Mr. and Mrs. Suleski would be reconciled. Muffy the Mutt would magically appear at Mrs. K's doorstep, and the cloud would lift from the Romanoff house and Mr. Ivan Romanoff would be out in the full light of day doing yard work.

Of course, the last one was dependent upon there actually being sun. And it had been so long since I'd seen more than brief glimpses of the sun I was beginning to wonder if it was a figment of my imagination.

My left leg twitched. My right elbow itched. And my eyes refused to stay closed no matter how hard I tried. I sighed and tossed the covers back. Maybe this was part of what it meant to be an adult. No more late sleep-ins. The world and all its responsibilities beckoned, refusing to let me be even in my dreams.

Fifteen minutes later I was showered, dressed, and measuring the ingredients for my morning frappé. As I shook my travel cup I looked around my apartment, from the blessed J.Lo perfume bottle that still sat on the kitchen table to where the remote was wedged between a cushion and the back of the couch. I squinted at where a thread stuck up a half inch from the thick pile of my new area rug. Still shaking my coffee, I walked over and tugged on the thread. One inch turned quickly into three inches. Scissors. I should really cut it. I remembered unraveling an entire sweater my grandmother had knitted for me when I was eight because I didn't put together that the yarn that was getting longer meant my sweater was getting shorter.

I added cold water to my frappé, inserted a straw into the cup, and took a deep sip, then got my scissors. *Snip,* and the stray thread was history. As was another one I spotted. And another.

On the fifth one, I froze on the rug. First fleas. Then the running dyes. Now the blasted rug seemed to be unraveling right before my very eyes.

And why not? The rest of my life seemed to be one catastrophe after another. Why shouldn't my rug mirror that?

I put the scissors away, put the J.Lo bottle in my purse, then headed out of the apartment lest I spot something else gone awry.

Still raining. I stood in the doorway watching as a small river ran the length of the curb and disappeared into a sewer drain, then I ran back upstairs and got my umbrella. I felt pretty happy with myself as I opened it and began walking toward the Romanoff house.

Let's say for a moment that I did occasionally give myself over to the belief that vampires walked—or flew—the earth with us. It was daylight and no sun-fearing vampire in his right mind would be up and about, would he? Which meant no threat for me. Well, okay, minimal threat. I had at least an hour before I had to go to my parents'. More than enough time to do a little private detecting, in the loosest definition of the phrase.

I barely paused at the squeaky gate, refusing to remember the way Rosie had run like a shot the other night when the creepy nephew had opened the door. I was up on the porch and knocking before I could entertain further thoughts of backtracking to my car and retrieving the weapons Rosie had given me yesterday. Truth was, I was afraid of what I would look like carrying a two-foot cross in broad daylight, and the wooden stake would be pretty hard to conceal in my jeans or shirt. And didn't you need a mallet or something with which to pound the stake through the vampire's blackened heart?

I gave myself an eye roll. Oh, get real. For one, the whole stake-through-the-heart angle made absolutely no sense at all. I mean, if it was true that vampires were neither living nor dead, then they didn't have a beating heart, did they? So putting a stake through it would accomplish what, exactly?

Or was I confusing vampires with zombies?

I knocked on the door again.

No answer.

I put my umbrella down on the partially covered porch, then leaned over and tried to peer through one of the windows. The curtains were drawn tight and there were no cracks that I could make out. I tried the door handle. It was locked.

Okay then. You couldn't say I didn't try.

But if I didn't at least try another entrance, what kind of PI would that make me?

The kind that was deathly afraid of vampires.

Looking down at my already wet shoes, I went down the stairs and around the side of the house, turning sideways when the way got narrow. I was in the overgrown backyard before I knew it. Was it just me or was it darker back here? A crack of thunder from above nearly sent me running back the way I'd come.

I climbed the steps to the back door and tried the same peering-through-the-curtains bit with the same result. Then I curved my fingers around the door handle.

Okay, it's locked too.

I released it and the door opened inward.

Oh, crap.

I waited for the creepy nephew to emerge from the darkness, but there was no sound aside from the low creak of the rusty door hinges. Didn't these people believe in oil?

I slowly pushed the door open, trying to make out familiar shapes in the gloom. A kitchen. A dark kitchen with a counter running along the right side, a faucet dripping into a sink that held no dirty dishes (of course there would be no dishes. Vampires drank, not ate. And I didn't think they required glasses for the drinking part, either). I stepped in and waited for my eyesight to adjust.

I opened my mouth to call out, but found I was incapable of any sound. I put my coffee down on the counter and edged even further into the room.

Since I'd never been inside the place, I hadn't known what to expect, but it wasn't what I was seeing. In contrast to the Gothic style of the house itself, all the furniture was starkly modern: black lacquer tables and furniture with silver lamps. I tried the light switch closest to me and nothing happened. Shocker. Why have lamps if you never intended to use them?

To lull fools like you into a false sense of security, a tiny voice answered.

I ordered my feet to move faster. I methodically looked through all the rooms on the first floor before starting on the second. Upstairs, three bedrooms with three neatly made beds. Clothes hung in the closet of one room, and a locked suitcase sat on the dresser of another, but everything looked somehow . . . too neat. Nobody was this tidy. Not even my mother, and she was the queen of clean.

I backtracked down to the kitchen, unable to get out of the house fast enough. I was reaching for the doorknob when I noticed another door.

I swallowed hard.

The basement?

Although I'd never had acupuncture, I imagined this is what it would feel like: like thousands of tiny needles inserted all over my flesh.

Okay, even under normal circumstances I'm not a big fan of basements. Even of basements that have been transformed into illegal apartments or rec rooms or anything other than a dark and musty place where you keep boxes of stuff you never intend to use again. Basements are home to creepy crawlies and smells you can't seem to get out of your nose no matter how hard you try. Basements don't have windows.

Basements would be the perfect place for vampires to hang out.

There was no way I was going down into this particular basement.

I'd come to the house. I'd come inside when I shouldn't have. I'd even looked through the whole place. I didn't need to go into the basement.

Even as I thought that, I was moving closer to the closed door, my hand seeking the handle. If there was no light, there was no way I was going down there.

The switch just inside the door activated a single bulb suspended from a cord at the top of the staircase.

You'd think I'd learn not to make deals with myself. I was no good at taking others up on a dare and I was doubly worse when it came to dares I made to myself—see exhibit A, the worm and bug shake incident.

"I dare you to wear that red Gucci dress."

"I dare you to marry Thomas-the-Toad."

"I dare you to move into that apartment building sans groom."

"I dare you to keep the groom's wedding gifts."

See. There was no end to the trouble I got into when I dared myself.

Yet here I was, again, ignoring common sense and descending into the very depths of hell itself.

Okay, so the bulb was strong, but it seemed to be the only source of light in the basement. I backtracked and looked through the many neat kitchen drawers. If there wasn't a flashlight, then I was just going to walk . . .

I found a flashlight.

Worse, I found a flashlight that actually worked and that I didn't have to hit on the side to get to shine.

I really needed to get psychiatric help for this condition of mine.

Back down the stairwell I went, the light from the flashlight not much help because, well, my hand was trembling so badly that I was probably providing the world's worst laser light show. The wavering beam illuminated no more than a foot or two of the pitch-black basement at a time. The air was thick and damp, that basement smell permeating every aspect of my being. There was a washer and dryer to the left, unused from what I could see although even vampires needed to change clothes, didn't they? I swept the beam to the right where metal shelves filled with dusty jars stretched to the low ceiling. I started to move toward the jars, then decided not to. I didn't see what good it would do me to know what was in them. Whether it was homemade jam or body parts, neither would help me find out what had happened to Mr. Romanoff. And since they weren't Tupperware, I didn't have anything to worry about.

I slowly edged my way to the right side of the basement. My feet made gritty, shuffling sounds on the dirty concrete floor, echoing loudly in my ears as I moved forward.

The flashlight beam caught the bottom of something long and made of wood, and I froze.

Okay, it wasn't actually physically possible for a person's heart to lodge in their throat, was it? I tried to convince myself of that as I slowly shifted the flashlight.

Oh. My. God.

It was a casket. It had to be. The wooden crate was pieced together, the length and width of a man's body, and inside were wood
shavings. The top was propped open like a violin case.

Wait till Rosie heard about this one.

Of course, I had to still be alive in order to tell her.

A sound from behind me made me turn so quickly I lost my balance and fell right into the wooden pauper's casket on the floor.
The top closed . . .

I was pretty sure the screaming I heard was my own.

Eighteen

CALL ME A COWARD, BUT being buried alive is one of my biggest fears. That and being submerged, headfirst, in a large body of water without being allowed to plug my nose. I didn't realize I had my eyes scrunched tightly closed or that I was screaming at the top of my lungs until I felt hands on my shoulders. And even then I kept screaming as I tried to make out the shadowy silhouette looming above me.

I pressed my chin into my chest, trying to make my neck the smallest target possible.

"Please, please, you are all right."

I was still holding the flashlight and jerked it around to shine on the face of the creepy nephew. I paid especially close attention to his teeth, although there seemed to be no sign of lengthening incisors.

"Oh, it's you," I croaked, my voice all but gone—no surprise considering how loud and long I'd screamed.

I clapped my mouth shut and allowed him to help me out of the box as if it were the most natural thing in the world for me to be in his basement, inside a casket.

This is how it all begins, I thought. The bizarre becomes the norm and before you know it you're cruising for easy victims with juicy-looking necks.

I busied myself with brushing myself off, the flashlight beam bouncing all over the place, until I realized I couldn't see the nephew so I shined it back on him.

"May I ask what you are doing in my uncle's basement?"

I raised my brows at him. "May I ask what you're doing with a people-eating casket in your uncle's basement?"

Vladimir Romanoff blinked at me several times, then grinned. "Casket. This is the English word for what you bury the recently deceased in, no?"

I nodded wildly and shuddered, hoping I wasn't about to fall into that category.

"Oh, my dear Ms. Metropolis. This is no . . . casket, as you say." He closed the top of the box and ran his pale, well-manicured hand over the length of the top. "I had this specially made to transport my cello here to America from my homeland."

Cello. I saw no cello.

"It is right here."

I hadn't realized I'd said the words aloud until Romanoff spoke. His right hand disappeared into the darkness from which he produced a cello.

"I just unpacked the piece this morning and was about to take it upstairs when I heard a sound."

He'd heard a sound? *He'd* heard a sound?

"Again, may I ask what you are doing in my uncle's basement?"

I tried to shrug off my fear and made a face at the unease that replaced it. "Looking for your uncle, of course." I cleared my throat. "You said I might come back to see him. I mean, I know I was supposed to come back a couple days ago, but I've been busy and I really haven't had the time and . . ."

I forced myself to stop babbling. "Anyway, I'm here for your uncle."

"And you're looking for him in the basement?"

"Nobody was upstairs and I heard a sound . . ."

I was so not explaining myself to this pale, scary ghoul of a man. "Where is he?" I asked.

"My uncle is being looked after by the finest in their field." He indicated the area of his chest. "He has . . . what do you call it? A chest cold."

"A chest cold doesn't require medical attention."

"It is in the more extreme version."

"Pneumonia?" I cringed when I realized I was helping him.

But for some reason, despite my nightmarish experience, I wanted to believe that Mr. Romanoff was, indeed, in a hospital, being treated for an illness that had nothing to do with vampirism.

"Yes, yes. That is it. How do you say it? Pneumonia."

He'd said it differently, making me wonder if Romanians used the same word we did, merely put the emphasis on a different syllable. The Greeks did that.

"Which hospital is he in?"

Vlad grinned again. "It is a private hospital."

"That's not a name."

"Excuse me if I do not give you the name. You must take my word that my uncle is improving and will return home soon."

He moved forward and I moved twice the distance back.

It was then I realized I was alone in a dark basement with this creepy guy and there was a casket, oh, excuse me, a cello case that I fit perfectly inside of nearby. If he didn't want to tell me which hospital, that was fine with me.

"Well, okay then. Just so he's getting better. Do you know when he'll be back?"

He shook his head, which appeared disembodied in the beam of the flashlight. "No, I do not."

Great.

"Okay, then, I'll check back in a day or two. If that's all right with you?"

His eyes seemed to glow at me. "It is more than all right. Perhaps next time we can enjoy a bite together."

I turned and scurried up the stairs.

"YOU'RE SOAKING WET," MY MOM said as I stood panting inside her kitchen doorway. "*Vrehei karekles.* Where's your umbrella?"

I remember the first time someone laughed at me for saying it was raining chairs, which was what my mother had just said in Greek. In English the saying goes "it's raining cats and dogs." But not in Greek. In Greek it rains chairs.

I'd always secretly wondered whether, if it's raining really hard, it includes tables.

At any rate, I didn't want to tell Thalia that my umbrella was still sitting on the Romanoff porch for two reasons: because she'd probably send me to my room for breaking and entering and because I didn't call her to come with.

"Yes, well," I said and nothing more.

I never had to wonder how Thalia kept in such great shape. One had only to watch her in the kitchen to know that whatever calories she ingested were easily offset by her busyness in that room I'd spent so much of my life in. Right now I watched as her right arm worked double time to whip egg whites into a froth, into which she then folded a cup of lemon juice and yolks before making a kissing sound with her lips while adding it to the top of . . . were those fresh *dolmathes*? Mmm.

I reached a hand in to snatch one of the stuffed grape leaves and she smacked it away without even looking. I'd always wondered if the woman had eyes in the back of her head hidden under all that black curly hair. I squinted. It wasn't all black anymore, was it? Gray was quickly catching up.

When had that happened?

"What were you doing snooping around the Romanoff place?" she asked me.

I nearly choked on the black olive I had substituted for the stuffed grape leaf. "Excuse me?"

"You heard me." She gave me a stern look. "I've told you never to go around that vampire."

I felt like I was five years old again, being lectured on why it wasn't a good idea to cross the street without looking first.

St. C's cathedral, a couple blocks up, chimed the hour and my mother crossed herself as she did every time the bells chimed or every time she passed the cathedral itself.

"Did you see him?" she asked as soon as she finished.

Just like my mom. Scold first, ask for gossip straight after. "No. His nephew"—I gave an involuntary shudder—"says he's in the hospital."

"Which hospital?"

"I don't know. Why, you planning to send flowers?"

She stared at me.

"And Muffy?" she asked.

Yes, Muffy. Rosie had called other shelters with no result.

"Nothing yet."

I perched on a bar stool next to the stove, peeking into each of the pots as my mother lifted the lids to add salt, to stir, or to add more water.

I'd always loved Sunday dinner. When I was younger, every day was like Sunday. We'd have dinner, the big meal of the day, at around three after we kids got home from school, then would nap for about an hour and have a light snack later on that night.

But as Kosmos, Efi, and I got older, and were rarely home at the same time, those daily sit-down dinners grew rarer and rarer.

Except for Sundays. On Sunday everybody made time for dinner at the Metropolis household.

I watched as *Yiayia* peeled potatoes at the sink and wondered if she'd finished her contraband yet.

"Anyway, how did you know what I was doing? Weren't you in church?"

Thalia looked affronted. "Of course I went to church. Mrs. Kapoor told me about your snooping."

"What else is new?"

She whacked me in the arm with a wooden spoon.

"Ow."

"Respect. If I've taught you nothing else, I know you learned to always respect your elders."

"Even when those same elders get me into trouble?"

"Especially when those elders get you into trouble. What? Do you think Aklima likes having to look after you?"

"What else does she have to do?"

I moved out of the way of the next spoon whack.

"Anyway, use the back stairs and go clean yourself up. You look like something the dog dragged in. If, indeed, we had a dog. Or if Mrs. Kapoor had hers."

I grimaced. I'd have to pay closer attention to my mom and learn how to do that. You know, make someone feel dirty and guilty and substandard all at the same time.

"Why? It's just us for dinner, isn't it?" I asked.

She pretended an over-interest in her *dolmathes* when we both knew she could make the dish with her eyes closed.

"Ma?"

She gestured toward the stairs. "Just go clean up. And see if Efi's got something . . . nicer you can borrow. Do you wear anything but jeans?"

"I like jeans."

"Yes, well, jeans don't like you." She waved the spoon at me. "And what's with those shirts? The hem isn't long enough. I can see your stomach."

"That's the style, Ma."

I resisted the urge to look in the other room to see if the "guest" who was going to join us for dinner had already arrived, thinking I'd get to see him soon enough. No sense in ruining my growing appetite for the food cooking on the stove. Although I had absolutely no intention of asking Efi to borrow anything. Hmm . . . maybe it wouldn't be such a bad idea if I came down in one of Efi's ultra-pink belly shirts with the word "Diva" or "Bitch" written across the breasts. The problem was I probably wouldn't fit into them. And it wasn't because of my breasts.

I fixed myself in the upstairs bathroom, plucking a wood shaving from my hair and wiping the smeared mascara from under my right eye. I stared into the full-length mirror on the back of the door. I did a side shot, then the other side, then grabbed the hand-held mirror on the back of the toilet and tried to get a good shot of my rear.

Ugh. My mother was right. My butt looked enormous in these jeans.

Maybe I would check to see if Efi had anything I could borrow. She might have one or two hand-me-downs that might do better.

I walked into the hall and ran smack dab into my brother, Kosmos.

Yikes.

"Hey, Sof," he said, giving me a peck on the cheek.

I always forgot how good looking my younger brother was until I was staring at him this close.

I'd also forgotten that I'd not only borrowed his high-end Olympus camera but that I'd busted it.

Rather, someone had shot it. "Hey, Koz. How's it hanging?"

He grimaced, never one for raunchier slang. How we had grown up in the same house and ended up polar opposites was beyond me.

"I'm fine, thanks for asking."

I began passing him on my way to Efi's room.

"Oh, by the way," Kosmos said, having paused at the top of the steps. "You wouldn't happen to know where my camera is, would you?"

"Camera?" I fairly choked.

"Yes, you know, the one Mom and Dad bought me a couple of years ago? I need it to get some shots of seniors at the nursing home for a piece I'm doing."

Okay, so I could feel worse than I already did.

"Nope, haven't seen it," I lied, then ducked into Efi's room.

As usual, my too-skinny sister was stretched across her twin bed, her left hand attached to her computer mouse.

"Hey, Sof," she said without looking up. "What did you do to Koz's camera?"

"Oh shut up." I looked through her drawers, checking sizes, before finally giving up and facing her. "Do you have any of my old jeans anywhere?"

She blinked at me. "Of course not. I took them all down to the church. They're too big for me anyway."

I scowled. "Do you have any idea who else is coming for dinner?"

Efi shrugged. "Not a clue. Ask me if I care."

I thought about her online guy and wondered which picture

she'd sent, but didn't say anything as I headed back into the hall. My brain was already on overload and I didn't think I could handle one more piece of information just then.

Back in the kitchen I found *Yiayia* making a salad. Mom was nowhere around. I lifted a lid and reached in to swipe a *dolmathaki*. *Yiayia* hit me in the arm with a wooden spoon.

"Ow." I glared at her. "Do you actually use that spoon or is it kept around strictly to swat me?"

She smiled.

"Dinner's on!" my mother called out, coming back into the kitchen.

My father wandered in from the living room, the Sunday paper folded back and tucked under his arm. I kissed him on both cheeks as I passed him on my way to the dining room with platters full of *mousaka* and *tiropitas*.

Before you could say *opa*, we were all seated at a dining-room table teeming with food. There were no interlopers present—no supposedly acceptable groom material. My parents sat at either end of the table, my grandmother between my sister and brother on one side and me and my grandfather Kosmos on the other. We each signed the cross and gave our own prayers, there was a pause, then we all dug into the food simultaneously. Even my brother Koz, who thought our eating habits were this side of barbaric, ripped into the freshly prepared flesh like a caveman.

"I heard you put in a few hours at your grandfather's the other day," my father said at my right elbow.

I blinked and pretended the comment held no significance, although everyone else's hands had frozen mid-swoop.

"Yes. I stopped by and he happened to be shorthanded so I offered to help out," I lied.

Truth was I'd been forced into slave labor, but to say so would only further aggravate the feud that had been going on between my father and maternal grandfather for as long as I could remember. Since before I was born, actually.

I'm not really clear on all the details, but while both my parents are from Greece and met here in the States, where they actually hailed from in Greece made all the difference in the world. Grandpa Kosmos, and thus my mother and the rest of the Kalamaras family, came from the island of Kalymnos, while my father and the Metropolises hailed originally from a small town in the western Peloponnese and had moved to Athens in the fifties. My grandfather had apparently not approved of my mother marrying my father; in fact he'd had her groom all picked out from his home island when my parents ran off and eloped and my mother came back from their weekend honeymoon in Florida pregnant with me.

So this bad blood went way back.

In fact, I still wasn't sure how in the world we all survived Sunday dinners together without the two of them killing each other. Mostly they just ignored each other or talked to a go-between, as my father was now doing with me when my grandfather was sitting on the other side of me.

"Isn't that nice?" my mother said across the table.

My father cut a big piece of pork and waved it. "She never stops by our restaurant. I was shorthanded this week, too. But no, she had to go work for the old man."

My grandfather grunted. "You've already stolen my best waitress and turned my Greek café into an American steakhouse. What more do you want?"

The waitress in question was my mother and the café was now the Metropolitan Restaurant, which my grandfather had grudgingly given to my parents after they named my brother after him over twenty years ago. My father had changed it from a Greek café to a steakhouse a few years back, spurring my grandfather to open another café, where else? Kitty-corner to my father's place.

Och.

In order to honor my grandfather's request that I not share his medal situation, I couldn't say exactly why I'd stopped by his place. And I couldn't use the excuse of the Muffy the Mutt posters either because I hadn't hung one at my father's restaurant. Mainly because I'd been forced into slave labor by my grandfather at his restaurant.

What a tangled web we weave . . .

"I do have a real job," I told them.

My grandmother made a sound of exasperation and the remainder of the family muttered things under their breath.

"What? It's a job. I get paid and everything."

My mother held up her hand. "We're not discussing this now. It can wait until after dinner."

At that everyone seemed to be looking at everyone else, obviously avoiding my eyes, before returning to their dinner. I squinted. Okay, what was up? Family arguments never ended that easily. Where were the insults and the inventive cursing? Was there a conspiracy underfoot to try to talk me out of working with Uncle Spyros and instead go back to my father's restaurant? My mother, my sister, and sometimes my brother—although less and less—all worked there. Certainly that was enough Metropolises in one place for an extended period of time for anyone's liking. It sure was for me.

"Okay, what's going on?" I asked, narrowing my gaze to Efi. I could always count on my younger sister to give it to me straight.

She blinked at me and shrugged. "Can't help you out on this one, Sof. I haven't a clue what's happening."

I sighed. If not even Efi knew what was happening, I was in trouble. Efi was plugged into everything, even though it appeared the only thing she was plugged into was her computer.

My grandmother said something about one of my cousins having a baptism in July and conversation swayed toward other topics, although my father seemed overly interested in his food and my grandfather kept clearing his throat as if there was something caught in there he wanted to get out but didn't dare in present company. I discreetly elbowed him and he looked at me and shrugged as if to say he was sorry.

Uh-oh. I could remember only one other time when I'd been the victim of one of these family conspiracies and the end result was my spending my thirteenth summer in Greece with relatives in a town the size of an Astoria block where chickens and goats ran free. All because I'd been caught kissing Alex Nyktas behind a See Foods grocery store. Okay, so maybe it hadn't been such a good idea. And I was only a week into thirteen when he was almost seventeen, both of us too young to be forced to marry. But he was cute and he was a damn good kisser.

Of course he hadn't been worth three months of cheese- and yogurt-making and being so bored out of my skull that I used to climb the mountain in back of my aunt and uncle's house and scream until I couldn't scream anymore.

Don't get me wrong. I love Greece. But my idea of Greece usually includes the sparkling blue sea and sugar beaches. (Imagine how upset I was when I found out the Ionian Sea and some of the most beautiful beaches in the world had been only fifteen minutes away from Aunt Maria's house during that long-ago summer. Hell, I'd have gladly walked if just to do something.)

I shifted in my chair. They couldn't possibly physically force me to go back to Greece again for the summer, could they?

I made a face. Of course they couldn't. I was twenty-six and could press charges.

So what, exactly, was going on?

Where usually I enjoy every bite of Sunday dinner, today I tasted nothing of it. All too soon it was over and my sister and my mother were clearing the table as I sat picking at my last *dolmathaki*, determined to enjoy it if it killed me.

The doorbell rang. I glanced in that direction and my mother took advantage of my distraction to swipe my plate.

"Sofie, why don't you go help *Yiayia* make the coffee?"

I stared at her. They usually kept me well away from making Greek coffee because it always boiled over onto the burner when I got anywhere near it.

But I dutifully did as asked, clearing the rest of the table as I went.

I stood next to my black-clad grandmother in the kitchen, watching as the liquid that looked like chocolate but tasted nothing like it began to rise in the *briki*, a small, long-handled pan. There was an art to making Greek coffee that I couldn't seem to master. You had to put it on low heat and allow it to rise to the lip of the *briki* and quickly remove it before it boiled over. Only when it reached the boiling point, "quickly" was the operative word.

Yiayia motioned for me to get it and I did, for the first time doing it right.

How about that. Maybe I'd have to make some for myself at home.

As I poured the liquid into tiny cups that sat on tiny saucers I counted them out. There were five more than usual. I frowned. Had my mother given up on parading potential grooms past me one by one? Was there going to be a bevy of guys in need of body waxing or hair transplants waiting out there, smiling up at me like a bunch of goat herders who hadn't seen a woman in three years?

Yiayia loaded a second tray with various sweets from a big box from the patisserie on 31st, Lefkos Pirgos. While most Greeks made their own desserts and sweet breads on big holidays, everything else was bakery bought and fresh.

Yiayia swatted me away when I tried to swipe one of the *louk-oumathes*, essentially honey puffs.

"Go, go," she said to me in Greek. "Take the coffee inside."

I rolled my eyes and walked into the other room . . .

And immediately felt like I'd entered the twilight zone.

Sitting around the living room were people I'd never expected to see gathered together in the same room—at least the same room in my family's house—again.

Thomas-the-Toad and the rest of the equally wart-worthy Cha-likis family.

If I were the fainting kind, I'd have fainted flat out.

Nineteen

THE HOUSE HAD BEEN NICELY warm when I came in but now it felt as frigid as a meat locker.

And I was the meat.

This was worse than sending me off to Greece for the summer. This was . . . this was . . .

I wasn't sure what it was, but I was sure that I didn't want to have anything to do with it.

It was only my years of experience as a waitress that kept me from dropping the tray before I put it down on the coffee table.

"Sofie," my mother said, overly cheerfully. "Isn't it nice that the Chalikises stopped by for a visit?"

My father muttered something under his breath and my grandfather watched me closely while my mother handed out the coffees. That's it. Quick, put something in their hands so they can't bolt for the door.

Efi refused a coffee and got up. "I can't believe this," she said. "I'm going upstairs."

I turned to follow her when my grandpa Kosmos caught me by the arm and grinned. "Isn't she as beautiful as ever?"

My almost in-laws seemed to look me up and down like a prize steer, and like any good financial planners I knew they were seeing nothing but dollar signs.

My gaze fell on Thomas, who looked as wary as I felt. But he'd known this was coming. He'd actually driven to the house and had stood outside waiting to be let in. He could have run at any time and hadn't.

But that didn't mean I couldn't. Or wouldn't.

"Excuse me, I have some more things to get from the kitchen," I said and jerked my arm from my grandfather's grasp, feeling betrayed and humiliated and like I had just cleaned and chopped a five-pound bag of onions.

I finally reached the kitchen and leaned against the counter for support, feeling ridiculously out of breath.

My mother was the first one to pop up. Not that I was surprised, since I was sure she had orchestrated all this right under my nose.

I stared at her wondering how a woman could do this to her own daughter.

"I don't get it," I said, my voice shaking and thin. "What are they doing here? I thought you'd finally accepted that I wasn't going to marry Thomas. Hell, you've been parading possible grooms by me for the past two months."

"Parading grooms by you . . ." my mother repeated as if trying to follow what I was saying.

I stretched an arm out. "Themios? Mitsos?"

"Oh! Oh," she said, the look of pity on her face more than I could stand just then. "Those men weren't for you, *agape mou*. They were here for Efi."

I felt as if the kitchen tile had just cracked under my feet.

I remembered the human Chia Pet making some sort of comment about my being too old. Now I knew why. He'd been expecting my nineteen-year-old sister, not an ancient, twenty-six-year-old spinster.

After my failed wedding attempt three months ago, I'd officially become a *yerotokori*.

This wasn't happening. This was much worse than anything I could have conjured up and, as evidenced by my run-in with the vampire earlier that day, I had a very vivid imagination.

"You're not young anymore, Sofia. Men want young girls who want to have babies. Not grown women who drink bug shakes and carry around a gun. You're lucky Thomas still wants you."

"Still wants your money, you mean."

I didn't kid myself into thinking my family was filthy rich. But they were doing well, despite the plastic-covered living room furniture and the ten-year-old cars my parents drove. They'd worked hard for the past thirty years and were well off. Well off enough to buy me an apartment building as a wedding gift. Well off enough to put my brother through seven years of college. Well off enough to pay for the entire family to visit Greece for a couple weeks every summer.

No, they didn't spend their money on big houses or big cars. They spent their money on their children.

And it was that money that Thomas' family wanted to get their hands on. Not that they didn't have enough of their own. But it was pretty clear that their thirty-year-old son Thomas wasn't going to make much of himself, so the next best thing was for him to marry someone who had money or access to enough of it that he wouldn't have to worry for the rest of his life.

That someone being me.

At the time I had thought I'd been the one making out better in the deal.

I somehow managed to make it over to the kitchen table and collapsed into a chair.

My mother patted my shoulder. "Thomas is very, very sorry for what happened, Sofie. Listen to him. Listen to us. We can work this out."

I opened my mouth to reply but she was already shooting for the door.

Yes, I'll admit, I fell for Thomas. Hard. He was tall and had the looks of a living, breathing Greek God. Jet-black hair, chocolate brown eyes and the kind of grin that was known to make the most conservative of women shimmy out of their panties whenever they saw it. (Of course, it wasn't until much later that I found out that he was collecting those panties.)

I'd started dating him because, simply, it pissed my family off. Not only hadn't they liked Thomas' family, they hadn't liked Thomas. But when it became obvious that not only had I fallen in love with him, but that we had—gasp!—slept together, the wedding date was set (hard to believe in this day and age that sex still means so much to the Greeks. At least when it includes other Greeks).

I hadn't really minded. After all, I was in love. Or thought I was. Now? I only felt sick to my stomach.

"Sofie?"

I nearly knocked the chair over I stood up so fast.

I'd expected my father next. Or even my grandfather. The last person I'd anticipated seeing in the doorway was Thomas himself.

Hadn't we just spoken on the phone? Hadn't we both made it clear that it was all over but for the rumors and the gifts stacked in my bedroom?

So what was he doing standing there looking like Adonis with a guilty conscience?

"This really wasn't my idea," he said, clearing his throat.

I couldn't look at him. It hurt my eyes. "Well it certainly wasn't mine, if that's what you're thinking."

I heard his quiet chuckle. "I had a feeling you were as much of a victim of this as I was."

"Then what are you doing here?" I asked, staring at him.

I had a hard time believing that it had only been three months ago that I had kissed him. That I had fussed over my wedding dress and called to confirm the tickets for our honeymoon. That we'd picked out furniture together and huffed and puffed to get some of it up to our . . . my apartment when the place wouldn't deliver, then ate Chinese food on the floor because we didn't want to get the new couch dirty.

That we'd broken in every room in the apartment, if you know what I mean, two days before our wedding.

"I don't know," he said. "My parents told me we were going to an old friend's house. By the time I figured out we were coming here, I thought, what the hell."

What the hell . . .

Well, that was something, wasn't it?

"You look good," he said quietly.

I didn't want him to say that. I didn't want him to say anything. In fact, I didn't even want him looking at me.

"I think the words are 'thank you,'" he said.

Oh, he had the second word right, but was way off on the first one.

I heard footfalls on the back staircase and watched as Efi came into the room, stared at Thomas, then took a couple of *koulourakia* from a plate.

"You suck, you know that, pinhead?" she said to him before going back up the stairs.

I don't know how I expected Thomas to react, but it wasn't with the unguarded chuckle he gave me. "Well, I guess we both know we won't have her blessing."

His use of the word "we" in reference to himself and me made me shiver. If only because I'd lived with the same word for so long and not enough time had passed to make me forget it.

He stepped closer and I automatically stepped back, only to find the table blocking my way.

"You know, Sof, it's funny, but I've actually missed you."

He missed me . . .

"And the farthest thing from my mind when I came into this house was reconciling with you . . ."

My throat was so tight I couldn't breathe.

"But seeing you . . . talking to you . . . I don't know . . ."

I didn't like the way this was sounding. I also didn't like the way my heart was pounding hard in my chest.

"I'm thinking maybe we should give this another try . . ."

Twenty

"AND I THINK YOU SHOULD go screw yourself."

I blinked. Then blinked again, unable to make myself believe I'd just said what I had. One minute Thomas' smile and laugh had softened me up and got me to thinking that maybe his one sin was forgivable . . . the next I was telling him to do the physically impossible.

Well, as far as I knew, anyway. Thomas, however, might know differently.

"I can't believe you're doing this," I continued, taking full advantage of his shocked face and tapping into all the words I would have liked to have said to him that day, and nearly every day since, but hadn't because I'd been the one in shock. "Give us another chance? We didn't break up because one or the other of us got cold feet, Thomas. Our relationship did not end because, like adults, we questioned whether or not marriage was what we should be doing right now." I now stepped closer to him and poked my finger into his chest. "It's over because I caught you *schtupping* my maid of honor on the day of our fucking wedding. In . . . the . . . church."

I must have raised my voice because the door opened and in spilled nearly every member of my family and his.

"I wouldn't give you another try if they stopped making batteries for my favorite vibrator and you were the only other option in town."

My mother made the sign of the cross and asked the Virgin and Christ for forgiveness, my father shook his head, Thomas' parents looked an inch away from stoning me and my grandmother grinned so widely I half expected her to applaud me.

Given her limited English she probably thought I'd said something else. Or given her gift of the see-through thong panties with lips all over them, maybe she understood perfectly.

I watched Thomas' face darken, the amusement gone from his eyes. "I want my ring back by tomorrow or you'll be hearing from my attorney."

He turned on his heel and stormed through the kitchen door.

I thought I heard his mother say something to mine about what happened to the apartment building now but my ears were ringing and I'd suddenly lost control of my knees. My grandmother put a chair behind me and I sat in it while my father started cussing at Thomas' mother in Greek by way of a response to the apartment building question.

I looked up to find Efi grinning at me from the spot she'd claimed on the stairs.

And I smiled back, for the first time in a long time feeling free and, well, damn good about myself.

Yeah, kind of.

TWO HOURS LATER I WAS back at my apartment under my kitchen sink, the toolbox I'd found in the maintenance closet in the basement open at my feet, my head under the garbage disposal. I grunted and puffed, trying to open it, as I had been for the past hour. I was going to get that ring out of there if I had to take a sledgehammer to the entire sink.

I lay back and sighed, thinking that a house looked completely different when you looked at the ugly underbelly. From musty basements to icky sink bottoms, I wondered why I hadn't noticed how everything was pieced together before. Maybe if I had, I might have noticed how everything else came together as well. Like my and Thomas' sorry excuse for an almost marriage.

Sex. Pure and simple. That's all it had been about. He'd wanted it. I didn't give it to him. When we finally did it, the sex was great. And we forgot that we didn't have anything in common and really, in the end, didn't even like each other very much.

Of course, the ultimate difference lay in the fact that I didn't go screwing the best man in the church's back room.

My arm was tired and I dropped it to my side. I guessed in some way I should be thankful for what had happened. I mean, imagine if I hadn't caught Thomas. He still would have screwed my maid of honor, my best friend whose name I hadn't said or thought since the event, but I would have been none the wiser. We'd have gone on our honeymoon to L.A., I wouldn't have done that lousy reality show, and we would have returned to this very apartment as man and wife.

I'm sure somewhere down the line I would not only have learned about what had happened on the day of the wedding, but there probably would have been several other women in between then and the moment of discovery.

Right this very minute I still might be living in married bliss, arranging dinners with his parents and my parents and going out with our married friends, and I might even be pregnant because, hey, that's the next thing you did after you got married, right?

Oh, God, I was afraid I was going to be sick.

Now I was under the sink of *my* apartment trying to salvage an engagement ring that might or might not still have the diamond in it. And I was trying to find my legs as a PI and nowhere on the horizon was a glimpse of a groom or a child or dinners out with my married friends.

In fact, I was questioning whether or not I was ever going to go to my own parents' for dinner again.

I crawled out from under the sink. Now, let's not be hasty. I'd probably starve to death if I didn't go to my parents'.

However, I decided that if I ever saw that . . . look on their faces again, I was scrambling out of the house double time.

Or at least I would dump the tray of hot coffee into the laps of our unwanted guests.

I don't know. I think the most disappointing part of the whole fiasco is Grandpa Kosmos' "boys will be boys" take on the situation. We weren't talking about Thomas bringing home a pet snake. We were talking about what he was doing—or rather where he was putting—his personal snake. And by rights—I smacked the stubborn garbage disposal—he shouldn't have been showing it to anyone but me.

I grabbed my cell from the counter and fished through my recent call directory.

"What can I do you for, Sofie?" Jake Porter's voice answered on the first ring.

"Where are you?"

"Down the street."

I pushed myself up and walked to the window. "Which way?"

"The other way."

He flashed the lights of his truck and I waved.

"What do you need?" he asked, his voice low and husky.

"You" was on the tip of my tongue. Exactly where I kept it. Wasn't my life complicated enough?

"You've proven yourself useful with cars . . . how are you with garbage disposals?"

"I'll be right up."

I closed my phone and put it back on the counter, just then seeing what a mess I was. I began moving toward the bedroom then stopped and sighed. This wasn't a date. This was a friend doing a favor for a friend.

Oh, and what favors I could conjure up.

Then again, no. Wasn't what had happened at my parents' enough for one day?

If that were the case, then what was I thinking calling Porter? I could have just as easily asked my father or my grandfather or my brother, or the three college students downstairs, to come monkey with my disposal.

Instead I'd called Porter.

I reasoned that it was because I was still really upset with the males of my family. And mostly because . . . well, I wanted to feel sexy. Not stripper sexy. Not even come-hither sexy. I just wanted Porter to look at me in that way that made me feel like a woman. And at that moment I needed that more than I needed anything else.

I suppose that's what happens when you're treated like a commodity from the day you are born; I'd been stamped with an expiration date that I'd never seen but was obviously already long past.

Had Thomas really ever wanted to marry me? Or had I been an acceptable adjunct to the lifestyle his parents refused to continue to support?

I shuddered as Porter knocked on the door.

I pulled it open and looked up at him.

"What do you need, luv?"

What I'd needed he'd just given me. In spades.

One look and I instantly forgot about Thomas and my family and the ugly words that had been spoken in my parents' kitchen.

Instead I thought about telling him exactly what it was I needed, which had nothing to do with monkey wrenches and everything to do with the king-size bed in the other room.

"I need to retrieve something from the garbage disposal," I said.

He reached out and rubbed at something on my chin. I watched as he drew his thumb along his tongue, then wiped again. "I take it you've been trying on your own."

I smiled, thinking of all the other things I'd like to have him do with his tongue. "Mmm."

"Is this the young man from the truck?"

I blinked to find Mrs. Nebitz standing in her open doorway.

I stood up straighter. "Yes, it is. Jake Porter, I'd like you to meet my neighbor Mrs. Nebitz."

"Pleasure," he said with that disarming grin of his, gently taking her hand and looking for a moment like he might kiss it.

Mrs. Nebitz blushed. I raised my brows.

"Nice to finally meet you, Mr. Porter. I'm glad someone's looking out for our Sofie here."

Looking out for me? I didn't need any looking after. Then I remembered the other night and the smack I'd taken to the head.

Okay, maybe I did.

"You wouldn't happen to be Jewish, would you?" Mrs. Nebitz asked.

"No, ma'am, I wouldn't."

She twisted her lips and seemed to give him a once-over. "Shame." She sighed heavily and I almost laughed. "Well, I won't keep you two. I just wanted to say hello."

I gave Mrs. Nebitz a little wave, then looked back at Porter.

"Lead the way," he said with a grin.

And I did.

Five minutes later my garbage disposal lay in bits and pieces on the kitchen floor and I was trying to keep my own bits and pieces together as I eyeballed Jake's washboard abs working under his T-shirt. The cotton of his old jeans molded against his thighs and other, more strategic areas.

"So how's Debbie?" I asked.

I heard a clank and wondered if he'd just hit his head on the sink. "Bugger. Pardon me?"

"Debbie Matenopoulos? You remember, the woman in the red dress from the motel?"

"I know who you're talking about."

Oh.

For a moment I'd hoped that the pretty blonde hadn't left much of an impression on him beyond that night.

Obviously I'd been wrong.

"You been going out long?"

He slid out from under the sink with a mechanism of some sort in his hands, his grin dirtier than his oil-covered hands. "Going out?"

"Are you going to answer all my questions with a question? Because if you are, I'm going to stop asking them."

"Promise?" He toyed with the mechanism he held, then blew on it. "Miss Matenopoulos and I are not going out, as the case may be. Our relationship is of a strictly professional nature."

Oh.

Oh!

"You mean you pay her?"

He stared at me. "Of course I pay her. She performs a job for me and is well rewarded."

Well. I wasn't quite sure what to do with that information. I suppose in the end he wasn't all that different from Thomas, except in Porter's case everything was worked out all nice and neat in advance. No gray area there. Whereas with Thomas-the-Toad word had it my maid of honor had fully expected Thomas to marry *her*.

"She work for you often?"

He shrugged. "I call her every now and again, you know, when she can be of use."

"God, all you men are pigs." I got up from the chair and yanked open the refrigerator door to stare at the contents.

His grin was entirely too self-satisfied. "I think we're getting our wires crossed here, luv. What services do you think I pay Debbie for?"

I took out a soft drink without offering him one and closed the door. "That's between you and Debbie."

I flopped back down at the table.

He got to his feet and leaned closer to me. "No, right now this is between you and me, I think."

I blinked at him as he pushed a stray strand of my hair from my cheek.

"I've never had to pay for the pleasure of a woman's company, Sofie, if that's where you're taking this."

"Then what do you pay Debbie for?"

"Probably for the same thing you pay her for. She plays decoy for me." His grin widened. "And judging by your reaction, she plays it well."

I felt my face burn.

He put down the mechanism and flattened his hands against the table in order to lean closer. "Rule number one in decoy selection: She must not distract you. Which is why you could never work for me as a decoy."

My tongue felt like it had doubled in size and I was filled with the incredible urge to lick his face. An urge I'd never felt before. "Never?"

He shook his head, his gaze moving from my eyes to my mouth then back again. "Uh-uh."

I thought he might kiss me. Prayed he might kiss me. Even licked my lips in anticipation of his kissing me.

Instead he drew back and pushed the mechanism toward me. "I think what you're looking for is caught in there."

I wanted to groan with frustration. Why was it Porter's eyes told me one thing, but his actions told me another? I wasn't used to that. If a guy wanted something, I was pretty used to his taking it. Or at least asking for it. But not Porter.

And what about me? I mean, I was by no means a passive woman. I wanted something, I took it. Well, before my engagement to Thomas, that is. Since then, I didn't seem to know the woman I'd become very well.

I looked down at the piece of the disposal in my hand and immediately spotted the mangled engagement ring, diamond intact and in place.

I released a long breath as I worked it free from the grinder. I examined the twisted platinum, wondering if the diamond was scratched or otherwise damaged. Not that it mattered. Thomas was going to get it back as is, along with detailed written instructions on what, exactly, he could do with it.

"Funny how accidents of that sort can happen."

"Hmm?" I looked up to find Porter, grinder in hand, sliding back under the sink, presumably to put the disposal back together.

"Your ring falling into the sink like that."

"Oh. Yes."

"Looks beyond repair to me."

"Very beyond repair."

"That go for the engagement as well?"

I stared at his hot body. Was he saying he cared whether or not I was attached? "The ring is in far better shape than the engagement."

His quiet chuckle. "Your grandfather seemed to indicate as much, but I got the feeling he was hoping otherwise."

I frowned and put the ring in the middle of the table. "Yes, well,

I think this is the only thing my grandfather and I don't see eye to eye on."

"Yeah, I'd say banging the maid of honor in the church on the day of your wedding is an unforgivable sin."

"Yeah." My frown deepened. I wasn't sure how I felt about Porter's knowing so much about me when I couldn't seem to dredge up a single shred of information on him.

"You want I should pay him a visit?"

Porter's Australian accent as he attempted a New York Italian one was enough to make me laugh. "Don't tempt me."

I didn't hear any sounds from him so I looked to find him watching my face from under the sink.

"Just say the word, luv."

I had the feeling he was serious.

Whoa. I'd never had a guy offer to beat up another guy on my behalf before. The feeling was . . . pretty cool, actually.

I cleared my throat and sat up. But, of course, I had no intention of taking him up on his offer.

I squinted at him. Would he really do it?

I saw the flinty expression he wore and guessed that he would.

Double whoa.

"Thanks, but I think his parents will spend every day of the rest of his life making him regret his mistake. Besides, if there is any visiting to be done, I'll be the one doing it."

Porter held my gaze for a long moment. "The offer's open. Always."

"Thanks. I think."

Twenty minutes later everything was back in order, Porter had washed up, and no trace remained of his having been under the sink other than the mangled ring sitting in the middle of the table. A ring Porter picked up and examined.

"Personally, I'd have left it where it was."

I raised a brow and took it from him. "It wasn't that bad. Well, until my wedding day."

"I'm talking about it being a fake."

I stared at him. "Is not."

He shrugged. "Okay then, it isn't."

I squinted at the diamond. "How do you know?"

"I worked at the Argyle diamond mines about two thousand kilometers outside Perth when I was fourteen, luv. I know my way around a rock."

Thomas had given me a fake ring?

Well wasn't that just the icing on the cake?

"Besides, you deserve a stone at least three times that size. A real one, of course." He took a soda out of the refrigerator, then headed toward the door. "Do you need anything else?"

I considered him long and hard before putting the ring back on the table. "Mmm . . . maybe."

His gaze narrowed on my face. "You're wearing that look again."

"Uh-huh."

Then I launched myself at him for round two.

Twenty-one

AH, YES. THAT'S EXACTLY WHAT I needed.

Jake Porter was granite hard exactly where a man was supposed to be hard. His mouth was firm as I devoured it like a woman denied a treat for longer than she could take, and no one with a wooden spoon was around to prevent me from having it.

Kissing, in my opinion, is grossly underrated. If a guy doesn't know how to kiss, then you need to show him to the door posthaste, because it is a good indicator that he won't be good at anything else either.

But Porter . . .

I sighed against him. His mouth fit nicely against mine and plundered it with just the right amount of pressure and pleasure.

He grasped my shoulders and for a second I was afraid he was going to push me away. Instead his fingers pulled me closer so that I became very aware that I was having the same effect on him as he was having on me. *Very aware.*

Chased from my mind was every stupid little thing that had happened to me that day. My falling into the coffin . . . no, cello case. My confrontation with not only my ex but my ex and his family. My failed attempt to retrieve my engagement ring by myself. Instead, I felt nothing but pure, unadulterated pleasure and . . .

Hope.

I caught my breath.

Yes, hope. Hope that this man was attracted to me. Hope that everything wasn't as bad I thought. Hope that he might allow me to lead him back to my bedroom where we could continue what we'd started, what had been sizzling between us for much too long.

The hands on my shoulders pushed me away.

I was more than a little hot and bothered as I stared at Porter.

"Oh no, luv. I have absolutely zero interest in being Rebound Man."

I blinked at him. "Who said you'd be Rebound Man?"

His hands began kneading my taut muscles and he gave me a grin tinged with more than a bit of regret. "I did."

He released me and turned back toward the door.

"I'll be up the road if you need anything."

I did need something, but he wasn't giving it to me.

I stood dumbstruck, staring after him even after he was long gone.

Then I gave a shriek of frustration and slammed the door so hard it seemed the entire building shook.

LITTLE SLEEP DOES NOT A happy camper make.

I rolled over and stared at the clock. Past nine.

I darted out of bed, hurried through my morning routine, made my frappé, and dashed out the door, barely awake.

So when I saw Porter under Lucille's hood during what looked like a brief break in the rain, I didn't know if I was awake or dreaming.

I scratched my head, watching as his arm muscles moved as he did something with a monkey wrench. Definitely awake. My dreams, no matter how vivid, weren't that detailed.

"Morning," Porter said, resting his hands on the hood and grinning at me.

I'm not sure, but I think I scowled.

He was the main reason for my restlessness last night. Despite what I'd said to Thomas, I didn't own a vibrator (I'd studied them once or twice at adult stores but could never muster the guts to actually take one up to the checkout counter), and somehow nothing short of Porter himself was going to do it for me.

I don't know, call me foolish, but when a guy turns me down flat one night, then the following morning shows up under the hood of my car . . . well, it was enough to make this girl batty.

"There's some croissants on the seat," he said, motioning inside the car.

Croissants? Okay, I could be upset with him later.

I opened the passenger door, snatched up the white bag inside, then slammed it again, causing Jake to have to hold the hood so it wouldn't close on him.

I smiled as I took a bite of the croissant, then held it out for him to take a bite. Would he? He didn't strike me as the type of guy who liked to be fed things by a girl. Then again, he didn't strike me as the type of guy who scared easily either.

He not only took a bite, he took the half that remained in my hand.

I gaped at him. "I thought they were for me."

He shrugged, chewing his mouthful. "You offered it to me."

"A bite." I pointed at him. "I offered you a bite. You ate half the damn thing."

I turned away. One croissant left. Ugh. I fished it out, determined not to be tempted to feed him any, no matter how good he'd look eating it. A girl and croissants were not to be parted.

"Aren't you running late?" he said, wiping his hands on a cloth, then closing Lucille's hood.

I glanced at my watch, only then realizing I'd forgotten to put it on. "I guess I am."

I polished off the croissant with gusto. "Thanks."

I climbed into the car, started the engine, and took off, happy to find the pavement dry enough to burn a little rubber. I watched as he stood in the street, arms crossed, staring after me.

Good. Let him make what he wanted out of that one. After all, a girl could only throw herself at a guy so many times before even she had to admit it was a lost cause.

Problem was, I wasn't quite at that point yet.

"FAKE? HE GAVE YOU A fake ring?" Rosie asked a little while later, staring at the mangled ring in question. "Oh my God. I mean, if a guy ever gave me a fake ring, I'd freak." She popped her gum. "What happened to it?"

I waved her away. "Long story. And I'm not one hundred percent positive it's fake yet. I'm going to the jeweler's later. Can you tell anything?"

Rosie squinted and I half expected her to take a jeweler's loup out from between her ample breasts, displayed this morning to their utmost flattering degree in a blue and white clingy shirt with a plunging neckline. "I dunno. But there's one way to find out."

She took the ring from me and walked to the front window.

"Whoa." I caught her hand before she could run it across the glass.

"On the off-chance it is real, I don't want to have to replace that glass. The lettering alone would throw me back a couple hundred."

"You're right. How about we do it on the bathroom mirror? Mirrors are glass, aren't they? And that sucker's already cracked anyway. Maybe breaking it would make Spyros replace it."

I twisted my lips. That was a thought.

We both stepped into the tiny closet that doubled as a bathroom.

"Go ahead," I said.

Rosie handed the ring back to me. "Uh-uh. You do it. It's your ring."

A minute ago she'd been all for destroying the front window.

"Seven years bad luck."

I gave her an eye roll.

"That's okay. I don't think my luck can possibly get any worse."

Rosie crossed herself. "What? The last time my sister said that she ended up pregnant and her husband ran out on her. A girl's gotta look out after herself."

Okay, fine. I lifted the ring to the faded mirror, found a point, then dragged it crossways down the surface.

Nothing. Not even a scratch.

"Oh my God, you broke it!"

I was staring at the mirror, but Rosie was scrambling in the sink for the sorry excuse for a stone that had survived a bout with my garbage disposal but lost against Spyros' bathroom mirror.

"Did you get it?" I asked, trying to see around her hair.

She held the missing gem up, giving me one of her deep-dimpled grins. "Got it."

I went out into the office and put both the ring and the stone into an envelope, then sealed it and slid it into my back pocket. If it did turn out to be fake, I didn't know what I would do with the information. Maybe take Porter up on his offer to pay Thomas a visit.

The cowbell on the front door rang and my grandfather Kosmos walked in wearing a suit.

I blinked at him. I could count the times I'd seen my grandfather in a suit on one hand. And it usually meant someone had died. Well, except in the case of my wedding, which really wasn't all that far removed from death when you thought about it.

"You ready?" he asked, tugging at a tie that had gone out of fashion three decades ago.

"Ready for what?"

Had we had a standing date for something?

"To talk more about getting back my medal."

Either Porter's kiss last night had knocked a few screws loose or else fate had decided to tie another kink in the already crooked rope that was my life.

I really didn't have the time to discuss searching for my grandfather's old war medal. But the earnest look on his craggy face and the way he kept smoothing his tie prevented me from saying so.

"Okay," I said. "But I have to make a stop first."

Let's see what *he* would have to say if the ring was fake.

Of course, with my luck it would be real . . .

"FUNNY AS A THREE-DOLLAR BILL," Antypas said twenty minutes later, examining the stone through his loop.

Antypas had been a top-notch jeweler in a past life. But after his partner had essentially robbed him blind, he'd been knocked down to pawn-shop dealer. He was also where I'd picked up the nine-millimeter Glock that sat in my locked glove compartment.

I felt both exhilarated and betrayed by his news.

Grandpa Kosmos looked over my shoulder. "What is it?"

I accepted the fake stone back and held it out to him. "The diamond from the engagement ring Thomas gave to me."

"*Ti les, file?*" He stared at the jeweler. "Fake? Are you sure? Look again." He shoved my hand back toward Antypas.

The other man shook his head and smiled. "I don't have to look again. It's cubic zirconia. Good CZ, but CZ nonetheless."

Silence as I pulled the mangled band out of the envelope. "What would it take to repair this?"

"What happened to it?"

I waved the jeweler away. "Long story."

He examined it and handed it back. "A miracle."

I spotted a camera similar to my brother's destroyed Olympus in the display case between us. "How much do you want for that?"

He named a price that would put a major dent in my savings account. Had Kosmos' camera really cost that much? I shuddered. "How far you willing to come down on it?"

"Depends on what you're willing to deal with."

Antypas wasn't talking anything sexual. He was gayer than the three-dollar bill he'd mentioned earlier.

"You're working for your uncle Spyros now, aren't you?"

If you could call what I'd been doing for the past three months "working." I thought it came closer to getting into a lot of trouble. "Yes," I said.

"Well, there's this little matter I might want you to look into." He looked pensive. "Actually, there are a few matters. Why don't you come back alone so we can talk about it? I'll see what deal I can work you up on the camera."

"I will."

I hadn't been paying close attention to my grandfather during the exchange so I was mildly surprised to find his face redder than I'd ever seen it. Far redder than it got when his favorite Greek soccer team, Olympiakos, was losing a match.

"*Gamoto horio sou mesa tha ton kano mavro apo to xillo, to paliopetho . . .*"

I started at my grandfather's impassioned outburst in Greek, wondering if he'd forgotten that the jeweler was also Greek.

"Thank you," I said to Antypas, then literally pulled my grandfather out of the shop as everyone looked on.

I watched as Kosmos paced back and forth on the sidewalk, shaking his fist in the air. I crossed my arms, ready to gloat, but when the rant continued, I grew increasingly concerned about his health.

"*Pappou*, settle down. It's not the end of the world. So he gave me a fake ring. All things considered, can you really say you're surprised?"

He stared at me, his eyes bulging. "Yes."

"Well, I'm not. It's just one more disappointment in a string of others just like it."

He took off in the opposite direction.

"*Pappou?* Where are you going?"

He angrily waved me away. I heard another stream of Greek curse words having to do with Thomas and a goat as he disappeared around the corner.

AFTER REASSURING MYSELF that my grandfather would be all right, I pointed my car in the direction of Suleski's repair shop, hoping that I'd finally be able to catch up with the man. I needed to figure out what was going on and I needed to figure it out now.

The problem was when I turned the corner onto Northern Boulevard I immediately spotted a familiar SUV and the two men attached to it.

I put on the brakes, then backed up into the closest drive before heading in the opposite direction.

Great. The FBI was at Suleski's.

So I headed back to Corona and Lynn Halsey's to see if anyone else had caught up with Mrs. Suleski yet.

To my surprise, Lynn answered the door looking almost chipper. Which I figured was bad news for me.

"She's gone."

"Why should I believe you? According to you she was never here."

Her smile widened.

She was gone.

Damn.

I held out another card. You know, just in case she had shredded the last one. "Please ask her to give me a call. It's important."

She tucked the card into her jeans pocket. "I'll pass it on the next time I talk to her. Which probably won't be for a while."

I pondered that as I walked back to the car. My guess was Carol had hightailed it out of town. But where? I'd had Rosie look up what family Carol had where. I guess now it was time to see what she'd come up with.

Twenty-two

"YOU DON'T THINK SHE'D GO there?" Rosie asked a short time later.

I was standing in front of two faded and frayed maps mounted on the wall, one showing the whole United States, the other just the metro area. I was considering the area just beyond the Delaware River in Pennsylvania.

"I hope not. If she's hiding from somebody, that's the first place they'll look."

"There" was a cabin in the Pocono Mountains, owned by Carol's parents. It was about an hour and half, two hours outside New York and was isolated enough.

It was also the most obvious place someone like Mrs. Suleski would choose to hide.

"Maybe that's why she's going there now. Maybe she figures they've already looked there and it's safe."

"Maybe."

My question was, why was she running to begin with?

NEWS AS GOOD AS THE fake ring was too precious not to share. The only problem was, there seemed to be no one around to share it with.

I stood in my parents' empty kitchen considering the leftovers in the fridge. My mother and grandmother were nowhere to be found. My father was at the restaurant. My brother was probably in class somewhere. The only one who might be home was my sister, Efi, whose ever-present headphones would block out the sound of a police siren. I grabbed a *tiropita* and headed up the back stairs to her room. A brief knock—which was probably an empty courtesy because she likely didn't hear it anyway—and I opened the door to find her stretched across her bed as usual. My mother was worried that one day Efi would come downstairs with two heads as a result of all the magnetic waves she absorbed spending so much time in front of a computer screen. Waves all the metal in her head and body intensified, of course. I lay down on the bed next to her and held out the *tiropita* for her to take a bite. She shook her head and pushed the right side of her headphones back slightly from her ear. I noticed that all other rings were on the subtle side.

"Going to work?" I asked.

"In twenty."

That explained it. Dad usually didn't comment one way or the other when he didn't like something, but if it interfered with his restaurant, he made his thoughts known. In this case, he was apparently requiring my sister to leave her many piercing rings at home.

"Yesterday was interesting," she said, looking at me. "How you holding up?"

"Okay. I just found out my engagement ring was CZ."

"Figures."

I shrugged and finished off the feta cheese pie. Efi had never been one to indulge in much gossip. In fact, nothing at all seemed to surprise her. I wasn't sure if it was because she'd been raised in such a dysfunctional family or if it was simply her nature. But I knew I wasn't going to get much satisfaction from discussing the ring situation with her, so I moved on.

"So which picture did you send to Jeremy?" I asked, skimming the posts in the chat room she was in.

She looked at me sideways.

"What? You thought I'd forget about that?"

"One could hope."

"So you didn't send him anything?"

I watched as she logged out and shut down her computer. "Just drop it, okay?"

"You sent him a blonde."

She rolled over, then vaulted to stand. "No, I sent the one you wanted me to send."

"And?" I rested against my elbows, watching as she changed out of her shirt into a white blouse. I still wasn't sure where she'd gotten breasts. Maybe every now and again the family gene pool gifted one offspring with the endowments the rest of us were robbed of.

"And what? He hasn't written since I sent it. Nothing. He hasn't been in any of the chat rooms. He's completely disappeared."

I stared down at my own less curvy chest. "You know, I always thought my life would somehow be better if I had bigger breasts."

Efi stared at me as she peeled off her black jeans and put on black slacks. "So get 'em done."

I gaped at her. "As in implants? Are you kidding me? Do you know what silicone does to a body?"

She gave me an eye roll. "They use saline implants now."

The way she spoke of plastic surgery without blinking an eye was cause for some concern. Then again, that's the way things are now, right? Don't like something? Change it. In this age of instant marriages and divorces and easily accessible plastic surgery, it's sometimes difficult to keep up with what is in and what isn't. Or is it that everything seems to be acceptable these days?

"You're joking, right?"

"No, I'm not. If you're not happy with your breast size, change it."

I wasn't happy with my breast size, but I was less happy with the thought of someone getting a knife—surgical or otherwise—near my person, unless the alternative was death.

"Have you tried writing to Jeremy again?"

Her movements slowed as she stuffed her discarded clothing into a laundry bag, tied the top, then hung it on the back of her bedroom door.

"I take it that's a no."

She glared at me. Oh, to be able to give those types of glares without worrying people would call you a bitch. "What do you think I am? Desperate?"

Why not? Maybe stuff like that ran in the family. After all, hadn't I virtually thrown myself at Porter—twice—only to be rebuked?

Funny thing was, I couldn't wait to throw myself at him again. After all, the third time might prove to be the charm.

I didn't know if I was a masochist or just plain stupid.

"The ring was really fake?"

I nodded.

"Jerk."

Not exactly the word I'd use, but it would do for now.

I followed her downstairs where my mother and grandmother were just returning home, apparently from the grocery store.

Efi told my mother the news about the ring, robbing the wind from my sails, before kissing her and my grandmother and leaving for the restaurant.

"Is it true?" my mother asked.

"Funnier than a three-dollar bill, Antypas said."

My mother and grandmother shared one of those looks I'd grown very wary of. But at least they were no longer questioning my judgment when it came to Thomas. Antypas, every Astoria Greek knows, knew his stuff. If he said a rock was fake, it was fake.

The telephone rang as I went through the grocery bags, liberating a peach. My grandmother smacked my hand and took the fruit as my mother picked up the kitchen extension.

Moments later she turned to me, wide-eyed. "It's your grandfather."

"He was there when they told me the news."

She waved at me. "It's not that. He's been arrested."

I DROVE—ALONE—TO THE 114th Astoria police station on Astoria Boulevard near 34th in a state of shock. My grandfather who, yes, had been known to curse up a blue streak and make a vocal fuss as often as he could get away with it, had been arrested for assault.

Assault.

The concept was enough to make my hands shake and it was all I could do not to floor the gas pedal.

I'd never known Kosmos Kalamaras, or any other member of my family for that matter, to raise a hand to anyone. Sure, my mother could work wonders with a broom to the backside, but this . . .

I pushed an autodial button on my cell. "Rosie, how much money can I get my hands on, like, five minutes ago?" I asked before her "hello" was all the way out.

She told me. "Why, what's going on?"

"My grandfather's just been arrested."

"Oh . . . my . . . God." I heard rustling on her end of the line. "Tell me it's the vampires."

I sighed. Although I wasn't sure what it was about, I was reasonably sure it had nothing to do with vampires and everything to do with Thomas Chalikis.

"Call me back and let me know what happened," Rosie said after I asked and she gave me the number for Fedor Petenka, the bail bondsman my uncle Spyros used.

I called Petenka, praying he was in.

It looked like my luck had taken a temporary turn for the better.

"I'll call you back in five," he told me.

In five I would be at the precinct.

I was searching for a parking spot on 34th when he called back. "They're transporting him to the courthouse for arraignment now."

"Isn't that fast?"

"I know people."

I didn't question him as he gave me an address on Queens Boulevard. "We'll be waiting for you to pick him up."

I disconnected, wondering where my uncle had found this guy, but thanking God that he had. The 114th could have held Kosmos for twenty-four hours before taking him before a judge.

The idea of my grandfather spending a night in jail made me shudder.

Or maybe my luck wasn't as good as I'd hoped. I reached to open the door to the courthouse just as Pimply Pino was coming out. We both stopped and stared at each other. Then I grunted and began to pass.

"Need your grandfather to defend your honor, Metro?"

"Piss off, Pino."

I strode down the hall, looking for what, exactly, I didn't know. I just needed to put as much distance between me and the NYPD police officer who irritated me no end, no matter the hanky he'd given me after I hurled outside the coroner's office.

"Miss Metropolis?"

I turned to find a man I could have sworn hadn't been standing there a split second before. Although how I could have missed the tall heavyset man in an overcoat was beyond me.

"Fedor Petenka," he said, and we shook hands. "Your grandfather should . . . ah, here he is now."

I was so relieved to see Kosmos I nearly hugged him for all I was worth. Instead I eyed him and asked him if he was all right.

He grunted.

What I guessed was an attorney stepped up beside him. "The judge set your hearing for next month. I'll send the information to your attorney as soon as you obtain one."

I barely registered as the attorney exchanged words with Petenka, then walked down the hall.

"What do I owe you?" I asked him.

He grinned. "Your uncle will take care of it."

"This isn't agency business."

"Your uncle will take care of it," he repeated.

"What were you arrested for?" I asked Kosmos.

He didn't answer so Petenka did.

"He's been charged with second-degree assault against one Mr. Thomas Chalikis."

I made a strangled sound in my throat.

Petenka extended his hand to Kosmos. "Keep out of trouble, old man. You're too wise to be trying to beat up a man a third your age."

"I don't know how to thank you for seeing to all this," I said, shaking Fedor Petenka's offered hand a little too long.

"Just so you know, the Chalikises are determined to press charges for assault with intent to kill and I wouldn't be surprised if they sued in civil court. Give me a call if you need any other help."

Kosmos grumbled something I couldn't quite make out as Petenka disappeared the same way the attorney he'd arranged for had.

Relief made my knees wobble as I finally gave in and hugged my grandfather, then led the way toward the front doors.

"What were you thinking?" I asked as soon as we were on the street, my harsh words in direct contrast to my warm hug inside. "Did you actually try to beat up Thomas?"

The reality made my mind swim. I'd wanted to prove a point when I'd taken him along with me to the pawn shop, but I'd never dreamed he'd take things as far as tracking Thomas down at his parents' travel agency and hitting him.

My grandfather was still wearing the three-piece suit he'd had on earlier, leading me to believe he'd gone straight from the pawn shop to Thomas. The suit looked a little worse for wear and I brushed a bit of grime from the right shoulder and smoothed out the left lapel. Where once my grandfather had been a giant to me, when I'd reached my current height he'd seemed to shrink a little, his shoulders slumping, his movements slowing.

I found myself smiling at him. "You could have at least called me so I could watch you do it."

The first sparkle I'd seen in his eyes since I'd sprung him. "I think I broke his nose."

I suppressed the desire to say "good" solely because I was afraid it might inspire him to do more damage and get himself into more trouble.

He looked at a spot over my shoulder, a strange, vacant expression taking hold of his ruddy features. "That diamond . . . it wasn't just any diamond . . ."

He could say that again. It had turned out it wasn't a diamond at all.

"It was from your grandmother's, my wife's, wedding ring."

The sky picked that moment to open up as I stood gaping at my grandfather. I took his arm, put him into the passenger side of my car, then ran to get into the driver's side. We both sat silently, the pounding of the rain on the soft roof a steady cadence.

"Did you know your top's leaking?"

I shook my head, not in response to his question, but rather to help clear my thoughts. "Explain what you just said."

He sighed deeply, then ran his meaty hand over his damp face. "When Thomas asked me and your parents for permission to marry, I was so happy I gave him your grandmother's wedding ring to have it re-set for you. I'd thought that you'd like that, you know, the tradition."

I hadn't even known. Thomas hadn't told me. And neither had anyone in my family.

I squinted at my grandfather.

"I was going to tell you on the day of your wedding, you know, right before your father walked you down the aisle. Make the day more special for you. Only . . ."

Only I never walked down the aisle.

I stared out at the rain. Now I wanted to go hit Thomas in the head.

Or take Porter up on his offer.

Kosmos was shaking his head. "When Antypas said the diamond in your ring was phony . . . I lost my temper."

I stared at him. "You can say that again."

He stared back at me. After long moments we both smiled and I even laughed.

"I'm sorry, *Pappou*," I said quietly, reaching out to touch his hand. "I know how much that ring, grandmother's ring, must have meant to you."

He patted my hand with his other hand. "It's not your fault, *agape mou*. It's mine." He shook his head. "I should have hit myself in the head for believing that boy had any redeeming qualities. After all, his family is from Crete."

I threw back my head and roared with laughter.

Of course, none of this answered the question of what had happened to the real diamond . . .

LATER THAT NIGHT, AT HOME, I lay across my bed staring at the ceiling, listening to the incessant rain outside my window. I hadn't spotted Porter's truck all day. Had he stopped following me? If so, why? Or had he merely gotten better at concealing himself, not wanting to complicate things more than he already had? Neither answer was particularly appealing.

I'd decided to head for the Poconos in the morning to hopefully finally get answers I was tired of looking for. Truth was, I was pretty much tired of everything at this point. Tired of looking for Muffy the Mutt. Tired of thinking about what had happened with Thomas at my parents' yesterday. Tired of worrying if I had what it took to be a PI.

Tired of being me.

I mean, let's face it. Being me was about as exciting as watching a fly get caught in drying paint. Oh, sure, stuff went on around me that might be amusing for, oh, about a nanosecond. But it was stuff around me, not stuff I was making happen. At the end of the day I was back to square one, staring at my bedroom ceiling as if it were Delphi and I was waiting for the Oracle to tell me what to do.

How easy life would be if someone actually told you what your role was . . .

Then again, no. Look where that had gotten me with my parents.

Of course, my parents weren't oracles, either. Hell, they couldn't even balance their checkbook.

As for my grandfather . . .

I rubbed my forehead, then pulled my hand down over my eyes. I still couldn't believe he'd given Thomas my grandmother's ring—a grandmother I had never met. My mother couldn't even remember her because she'd died when Thalia was two. And Thomas had done something with it other than give it to me.

I'd planned to drive to the Poconos today to get the answers I sought but had been knocked off track by what had happened with Kosmos. Tomorrow. Maybe tomorrow I could get some much-needed answers. More specifically: Who was the dead guy Harry Brooks, why was Carol Suleski hiding and who was she hiding from, and just what in the hell had been in that damn bedspread Porter had carried from the room anyway?

There were other questions, of course. But I'd settle for the answer to those three first.

There was a knock at my door. I pushed myself up to my elbows, staring down at the old Amazin' Mets T-shirt I had on. Maybe whoever it was would go away. Another knock. I got up and put on a pair of shorts, pushed my hair from my face, and went to the door. If it was Porter, tough. I wasn't in the mood for making a fool out of myself again so soon after the last time.

Mrs. Nebitz stood outside my apartment, holding a plate. "I made some *latkes* and thought you might like some."

It was ten P.M. and the old woman next door was making me potato pancakes from scratch. I smiled and accepted the plate. The constant offerings made her rent control well worth it.

"Are you okay? I don't hear your television and you don't look so good."

I nodded. "I'm fine. I'm just . . ."

I realized I was about to tell her I was having a hard time convincing myself I had what it took to be a PI. Then I went ahead and told her anyway, figuring at this point it couldn't hurt. I couldn't exactly talk to anyone in my family about it, Efi aside.

Mrs. Nebitz was nodding as I finished. "My husband Noah went through stages like that. He was an attorney, you know."

I knew.

She waggled her finger. "No, I used to call him. No, if you want your dreams to come true, don't sleep."

I squinted at her. Since Noah had become a prominent attorney, was Mrs. Nebitz telling me that he hadn't slept?

I didn't get it.

"Thank you, Mrs. Nebitz. I really appreciate the *latkes*. And the advice."

I began to close the door.

She held it open. "Oh, and it couldn't hurt if you entertained some nice gentlemen like that Mr. Porter every now and again. Would you like I should fix you up with one of my grandson's friends?"

I shook my head. "Thanks, but no thanks. Right now I'm considering swearing off men altogether."

"Even that nice Mr. Porter?"

Especially that nice Mr. Porter. "We're just friends," I said.

"Oh."

"Goodnight, then."

I closed the door, smiling. I wasn't sure which amused me more, Mrs. Nebitz's cryptic advice, her offer to matchmake for me, or her shocked expression when I told her I might swear off men.

I shook my head, thinking it was a sad state of affairs when your eighty-something next-door neighbor was giving you advice on your sex life.

Twenty-three

THE FOLLOWING MORNING I STEPPED out of my building onto the sidewalk and watched Porter tinkering under the hood of my car again. I leisurely sipped my frappé. This was something that would be easy to get used to. Too easy.

I walked over and slammed the hood, just missing his hands.

"Easy there. You're liable to take off a digit or two."

I smiled at him then climbed into my car. He leaned on the door when I opened the window.

"Can I ask where you're heading this A.M., mate?"

I squinted at him. We were back to "mate" now, were we? "To work."

"The office?" He looked doubtful.

I didn't know how he knew, but I had a feeling he knew my destination was the Poconos. "In a manner of speaking. Did you put a bug on me somewhere?"

He grinned at me.

I rolled up the window and started the car.

He knocked on the window.

I rolled it back down.

"Can it wait till tomorrow?"

I shook my head. "Nope. I already cleared my schedule for today."

"Shame. I could have come with you tomorrow."

The thought of being in the same car with Porter for nearly four hours, round trip, made my mouth water. "A real shame." He reached for my coffee and took a sip.

"So what do you have on tap today?" I asked casually.

He grinned again.

I scowled. "You know mystery is good in a man up to a point. And you passed that point a long time ago."

"Do you think?"

"Mmm."

He leaned in and kissed me. I was so shocked, I didn't have time to even think of kissing him back. "Anything I can do to talk you out of going today?"

More of that, I thought. "No," I said.

He held my gaze for a long moment, then stood up and tapped the top of my car. "Well, promise you'll be careful."

"And here I had planned to be as reckless as I could."

I smiled and waved as I pulled away from the curb. My car was running better than she ever had. I wasn't running badly either as a result of Porter's attention. This and he hadn't gotten anywhere near my dipstick . . . yet.

Normally I'm not a big driver. Most city dwellers aren't. The public transportation system pretty much takes you wherever you want to go up to a two-hour radius surrounding the city. Between the trains, the subway, and buses, you're pretty much covered. Anything beyond that, most natives rent a car, especially if they live in Manhattan. Parking rates there were atrocious, to say nothing of sky-high insurance rates.

I eyed the steel gray sky. It was hot and it looked like rain . . . again. But it wasn't raining now and I missed having the top down. So just before the Grand Central Parkway on-ramp, I pulled to the side of the road and put the top down, checked to make sure my cell phone was fully charged, then headed for the Poconos.

OKAY, THIS WAS AS FAR outside the city as I'd ever gone. Well, within the U.S. anyway. L.A. didn't rate because, well, it had been a two-week aberration I was determined to obliterate from my memory, if only because of the bug-and-worm shakes. Greece didn't count because we left from Kennedy in Queens and came back to Kennedy in Queens, and Greece wasn't merely a destination, it was another planet.

From what I could see Pennsylvania didn't look all that different from northern New Jersey, the exception being the mountains. I looked up at a particularly majestic one and got nailed right in the eye by a raindrop.

Aside from a few sprinkles outside Newark, the sky had remained overcast but had spared me from a full-out downpour. I supposed I should be grateful. I put the folded map on the steering wheel and drank the last of my coffee. If I turned right here, that would put me on the road that would take me to Carol Suleski's parents' vacation home.

I knew little about the Poconos except that in the winter people skied there and in the summer they honeymooned there. I'd once seen a picture of a mammoth champagne glass that was a Jacuzzi and wondered why people would want to soak in such a monstrosity. And just how did you go about getting into and out of a mutant champagne glass anyway?

Porter intruded on my thoughts and for a moment I entertained the idea of trying.

Then again, if Porter had been around when I'd gone to L.A., maybe things would have turned out much differently than they had.

What was I talking about? I couldn't seem to get Porter into my bedroom, much less onto a plane.

I'm not really sure why I'd picked L.A. as a honeymoon destination. Probably my fascination with television and movies and, well, all things Hollywood. Astoria was considered Hollywood East, what with the American Museum of the Moving Image on 34th, where I went to see classic and foreign films every now and again, and Kaufman Astoria Studios on 36th, which was still active. There, *Sesame Street* was shot and *Angels in America* had been made (I'd actually seen Al Pacino walking to the studio one morning and I had stopped dead in the street, gaping like a dumbstruck teen, the line from *Scarface* streaming through my head: "Say hello to my little friend"). But it wasn't *Hollywood.* Too many people saying "yo," I think.

What I hadn't been prepared for was all the plastic in L.A. I don't know why. I mean, I'd caught a couple of those shows where they cut up people who wanted to look like stars. I remembered I'd been eating popcorn during the first one and after they'd showed liposuction being performed I'd chucked the bowl and its contents and changed the channel. As we've already established, I know the definition of the word "desperation" well, but not even I would go under a knife. I stared down at my modest chest, remembering Efi's suggestion. Not even to get bigger boobs. Not even if you told me Porter would dive straight into my bed if I got 'em. The way I saw it, you were either born with them or you weren't. Besides, there was beauty in variety. At least that's what I told myself when I looked in the mirror every morning.

In L.A. I'd been mapping out the stars on the Hollywood walk of fame when I stumbled across a movie premiere in full swing. It was for one of those cool action flicks that I usually got into unless they went too far into animation mode. Too much animation made me feel like I was watching a cartoon. Somehow that just didn't do it for me. I couldn't relate.

Anyway, I'd stood with the mob of tourists in my new cargo shorts and tank top holding my map and I'd started noticing a pattern. It seemed every woman had the same set of boobs. Jutting, overstuffed boobs that weren't in danger of popping out of their tops because they didn't move, period.

That made me remember hugging one of my mother's cousins once. It had been rumored that she'd had her breasts done following a full mastectomy. Hugging her had been like holding two round and smooth rocks between us. I'd been half afraid they'd drop onto the floor after I let her go.

Then there were those Botox parties . . .

I swerved to avoid hitting a squirrel that had wandered into the middle of the road. Stupid squirrel. I read a nearby sign and realized that in the midst of my mental blathering (funny, the stuff you thought of when you had nothing else to do), I'd passed my turnoff.

There were no cars around so I did a U-ie, a thing of beauty if you have the room and a Mustang. It was almost as good as sex.

Well, okay, maybe only better than bad sex. Good sex . . . well, nothing beat that.

Which made me think of Porter again.

I hunched forward, reading the road signs. It didn't look like anything but squirrels lived here, given the thick forest, but if there were numbers, there were houses somewhere. At least that's what I was banking on. Frankly I'd never been around this much wilderness before and it kind of made me itch.

Two-thirty-seven . . . two-thirty-nine . . . two-forty-three . . .

I frowned. Okay, I was missing a number. And it happened to be the number I needed.

I looked in my rearview mirror. Still no cars behind me. So I stopped, put Lucille in reverse, then backed up to the unmarked drive.

The trees surrounding me looked as old as Methuselah. I felt like I had been driving in the dark for about a quarter of a mile before I finally came to a clearing and a sprawling log home. Whoa. I stepped on the brake pedal. Who didn't dream of at least renting one of these babies, much less owning one? Where there wasn't golden wood, there were windows overlooking the surrounding forests and, I guessed, the mountain in the back.

Paradise.

I swatted at a mosquito. Paradise with bugs.

I was still officially in the drive so I backed up, as much to block the narrow driveway as to conceal my presence. I put the top up on the car—you know, in case it decided to rain—climbed out, quietly closed the door, then began hiking the short distance toward the house. There was a carport visible on the left; in it was parked the Cadillac with the crown air freshener in the back window and the Giants bumper sticker.

Looked like Rosie had come through for me again.

I edged around back. A huge wooden deck was attached to the house. It was the middle of the day and there was little for me to hide behind. So rather than try to slink up like a fool, I casually walked up the stairs and approached the open French doors.

And there was Mrs. Carol Suleski in the kitchen, making lemonade.

"Come in, Miss Metropolis. I've been expecting you."

I froze in the doorway. She'd been expecting me? All that sneaking around and hiking halfway up the drive for nothing?

I had the feeling she was speaking of more than just my arrival at her house. I suspected she'd known I was coming before I pulled away from the curb this morning.

She stirred the contents of the pitcher, then filled two glasses, holding one out to me. "Try it," she said when I hesitated. "The recipe's been in my family for generations."

I walked the rest of the way in and took the glass. I took a sip and tried to hide my shudder at the sourness. "It's, um, good," I said through my tight throat.

"It sucks." She took a sip and made the expression I would have liked to make. "But it's tradition. I always make it on my first full day here." She sat down on a stool and motioned for me to do the same.

I did.

"Why were you expecting me?" I asked.

She smiled at me. "He said that would be your first question."

Porter. It had to be.

"You were what was in that bedspread that day at the motel," I said.

Her smile widened. "He said that would probably be the second thing you'd say."

I resisted the urge to scratch my head. "I don't get it. I mean, if he was in on this the whole time, why not just tell me?"

She shrugged and put down her glass. She reached across to get a paper towel, tore it into two pieces, then put one under her glass and one under mine. "I don't know. I didn't even know you two were connected until he called this morning."

Connected. Well, that was an interesting way to describe me and Porter.

She sighed heavily and I looked at her closely for the first time.

Ten years ago she'd probably been a knockout. She had blond hair and dazzling blue eyes and teeth as smooth and bright as Chiclets. But time, and children probably, had taken their toll. She probably still cleaned up pretty well, but there was a . . . I don't know, maybe a rundown feel about her that made her look older than she was.

"I don't get it," I said, speaking my thoughts aloud. "I mean, one minute you're meeting your lover, the next all hell breaks loose."

She looked at me, startled. "Lover? Is that what you think all this is about?"

I squinted at her.

"He really hasn't told you what's happening, has he?"

Neither of us had said Porter's name yet and I was getting more than a little ticked that she appeared to know more about him and what was happening than I did.

"That's all right. He's probably doing it to protect you."

It wasn't all right. I didn't want to be protected. I'd been hired to perform a job. And when that job went south, I was determined to figure everything out until the bitter end.

Was this the end?

"So if you weren't meeting a lover, who were you meeting?"

"An FBI agent, of course." She looked back at her lemonade. "At least I think he was FBI. It's hard to tell nowadays, with so many branches of law enforcement."

So she thought she'd been meeting with the FBI. Harry Brooks was an FBI agent? Or maybe the guy who had opened the door?

And how was Porter, the sometime bounty hunter, tied into the FBI?

"Okay, so you go there to meet this FBI agent and a gunfight breaks out," I say, almost to myself. "But the coroner reported a knife wound as the cause of Harry Brooks' death. Who brings a knife to a gunfight?"

Carol seemed overly interested in her glass of lemonade. Probably she had just taken another sip. Probably it was choking her.

I heard a branch crack outside. Likely another pesky squirrel, but I turned to look anyway. What I saw wasn't a squirrel. Not unless he'd taken some major steroids, donned a black ski mask, and learned how to aim a sniper rifle.

"Look out!" I shoved Carol Suleski to the floor, landing on top of her as the glass from the balcony doors shattered, reminding me a little too much of that night at the motel. Only it wasn't Queens Boulevard outside the window, but the wild, wild west. And my damn gun was in my car.

I got off Carol. "Run. Hide. Then get out. My Mustang's in the driveway."

She didn't need to be told twice. She scrambled on all fours into the connecting hall and out of sight. I crawled to the other side of the island. I didn't have a clue what the hell I was going to do once I got there, but I figured it probably wasn't a good idea for me and Carol Suleski to stay together. Hopefully, we stood a better chance apart.

I realized I'd left my purse—and my mace and expandable baton—on the counter and cringed.

I heard footsteps on broken glass. The gunman had entered the house.

My heart sounded unusually loud in my ears, probably because I was holding my breath. Another crunch and I sucked in air and blindly felt around one of the kitchen drawers to my left. Towels. I tried another. Bingo. I pulled out a wood-handled butcher knife. I stared at the shiny blade, wondering just what in the hell I was going to do with it against a gun.

A knife against a gun . . .

The word "eureka" exploded in my mind. Carol's odd, evasive expression when I'd asked her about Harry's demise by knifing wasn't a result of bad lemonade. It had been because she'd been the one carrying a knife in that motel room that night.

A knife was the first thing I'd gone for when I'd found myself without anything to use for defense.

Is that what Carol had done? She was meeting an FBI agent for Lord knew what, and was probably more than a little scared, so she slipped a knife into her purse as an afterthought. A knife is better than nothing. Then all hell broke loose and bullets started flying and . . .

Carol Suleski stabbed Harry Brooks.

My moment of revelation was interrupted by more shuffling footsteps. I peeked around the corner of the island. The gunman was skulking down the hall in the same direction Carol had gone.

Oh, boy.

I stared at the knife in my hand. Just what the hell was I going to do with this, anyway? I didn't even like cleaning chicken.

I dropped the knife and ran full out through the shot-out balcony doors and around the house, sprinting for my car and the gun in the glove box. I opened the driver's door, my heart pounding a million miles a minute. Carol Suleski was nowhere to be seen. I heard a loud bang and my car lurched forward, throwing me face-down across the seats. The car stopped moving. I popped my head up to see a big, black, angry-looking SUV backing up. It stopped and I could hear the engine revving.

Oh, shit.

I scrambled into the driver's seat and shoved my key into the ignition, outgunned for the second time in as many minutes.

This just wasn't my day.

I was finally able to start my engine. With trembling hands, I put the car into gear. At that moment, the SUV smacked into the back of my Mustang. When the SUV stopped pushing, I pressed the gas, doing a 180 not because I was enjoying it but because I had to. I sat facing the SUV, some twenty feet away, unable to see through the fully-tinted windows of the monster vehicle. The engine growled.

This was not looking good.

Okay, I'll admit it. I've never been good at playing chicken. Dare me to do something, and it's a pretty good bet that I will. But playing chicken was never quite my thing.

I looked behind me. Nothing but the house. In front, the SUV blocked the narrow drive.

I spotted something in my rearview mirror. Carol Suleski was running into the thick woods to my right, the gunman nowhere to be seen.

The SUV lurched forward.

"Shit!"

I hit the gas. At the last minute I yanked my steering wheel to the left, then right, practically screaming a prayer as the car finally steadied and I found myself speeding down the driveway.

Yes!

I frantically looked to my right, trying to catch sight of Carol. There! She was getting into another car and a moment later was speeding down a parallel driveway. We reached the road at the same time.

She waved and took off to the left. I gunned the motor and turned to the right, not stopping until I'd hit the main highway.

The great thing about having a car like mine is that it's one of a kind. The crappy thing about having a car like mine is that it's one of a kind. Easily located in a sea of other cars. And, of course, it didn't help that there wasn't any sea of cars to be had in eastern Pennsylvania.

So I headed for a used car lot I'd spotted on the way in and parked in the back, behind a couple of trucks. I took the Glock from my glove compartment, stuffed it into my purse, and climbed out just as a salesman started toward me. "For parking," I said, slapping the crisp fifty I had in my pocket into his hand. "I'll be back in a little while."

At the McDonald's across the street, I got a coffee and a small order of fries. I sat near the front, where I could watch the road.

Within a few minutes the SUV slowly went by. I assumed that whoever was inside was studying both the fast food parking lot and the used car lot. It didn't stop.

I didn't fool myself into thinking that was it. That SUV would be back when he figured out I wasn't farther down the road. So I snatched a newspaper from an empty neighboring table and began reading it, keeping an eye on the road and hoping that neither I nor my car would be spotted.

Twenty-four

THE DRIVE BACK TO ASTORIA wasn't as carefree as my drive out. I spent half the time staring into my rearview mirror, waiting for the black monster SUV to pop up behind me. Couple that with Porter's not answering my repeated calls and, well, I was both happy with my success at avoiding said SUV and the gunman, and majorly ticked that I didn't know what was going down while Porter did. Excuse me if I was wrong, but things like that tended to bother me.

Okay, so Carol Suleski had been in that rolled-up bedspread Porter had carried out of the motel room. But what was the extent of his involvement in what had started as a simple cheating spouse case and then went terribly wrong?

"So was she there?" Rosie asked, springing from her chair the instant I walked into the office.

"She was there."

"And?"

"And I'm more confused now than before I went out."

She popped her gum. "I'm not following you. If she was there and you talked to her, how does that make you more confused?"

"I'll explain later."

"Okay. Oh, Spyros called again. He wants to talk to you. He says he's going to call back tomorrow, same time."

Great. My uncle, the owner of the agency, my boss, wanted to talk to me. I had the feeling it wasn't going to be good.

I LET MYSELF INTO MY dark apartment and cautiously turned on a light, afraid of what I mind find waiting for me. While I was pretty sure the gunman earlier had been after Carol Suleski and not me, there was no sense taking chances. Not with the way my luck had been running lately.

Then again, maybe luck had been working in my favor more than I thought. After all, I hadn't taken a bullet that first night at the motel. The FBI had yet to catch up with me, although it wasn't from lack of trying. And in the Poconos I could have easily ended up as dog food.

I fished my cell phone out of my purse and called Porter—again. He didn't pick up. I got the sneaking suspicion he was ignoring me. If I were him, I'd be avoiding me, too. The blast that was coming his way wasn't going to be pretty.

I hadn't spotted his truck all day. I'd known he wasn't going to follow me to Pennsylvania because he'd told me he wasn't. But what about after I rolled back into town?

I disconnected, then called Lynn Halsey. I wanted to make sure Carol had made it out. Lynn told me she hadn't heard from Carol. I didn't know whether or not to believe her.

I pressed disconnect and checked my messages—again. The one I wanted—Porter's—wasn't there. Instead, there were six messages from my mother, left throughout the day, asking me to call her as soon as I could. The last one, left about an hour ago, told me it didn't matter how late it was.

I pressed my index fingers against my closed eyelids until I saw stars. I really wasn't up to my mother right now. But while she was known to pester me for myriad reasons, her last message sounded urgent.

I absently scratched the side of my right hand as I placed the call.

"Thank God, I was worried sick," was Thalia's greeting. No hello, how are you.

"Sorry. I had to drive to Pennsylvania and lost my cell phone signal." A lie. But Thalia wouldn't know any better. "What's wrong?"

"It's Mrs. K."

"I haven't had time to look for Muffy today."

"No, no, it's not that. I mean it is that, but it's not."

I frowned and stared at where my hand itched badly. The dog bite. Of course. Itching was good, right? It meant that the wound was healing. Only I shouldn't be scratching it.

I stared at it harder.

"I'm worried about her. She didn't look good earlier. She said it was just indigestion, and given the food she eats, well, I could understand that, but it was something more. Something that doesn't sit well with me."

I barely heard her, my attention focused on my dog bite as an idea did a Greek *zembekiko* dance around the edges of my thoughts, then slid to take center stage with a dramatic sweep of a phantom arm.

"Mom, I think I've figured out where Muffy is. Give me half an hour and I'll call you right back."

I hung up.

Twenty-five

I KNOCKED AT BARB QUAKENBOS' door, aware that it was after eleven and that she might just as soon call 911 as open up to me.

I was surprised when the door swung open and she looked at me in almost comical relief.

"Thank God. I was afraid you'd never figure out I kidnapped that stupid dog." She yanked me inside the house, nearly pulling me out of my Skechers. "He's in there. Get him."

"Whoa, hold on a minute." I held my hands up. I'd already been bitten by a Muffy look-alike, I was in no mood to be bitten by Muffy himself so soon afterward. "What makes you think I'm taking him home?"

"What? What?" Mrs. Quakenbos repeated, her voice growing higher. "This is what what!"

She held up both hands. They were covered in Band-Aids.

I held up my own hand. "That's how I figured out you were the one who took him. What I want to know is *why*."

"Why? Because Aklima wouldn't stop making fun of my cooking, that's why. I warned her. I told her that if she insulted my coffee cake one more time she'd live to regret it. But did she listen to me? No. So I knew in the morning while she's making that tongue-scorching tea of hers she's not paying attention to the dog outside, and I took him."

It looked like Barb was the one living to regret her actions.

"He's locked in the kitchen."

I looked around the living room. Stuffing was out of cushions, plants had been knocked over, the wastebasket overturned, and everywhere you looked were little steaming piles of doggie doo.

I shuddered at the sight and the smell, then made my way down the hall to the kitchen.

"Well, what are you waiting for? Get him out of here!"

"How I'm I supposed to do that?"

She waved her wounded hands. "I don't know."

I pressed my hand against the swinging door, then withdrew it. "Do you have a blanket or something?"

"A blanket? Whatever do you need with a blanket?"

The thought of a bone-marrow extraction was preferable to suffering one more trying exchange with this frazzled woman. "Just get me one, okay?"

A moment later she handed me a lightweight blanket. "What are you going to do with it?"

"I'm going to throw it over Muffy and wrap him in it so he can't bite me."

She grabbed the blanket back. "That's not going to work."

I yanked at the cloth. "Try me."

She sighed heavily and went back to the linen closet. "At least let me get you another blanket. An older one."

At this point it looked like a ruined blanket should be the least of her worries, but hey, I wasn't going to argue with her.

"What about his blankie?" Had I really just said "blankie"?

"It's in there with him."

Another blanket in hand, I opened the swinging door a couple of inches. "Here Muffy, Muffy, Muffy."

I heard growling and jumped.

Why were there no lights on?

I felt the dog before I saw him, more specifically I felt him attach his teeth to the bottom of my jeans.

"Yeow!"

In response to my shriek Barb ran down the hall and I heard her footsteps on the stairs. A moment later a door slammed.

Fat lot of help she was going to be. I ought to just shove the dog back in the kitchen and leave.

"Nice doggie," I said through clenched teeth, beginning to crouch.

He readjusted his hold on my jeans, ripping the denim and getting uncomfortably close to my skin.

Wrapping my vulnerable hands in the blanket, I covered the unappreciative canine with fabric, trying to work it between his sharp little teeth and my flesh. The Jack Russell terrier wasn't having any of it, even though the blanket was now impeding his vision.

I gave his hindquarters a gentle pinch. He yelped and I yanked and just like that my arms were full of blanket and the growling, wriggling hound from hell. I had the presence of mind to grab his blankie from the floor before leaving the room.

"Is it safe to come out now?" Barb called from upstairs.

I adjusted my hold on the blanket and the dog, making sure there was no possible way he could bite me.

"No!" I called up, doling out my own brand of punishment. What was the world coming to if it was okay for best friends to petnap each other's dogs? "Muffy's loose in the house, so I wouldn't recommend you come out until I tell you to," I lied.

The upstairs door slammed again as I opened the front door. For long minutes I stood beside my car. I had no idea how I was going to work this. For starters, I was sure what I was doing would be looked upon as cruelty to animals. Next, just what was I supposed to do with him, put him in the trunk? Then I'd really be in trouble.

I folded back a corner of the blanket, exposing Muffy's face. Truth was, I felt sorry for the little mongrel. I mean, to be taken from your nice, safe, familiar backyard and held hostage in a stranger's house for days on end was enough to make anyone a little angry.

"Okay," I said to him carefully. "I'm taking you home to Mommy." Had I really just said that? "Do you understand? I'm taking you *home*. Where the streets will no longer be safe with you running them and where your owner will spoil you rotten and sic you on me."

He was still growling, an incessant hum that sounded a bit like a motor engine that was in need of a tune-up left on idle. But once I'd uncovered his face and started talking to him, the sound seemed to moderate a bit. He even took a brief time-out in order to lap his drying chops before going at it again.

"In order to take you home"—I kept putting the emphasis on "home," praying this would be the magic word—"I need to put you in the car. A car I'm going to have to drive home, so I won't be able to hold you." The idea wasn't looking very good to me. "Do you think you can be a good boy and sit in the back seat?"

More growling.

I had the bad feeling this wasn't going to work. But what were my alternatives? It was almost midnight and I couldn't exactly call in the cavalry.

I drew in a deep breath, opened the door, then slowly put Muffy into the back seat, still wrapped in the blanket. I quickly got into the car and closed the door.

Barb had been right about the blanket. It was going to be history in two seconds flat given the amount of tearing I heard.

I started the car, switched off the radio lest it irritate him further, then put pedal to metal, my objective twofold: get to Mrs. K's as soon as humanly possible . . . and keep the hound from hell off balance so he couldn't rip me to shreds along with the blanket.

Five minutes later I was still bite-free, even though a glance into the readjusted rearview mirror told me Muffy had long since made history of the blanket. He sat there staring at me uncannily in the mirror, his growling growing louder whenever I met his gaze.

I turned onto my street, immediately spotting flashing lights two blocks up. Lights that belonged to cop cars and, I realized as I drove closer, paramedics.

Oh, boy.

I pulled to a stop and jumped from the car, slamming the door quickly shut after me as I hurried up to where my mother stood to the side of an ambulance.

"What is it? What happened?"

She wiped her eyes. "It's Aklima. She's had a heart attack."

I blinked at her. Mrs. K was too ornery to have a heart attack.

I watched as a gurney was carried out of Mrs. K's front door and rolled toward the waiting ambulance. Her face was pale against the white sheets and, well, she didn't look too good.

She reached a hand out from under the blanket and caught my wrist, pulling me along with her because the paramedics weren't stopping. "Did you find my Muffy?"

I nodded. "Yes. He's in my car now."

Her face seemed to relax. "Good. Good. You good girl, Sofia. Take care of my Muffy till I get home."

I stood rooted to the spot as the gurney was lifted into the ambulance, the door was closed, and the ambulance sped away, siren wailing.

I glanced from the chaos to my car to see Muffy with his front paws against the steering wheel, barking. I had the feeling that I might be the one wishing I were being carted away in a couple of hours.

OKAY, SO IT MIGHT NOT HAVE been the most sensitive thing to do, but after the ambulance pulled away I tried to foist the dog on my mother. If not my mother, surely one of Mrs. K's three kids could take the mutt.

She looked at me as if I'd gone insane. "Keep the dog until Mrs. Kapoor gets well, Sofie. How difficult can it be?"

I stood alone on the quiet street half an hour later, watching as Muffy still leaned his paws against the steering wheel of my car, barking his little head off.

How difficult could it be, indeed.

The dog had to exhaust himself at some point, didn't he? I mean, it couldn't be that long before lack of nourishment and water caused him to tip over and fall asleep, right?

I went inside my building and up to my place, trying to figure out where I was going to put him. Where could he do the least amount of damage? The bathroom.

I filled the bowls my mom had gotten from Mrs. K's house with water and dog food—also from Mrs. K's kitchen—and put them in the bathroom. After a moment's thought, I topped the nasty canned stuff with a cut-up leftover pork chop my mother had given me. I was about to go back downstairs when I realized that what went in eventually had to come back out, so I lined the bathroom floor with old newspapers.

Again I stood outside the car where Muffy was still looking like he'd commit grand theft auto if only he had the keys and his back paws could reach the gas pedal (although I wouldn't have put it past him to do a back and forth routine). I'd brought another blanket down with me and I had oven mitts on. The oven mitts Thomas' brother had given as a wedding gift. They'd come in handy after all.

"Okay, Muff, it's one o'clock in the morning and I'm fresh out of patience and goodwill. So be a good little dog and maybe we'll both get some sleep tonight."

Blanket held strategically, I opened the door, and Muffy zoomed out and ran straight for Mrs. K's.

Of course, it probably didn't help that I was holding the blanket more to protect myself than to catch the dog.

I groaned and ran after him, the irony of the situation impressing me not at all. Wasn't it usually him chasing me?

Muffy zipped through the gate left open by the paramedics. I hurried after him, closing the gate behind me. I found him on the front porch, back to growling like something out of a Stephen King novel.

Okay . . .

"Here, Muffy, Muffy, Muffy," I said, holding the blanket out at arm's length.

He caught the edge of the blanket in his teeth, then shot out to the soggy front yard, not so much running from me as pulling me after him. I found out why a split second later when I tripped over a garden hose and went sprawling headfirst into the mud.

I wasn't sure, but at this point I think I was doing a little growling myself.

Muffy continued to pull on the blanket as I wiped mud from my eyes with the hand I'd yanked out of an oven mitt, the slime sucking at me as I got up. I eyed the dark house, wondering if there was some way for me to gain access and leave the mongrel inside. I'd bring him water and food.

Speaking of food.

I reached inside my mud-caked front jeans pocket, where I'd

tucked a bit of pork. I put it in the other hand, then put the oven mitt back on and crouched down.

"Are you hungry, boy?"

I waved the pork as if he could see it in the dark.

I edged a little closer and he barked, putting so much energy into the action that he bounced a foot backwards.

Thankfully there was only so far he could go, what with the fence and all. I continued edging slowly forward, muttering what I hoped were comforting words. But, hey, if I'd gone through what he had over the past week at Barb Quakenbos' house, I probably wouldn't trust anyone either.

Finally my hand was close enough for him to bite me, although I personally hoped he'd settle for the pork instead. I stayed perfectly still, watching his little body vibrate from snarling so hard. He sniffed the meat, then snatched it, along with a piece of the mitt. While he was chewing, I plucked him up, holding him at arm's length, the blanket a lost cause in the mud nearby.

Who knew a dog so small could be such a handful?

I hurried back to my place, where I'd propped open all the doors so I wouldn't have to worry about them, and before I knew it Muffy was in the lighted bathroom, the door firmly closed behind him.

I leaned against the wood and slid down to sit on the floor. The door jumped behind me and I started wondering if it was possible for him to knock it down.

Okay, I thought, raising a hand. From here on out I promise never, ever to question the luck gods again.

The problem was I had a sneaking suspicion they weren't finished raining down bad luck on me just yet . . .

Twenty-six

I WOKE WITH A START, my T-shirt drenched in sweat. In my dream I'd been running from masked gunmen. As a bullet made its way toward me in slo-mo, the man who had fired it peeled back his mask to reveal Porter's face.

Usually my dreams about Porter were of the wet variety. I stared at my T-shirt. I preferred the other way.

Filled with an incredible urge to pee, I dashed for the bathroom, only distantly registering that the door was closed. I threw it open and stood face to face with a still growling Muffy.

Oh, shit.

I slammed the door shut.

I'd forgotten about the damn dog. How was anybody's guess, because his barking had kept me awake for the better part of the night. I'd even received a call from Mrs. Nebitz wondering what the racket was. Once I'd explained the situation with Mrs. K, Mrs. Nebitz had asked if there was anything she could do. Now there definitely was—allow me use of her bathroom. I hoped it wasn't too early to wake her.

I rushed into my bedroom and pulled on a pair of shorts. I ran across the hall, squeezing my thighs tightly together to keep from making any smelly puddles, and knocked on her door.

She opened it and with a quick exchange I ran for her bathroom.

As I relieved myself, I looked around the frou-frou bathroom, complete with powder and a powder puff. I cleaned up and flushed the toilet. I stared at myself in the mirror. Not a pretty picture.

I cracked the door a bit. "Mrs. Nebitz, do you mind if I use your shower?"

"No, dear, go right ahead. There are towels in the cabinet."

I thanked her, using her products as I scrubbed myself clean of the lingering mud. I'd have to call my mom as soon as I went back to my place and see when Mrs. K was due to be released. It was bad enough I'd been turned from pet detective into petsitter without being paid. Now I was locked out of my own bathroom, which wouldn't do at all.

I thanked Mrs. Nebitz, stuck a fresh bowl of food and water into my bathroom quick-like while wearing fresh oven mitts (I'd taken great pleasure in dropping the ones from Thomas' brother into the trash can), then climbed into my Mustang, my destination Bud Suleski's auto shop.

Halfway there I threw my useless cell phone onto the passenger seat. I'd had to leave messages for my mother, Porter, and Lynn Halsey, and I was convinced the last two were avoiding me.

I noticed the CLOSED sign in the window of the shop after I saw the closed bays and empty parking lot. Figured. Muffy aside (and I wasn't counting that a success yet), I always seemed to be a day late and a dollar short.

I parked anyway and walked up to the shop, pressing my hand against the glass to peek inside. Miracle of all miracles, I saw movement. I knocked on the glass, then peeked again.

Nothing.

Hmm. That was funny. I could have sworn I saw something.

I leaned back and looked at the closed bays, then back in the shop. There were no cars parked in the lot and none close by aside from Lucille. I eyed the lock. Maybe this was just the opportunity I was looking for.

I took out the lock-picking kit I had in my purse. I'd bought it on a whim when I'd purchased the baton and mace a couple months back and had practiced on my lock at home for three days before finally popping it. While I was by no means an expert when it came to professional locks (although I could open the one on the inside office door with my eyes closed), I was pretty sure I could do this one.

Ten minutes later I had a crick in my neck and was waiting for Pino to pull up any second and ask what I was doing, when finally the lock clicked open. Thank God. I was just about to pack it up and go home.

I glanced around, probably looking about as inconspicuous as those idiots you saw in those *World's Dumbest Criminals* videos. But I comforted myself with the fact that I wasn't there to steal anything. I just wanted to have a look around.

I closed the door after myself, making sure it didn't lock, then stepped quickly to the office door. This one I didn't have to pick; it was already open. I wrinkled my nose at the scent of gasoline coming from the garage, then walked inside. There were boxes all over and a couple of things had been taken from the back wall, as evidenced by the squares of faded paint. Looked like Bud was officially closing up shop. I moved to the empty filing cabinet, then rifled through the desk drawers. Nothing. Of course, I didn't know what I was looking for, but I felt I'd know when I saw it.

I looked through one box then pulled over another, this one marked "Personal." And right on top I saw exactly what I'd been looking for: an insurance policy.

I bit the inside of my bottom lip. Correction: plural, insurance policies. I counted four different sets of papers. The first covered the shop. The other three had been taken out in Carol Suleski's name and the payout added up to one million two hundred thousand.

I hiked a brow, the last puzzle pieces audibly clicking into place.

"I was wondering when I'd catch up with you again," Bud Suleski said from the door.

It hadn't been imaginary puzzle pieces I'd heard click. It had been the sound of the keys fastened to Bud's belt.

I stared at him, wondering how he'd gotten in without my seeing him. Then it occurred to me that he hadn't just come in, he'd already been inside. That's why I'd seen movement when I'd first arrived. I looked down at the box in front of me. He'd probably been collecting the last of his stuff when I got there and had ducked out of sight when he saw me.

I quickly put the papers back in the box and closed the flap.

"You look like shit," he said.

I scowled, becoming more and more sold on the idea of growling as an acceptable response. I wondered if it would work on my mother. Probably not. Probably she would cuff me on the back of the head if I growled at her.

"You and me need to have a talk," I told Bud.

I'd pretty much figured out that my own client was responsible for the blow to the head I'd taken a few nights before. I mean, who else would break into my place and not take anything but a stale knish? He hadn't expected me to be home.

For that reason, I'd come prepared. In the purse I squeezed

against my side were my mace, the safety off, and my expandable baton, ready to whack a few bones if the situation demanded it.

Bud pulled the box I'd been going through in front of him. It didn't take a genius to know what I'd been looking at.

"You haven't asked me about your wife," I said, gauging the distance between me and the door.

He threw me a scowl of his own. "A little late for that now, isn't it?"

"Depends on what you mean by 'late.' But judging by your reaction, I'm guessing it means she's still alive and there's no way in hell you're going to get close enough to kill her now."

His hands slowed where he was closing the flaps of the box and folding them under to secure them.

"Oh, yeah, I pretty much figured everything out. You hired me not to prove your wife was committing adultery but because you wanted a plausible eyewitness who would also provide you with an alibi when she was whacked. A hit you arranged so you could cash in on the three life insurance policies I saw in that box. That money would save both your shop and your home and finance your gambling habit."

He was staring at me now and I wasn't liking the look in his eyes. "You think you have it all figured out, don't you?"

I thought I did. But now he was making me wonder. "What I want to know is why you chose me as the patsy?"

He laughed at that. "Nothing personal. I closed my eyes and poked a finger in the phone book."

Well, that was nice to know. And not surprising, really. I mean, only I could have been the one his finger landed on, the way my luck was running. Of course it would have been Uncle Spyros' name in the book, not mine, but since I was the only full-time investigator presently at the agency . . .

"What did the FBI want?" I asked him.

He stared harder at me. "You ask a lot of questions."

I shrugged. "So sue me. I've been shot at—twice—had my apartment broken into—thanks for the bump on the head, by the way—and my life has generally been a living hell ever since you walked through the agency door a week and a half ago. I think I deserve a few answers."

I'd put my right hand into my purse and had my fingers closed around my mace.

Bud said, "The FBI were following up on my missing persons report."

I hiked a brow and watched as his scowl turned into a dark grin.

"It seems that after all this, my devoted wife Carol has been killed. The problem with the whole scenario is that I'm suspect number one."

Carol Suleski was dead? The gas smell suddenly made me dizzy.

While I'd been around dead people before—see previous employment—I'd never personally known anyone who'd been killed before. I swallowed hard. Okay, so I didn't really know Carol Suleski either, but I had become somewhat acquainted with her. And I'd liked her. Until a sniper shot through her window.

Is that what had happened? Is that how she'd been killed? Had the men in the SUV caught up with her?

I thought it was long past time I had a little chat with the FBI.

I started edging toward the door, which meant I'd have to get past Bud. I wasn't at all surprised when he grabbed my arm. "Where do you think you're going?"

To the FBI to help nail your hairy butt to the wall, I thought. "To the hospital. My neighbor had a heart attack last night."

Was it me, or was the smell of gasoline stronger near him?

He stared at me hard. In his face I saw all the anger that had likely been channeled into wanting his wife dead. Reasons probably not limited to life insurance money.

His grip tightened and I made a little noise of discomfort. He snatched my purse out of my hand, stared inside, then tossed it into the corner of the room. "What, no gun?"

"I hate guns." I hoped he wouldn't notice the can of mace in my hand; I'd still been gripping it when he took my purse.

"You know, you'd have been better off keeping your big mouth shut."

I can't tell you how many times I'd heard that in my lifetime. Now I wished I'd listened.

Bud grinned. "I should have hit you harder."

Now that pissed me off. Waking up with a pounding headache and my cheek pressed against my cheap rug because of a smack in the head given to me by my own client was not my idea of a good time.

I hit him with the oldest female trick in the book, kneeing him in the balls and spraying him point-blank in the face with my mace. Only I discovered that it wasn't mace I was holding but the bottle of J.Lo perfume Rosie had given me. I'd just "maced" Suleski with holy perfume.

I shrieked and ran for all I was worth.

I'd gotten into my car and started to pull the door closed when he caught it in his hands and wound something around my neck. I knew enough to put my left hand between the thick metal cord and my throat before he could tighten it, but I was afraid it would not only cut through my fingers, but completely decapitate me. I coughed, my eyes flooding with tears. So far gone was Bud that he didn't care that he was strangling me on the street in the middle of the day in full view of God and everyone.

I kicked at Bud's knees with my left foot, gaining a bit of leeway that I used to lean farther into the car, my right hand groping for the glove compartment.

He pulled tighter and my vision went black for a moment.

Oh, boy.

I grabbed the Glock. I thumbed off the safety and shot Bud in the knee.

He howled and released the garrote, falling backward onto the street.

"I said I hated guns, not that I didn't know how to use one." I reached for the phone to call 911.

Twenty-seven

PINO LEANED AGAINST THE DOORJAMB of the examination room at Astoria General, arms and ankles crossed, shaking his head at me. It figured he'd be the first cop to show up at the scene.

"You should have called the police before you went over there."

The nurse cleansed my neck wound. I hadn't gotten a good look at it yet, aside from what I'd been able to make out in my rearview mirror. I wasn't sure I wanted to get a good look at it either. I was just grateful I didn't need stitches. It was bad enough that I felt like the ex-bride of Frankenstein, I didn't want to look like her, too.

I heard a man's shout. Pino looked down the hall. Bud Suleski had been brought into the same hospital and was being attended to down the hall. With the evidence I'd provided the NYPD, I was convinced there was a pretty good case against Bud, even without a body.

I shuddered, feeling cold to the bone.

At the very least my ex-client would serve time for having assaulted me. I was also pretty sure that Suleski had been about to torch his own shop when I'd interrupted him, which would tack a few more years on to whatever sentence he received.

Pino's gaze sharpened on me. "By the way, do you have a permit to carry concealed?"

"I wasn't carrying concealed. The Glock was in my glove box." I cringed away from the nurse who was approaching me with gauze. "Do I have to have that? Is it all right to leave it exposed?" It was bad enough to have the wound, but wearing gauze like a bad turtleneck with summer around the corner didn't appeal to me.

"I have some flesh-colored tape."

I nodded. That would do. Anything but white gauze.

Pino was waiting for a straight answer to his question. I didn't feel like giving him one. "What do you think?" I asked.

"I need to confiscate your gun."

I smiled. "I have a permit."

He lifted his right hand and scratched his head, looking disappointed. "Another thing: Do you know where we might find Mrs. Suleski's . . . remains?"

Me and missing bodies. Seemed to be a theme lately. "No. Sorry, I don't. Could be anywhere between here and the Poconos." I gave him the address of Carol's parents' cabin.

He nodded. "Okay. You need a ride home?"

I'd driven my car to the hospital despite the protests of the paramedics. "No, I think I'll be fine."

Anyway, home was the last place I wanted to be right now. I wanted to go to the office and share my exploits with Rosie, whose animated face I could already see, eyes wide and gum popping.

I'D BEEN LEAVING MESSAGES FOR my mom all day. Not because I wanted to share my Suleski story (although I knew I'd have to say something about my new piece of neck jewelry), but rather because I wanted to find out when I could take Muffy home. I didn't relish the thought of being locked out of my bathroom for another night.

After entertaining Rosie, I squinted at the threatening clouds, wondering if it was ever going to stop raining, and called Porter. Of course, I didn't get him. But I did leave a message. "Meet me across from the motel at nine tonight."

I didn't tell him which motel. I was pretty sure he'd know. I stepped outside, onto Steinway.

Home.

Everything about Astoria was familiar to me. From the layout of the streets to the myriad smells to the eclectic collection of people living in harmony together, everywhere I looked made me feel a part of something . . . I don't know. Bigger than me, maybe. Like I was meant to be there. Like somehow I would be missed if I were to leave or, God forbid, something should happen to me.

I found myself toying with the tape around my neck. I opened the agency door and told Rosie I'd be back in a while. She asked me to pick her up a Danish from the bakery up the block while I was out.

I'd decided to walk over to my parents'. Because of her limited knowledge of English—or rather her inability to be understood in English—my grandmother never answered the phone, but it was a pretty good bet she'd be home. Maybe she would know something about Mrs. K's condition.

It was a good ten-block walk. While cloudy, it wasn't raining, and the warm June day was pregnant with the smells of summer. Trees seemed to spring out of the cement sidewalks, symbols of the ongoing man-against-nature battle that would probably rage on forever, but had found a nice balance in Astoria. Maybe I'd check in on Muffy, too, see how the mongrel was doing. Pick up some more dog food for him. Or maybe a *souvlaki* sans *tsatsiki* and onions. If he was going to be my houseguest, he might as well get used to Greek food. The sooner the better.

A short while later I left my apartment building after risking serious injury by throwing food to the ungrateful mutt that had taken possession of my bathroom. I began to turn toward my parents' when a dark, gleaming car some thirty years old with rear doors that opened backward slowly drove by. I watched as it stopped outside the Romanoff house. I drew to a halt and stared as the creepy nephew got out from behind the wheel, shielding himself with an umbrella though it wasn't currently raining, then helped someone out from the back.

Ivan Romanoff.

The master vampire lived.

I squinted, trying to see him better. He still had that pasty look about him, and seemed to be moving a little slower than usual, but was still on this side of the ground (which I wasn't sure was a good or a bad thing) and not packed away in dozens of Tupperware containers as Rosie had feared.

And he was out in the daylight.

I made a face. Okay, so the dark clouds made it look like dusk. And the huge, black umbrella the nephew was using made them look like they were walking shadows. And both of them wore long, dark raincoats, boots, gloves, and sunglasses. But that they were outside in daylight was all that mattered to me. Umbrella or no umbrella, it meant they weren't vampires.

I think.

The elder Mr. Romanoff took off his sunglasses and looked directly at me, almost as if sensing my attention, if not my thoughts (don't be stupid). His eyes seemed to flash red briefly. Then he smiled and continued on into the darkness of his house, long coat flapping out behind him.

Yikes.

I gave a mammoth eye roll, then headed for my parents'. There were no such things as vampires.

Of course it was easier for me to say that now that Romanoff had officially been found and there was no longer any reason for me to snoop around the dark castle that was his house.

And, of course, if I chose to forget about the casket—cello case—in the basement, well, that was nobody's business but mine.

I let myself into my parents' house with my own key, calling out for anyone that might be home. I found my grandmother and my mother in the kitchen. My neck wound started aching when I noticed my mother was crying.

I could count the times I've seen my mother cry on one hand. Actually, two fingers would do the trick. The first time was when Princess Diana was killed in that awful accident in Paris.

The second time was now.

I wondered if I could back out of the house without being seen; the precedent didn't bode well for what was the cause of her tears now.

My grandmother caught my gaze, looking pale and somehow frailer in her black dress, a color she'd worn ever since my father's father died when I was five. That's what old Greek women did: Their husbands died; they were widows for the rest of their lives and wore black.

I wasn't liking the direction of my thoughts. Especially when my mother looked up, her face full of a type of pain that made my stomach ache.

I didn't want to hear what she had to say. Didn't want to face what she obviously was facing. But I didn't think there was much I could do to keep her from saying it.

"Aklima is dead."

My throat closed off. There it was. The news I'd dreaded the moment I spotted her crying. Mrs. K had kicked the proverbial bucket and had moved on to the big Hindu heaven in the sky. Or did they believe in reincarnation?

Either way I felt the intricate patchwork of the neighborhood I had been considering just a few minutes ago give a subtle but very noticeable pull as a rip appeared.

And I was pretty sure I, too, was about to cry.

Twenty-eight

THE GOOD NEWS WAS MRS. Kapoor hadn't suffered much. At least that's what my mother said, although I wasn't sure who she was trying to reassure, me or herself. Shortly after being transported to Astoria General, Mrs. K had gone into full cardiac arrest. The doctors had revived her, only to have her arrest again about an hour or so later. She'd lost consciousness in the ambulance while being transported to the hospital and it was generally believed she'd been unaware since then.

Mrs. K was gone . . .

The news had hit me with all the force of a two-by-four, upsetting me far more than the "necklace" I now wore. Mrs. K and I had had a symbiotic relationship my entire life. So long as I knew she was around to keep me in check, I had license to do whatever I wanted.

Now that she was gone . . .

I was having a hard time wrapping my mind around the idea. Somehow I had never considered she might die. She'd been too stubborn to die. To give in just like that. But I suppose that was death for you. It didn't send out engraved invitations. It visited in the dark of night—or in broad daylight when you weren't looking—and changed everything with a simple snap of its skeletal fingers.

If her going had shocked me, it had completely devastated my mother and Barb Quakenbos. They and Mrs. K . . . well, they'd shared more than age in common and had been far more than just friends. They'd been allies in a place that had been foreign to them all when they'd first arrived in Astoria many years earlier. They had supported each other when the going had gotten tough and one or the other had wanted to pack her bags and return to her homeland. They'd been through the birth of each other's children, had shared good times and bad, finding common ground where one would think there was none to be found.

The only thing keeping my mother going was taking care of Barb, who was afraid she'd caused Mrs. K's heart attack by dognapping Muffy.

Then again, there appeared to be enough guilt to go around as I wondered what would have happened if I'd figured everything out an hour or two earlier.

I didn't know how I was going to pass Mrs. K's house, knowing she wasn't inside, peeking through the crack in her curtains to catch me in the middle of my latest escapade, her finger hovering above the autodial for my mother.

I stood in the middle of my apartment, arms straight at my sides, my eyes registering nothing. I blinked everything into view, mildly surprised to find that I hadn't moved since coming home twenty minutes ago.

If the good news was that Mrs. K hadn't suffered, the bad news was that I now had a new roommate in an apartment building that didn't allow pets (ignoring the fact that as the owner, I could change the rules).

I looked at the closed bathroom door. The problem was, it was no longer closed.

I stared at the slight opening, then walked toward it, opening it the rest of the way. No food. No poop. No Muffy. The T-shirt hanging from the inside doorknob bore rips and tears consistent with a certain furry someone's teeth. The little monster had probably used it to help him open the door.

I jerked around. That meant he was loose in the apartment . . .

Oh, boy.

I dropped the ruined T-shirt to the floor and stepped warily forward, although I wasn't really sure why I was being cautious now. I mean, I'd been home for almost a half hour and hadn't been attacked yet. But there was something about knowing the hound from hell, who had a taste for Sofie flesh, was hiding somewhere, watching me, that made my skin crawl.

"Here, Muffy, Muffy, Muffy . . ."

I started in the living room. The dog was small enough to hide just about anywhere. But why he would, I didn't know. I mean, if our roles had been reversed, I'd probably have attacked me already.

I looked toward the main door. Or maybe he was biding his time, waiting for me to go out so he could make another break for it.

Great. I could just see myself chasing the wiggly fur ball up and down two flights of stairs all night.

I was looking under the sideboard in the dining room when I heard growling practically in my ear. I started and almost knocked over a chair. Muffy sat in the open window, his teeth bared as he looked between the fire escape behind him and me in front of him. I guess his ultimate decision would depend on how hungry he was.

Not daring to breathe, I began backing up toward the kitchen where I'd left the oven mitts. The moment I moved, Muffy turned around and jumped to the fire escape.

"Oh, shit!"

I ran to the window and poked my head out, watching the dog's little butt as he ran up the iron stairs.

He was going to the roof.

And I was going after him. I started to swing my leg out the window, then pulled it back in. Maybe not this way.

I hurried out into the hall with my keys, careful to close the door after myself, then went up the indoor stairs to the roof access. I slowly opened that door, then edged out onto the roof, quickly closing the door behind me. There, in the corner. I watched as Muffy lifted his pint-sized leg on an empty old flowerpot, then turned around and crouched.

Cripes.

When he was done, he scratched his back legs against the roof in an effort to cover up his business, then ran around a bit, barking, before sailing off the roof back to the fire escape.

I stood there for a long moment, wondering if I was imagining things. I hadn't seen any yellow spots or steaming piles in the bathroom. Had Muffy really held it all that time? Waited until he had access to the outdoors to relieve himself? Couldn't be.

A minute later I stood back inside my apartment, blocking the door to keep Muffy from getting out. But it turned out my efforts weren't necessary. I immediately spotted the Jack Russell terrier, sitting next to the refrigerator and barking. Not in threat, but as if to tell me, "All right, time to refill the old stomach."

"Okay . . . all right . . . we can do this," I said aloud. "Just be a good boy, you hear, and maybe we'll both make it through this alive."

I eyed the oven mitts on the counter, then watched as Muffy backed away from me and the refrigerator, apparently determined to stay in the kitchen.

Humph. It seemed hunger did strange things to both people and dogs.

"You know what, I'm a little hungry myself," I said, for some strange reason believing that so long as I kept talking, Muffy would keep his distance. I slowly opened the refrigerator door, keeping one eye on the terrier as I took inventory. There was another pork chop on the top shelf I'd been saving for myself along with a bit of homemade *rizogolo,* Greek rice pudding. I took out both and with measured movements cut the meat into terrier-size pieces, then dropped them into a low bowl.

"There. Is this what you're looking for?"

I put the bowl down and nudged it across the tile in Muffy's direction. He growled for a few moments, stepped forward, then drew back and started the whole process over again.

Finally he was eating, although how he could eat and growl at the same time was beyond me. I worried he'd get indigestion.

I smiled faintly, finding a bit of joy at his show of faith. Faith not only that I wouldn't poison him, but that I would take care of him. I gave the apartment a cursory glance, remembering Barb's place. I also counted myself lucky that he hadn't gone to town on any of my belongings. Lord only knew how long he'd been out of the bathroom and how long since he'd found access to the fire escape.

The hound from hell otherwise engaged, I went into the bathroom, gathered up the clean newspapers, and shoved them into the recycling bin in the kitchen, then picked up Muffy's water bowl. After refilling it, I set it down next to the now empty food bowl. Muffy began drinking.

"That's a good boy," I murmured, reaching out to pat his head.

He bared his teeth at me and snarled.

I snatched my hand back. "Okay, so I was stupid to think it would be that easy. I can adjust."

I watched as he padded out of the kitchen, his nails clicking against the tile, then jumped on top of the Barcalounger. He jumped down, pulled his blankie from the bathroom doorknob where I'd hung it while tidying, then jumped back up onto the chair, tugging the threadbare, plaid material until it was under him. Around and around he went, then lay down. His entire compact body seemed to shudder as he took a deep breath, then rested his head on his paws, his big watery eyes watching me.

I heard a sound and realized it was my own quiet laughter. "All right, if you want it that badly, it's yours."

As I stood watching a dog that had never been in my house before, a dog who'd just had his entire life turned upside down without knowing how or why, make himself at home, I began to believe for the first time this might work.

"Well, Muffy, I guess it's just me and you, kid."

And it was, wasn't it? Here we were, two grown . . . entities, out in the world on our own for the first time. He was supposed to have curry-flavored doggie biscuits for the rest of his natural life and I was supposed to be happily married and looking forward to a future that included kids and christenings and lots of visits to Lefkos Pirgos. Instead fate had snatched all that away from us and left us staring at each other warily, trying to forge a new path.

The difference was I could pick up the phone and call my mother. He couldn't. He would never see Mrs. K again.

I found myself taking a deep breath. The way Muffy was looking at me, I almost thought he knew what I was thinking.

Muffy . . .

I waggled a finger at him. As soon as things settled down a little, when the idea of Mrs. K's passing wasn't so raw, the first order of business would be to give him a name more befitting a male Jack Russell terrier. Maybe something like Jack. No, no, that reminded me too much of Jake. I considered other choices: Muffy the Mutt . . . Hound from Hell . . . H.H.? No, that didn't sound good. M.M.? Wait. Eminem. Muffy was scrappy and had short blond hair and a snarling demeanor just like the Motown rap star.

Yes, maybe Eminem. Nem for short.

Muffy started growling anew. Then again, maybe not. Maybe I'd just have to accept that some things aren't changeable.

AN HOUR LATER I WAITED in the Wendy's parking lot where everything had begun. I hadn't heard from Porter after having left my message earlier asking him to meet me here, nor had I expected to. Either he would be there or he wouldn't. At the moment I wasn't sure which I preferred.

My passenger door opened and I jumped.

"Jesus, you scared the hell out of me," I told Porter as he climbed in next to me.

His eyes narrowed in the dim light. My breath caught in my throat as he reached out and ran his fingertips over the bandages covering my neck. "Talk about scaring the shit out of someone."

I smiled shakily. "Yeah, but I busted his kneecap." I glanced toward the glove compartment where my gun was one bullet short. Hopefully I wouldn't need another one any time soon. Then again, any time I had to touch that gun was too soon for me.

Porter grinned at me and his fingers moved from my neck to my cheek. "That you did."

I didn't know how much he knew. I didn't want to know how much he knew. Truth was, I didn't want to learn how connected he was to everything going on around me. To merely consider it seemed to rob my life of mystery. And I'd decided I liked mystery.

For now.

He must not have liked the look on my face because he removed his hand. "What did you want?"

I battled back disappointment. Couldn't anything in my life go the way I wanted for once? Couldn't Porter kiss me in a way that made me want to shuck my panties? Couldn't he profess his undying love to me without my having to ask him to do it?

"I don't know. A few answers might be nice."

At least he could give me that.

He crossed his arms over his wide chest, the top of his head nearly brushing the roof of my car, his gaze on the rain beginning to fall again against the windshield. "Shoot."

Considering what had gone on that day, his choice of words didn't amuse me. "How's Carol Suleski?"

He slid me a sidelong gaze.

"Don't try telling me she's dead, because the last time I saw her she was very much alive."

"Then that's all you need to know."

I nodded. So she was alive. Maybe in protective custody. The witness relocation program, where her kids—Pino had told me they were with her parents in the city—might join her in a few months, after their father was in prison and things had cooled down a bit.

I didn't need details. Just then it was enough to know that she was okay.

"And the other guy from the motel room? The FBI agent Carol was meeting? How's he?"

I'd figured out from the pictures I'd taken that there had been two guys in that room that night. And they hadn't been there for a ménage à trois. Carol Suleski had been there to meet the mystery FBI agent and pass on what she knew about her husband's connection to the new-and-improved NYC mob. Harry the Hitman—Harry Brooks—hired by Carol's own husband to kill her, had interrupted the meet, shooting at everything that moved, which happened to include me, standing outside the window.

Then Carol Suleski had stabbed him with the butcher's knife she'd stuck into her purse before leaving home.

Speaking of which, I needed to go to the pawnshop tomorrow to pick up my brother's replacement camera and find out what Antypas wanted me to do for him PI-wise in return.

"Recovering," Porter said in answer to my question.

Good. I shifted in the driver seat. At least he wasn't lying to me anymore. Wasn't looking directly at me and saying, "What FBI agent?"

While it wasn't panty-shucking material, this was a new level of trust and it made me feel good. If only because this meant that our relationship, whatever it was, was progressing in the right direction.

"And Mrs. Suleski *was* the person in the bedspread." I said it as if I were certain.

He didn't respond, which I'd pretty much expected.

"Fine. Just tell me, do I have to worry about the FBI looking for me anymore?"

"Nope."

I shifted. "Okay. That's all I need to know."

I felt his gaze on my profile.

"That's it?"

I looked at him. "Unless you want to come back to my place and finish what we started the other night."

His grin made my toes curl in my Skechers.

Without saying another word, he climbed from the car and began walking toward his truck on the opposite side of the lot.

I opened my car door and stood outside. "Hey!" I called.

He turned to look at me.

"Will I see you again?"

He didn't say anything, merely stood looking at me.

I knew a moment of panic. What if he said he was heading back Down Under? That his business with me, whatever it had been, was done?

His grin made me feel like he was standing directly in front of me instead of halfway across the parking lot.

"Oh, I'm sure our paths will cross again, Sofie Metropolis."

Suddenly I didn't care that there was rain running down my face, ruining my makeup and drenching my clothes.

As I watched him get into his truck and pull away I thought of the advice my grandfather Kosmos had shared with me over food from the Chirping Chicken:

"There are three things you need to learn in life, Sofie. First, how to dance like you're alone. Second, to love like you mean it. And third, you need to learn to laugh at the rain. Learn how to do those three things, and you'll be happy, always."

I turned my face up toward the sky, reveling in the feel of the fresh, cool drops against my skin.

Suddenly they stopped.

I blinked open my eyes to find the clouds quickly thinning. Behind them, the moon and stars seemed to beam for the first time in nearly two weeks.

I smiled and gave an eye roll. Figured.

Then again, maybe I had to figure out the first two in order to give the third one the respect it deserved.

And maybe, just maybe, for now it was okay for me to be happy right this minute . . .

Telos

Recipes

Dear Reader,

We thought you might like to sample some of the foods Sofie waxes rhapsodic over, so here are a couple of traditional Greek recipes from our own personal files, as well as one that is all Sofie. For more delish recipes, visit our Web site at www.sofiemetro.com. *Kali Orixi!*

NESCAFÉ FRAPPÉ

Add 1½ teaspoons of Nescafé instant coffee, sugar to taste (generally 2 teaspoons), and an ounce of very cold water to a glass-size shaker (travel cups work well for this) and shake until the mixture becomes foam. Then add additional cold water (4 to 6 ounces depending on how strong you like it), milk, ice cubes, and a straw. *Sten eyeia sas!*

KOULOURAKIA (Traditional Greek Easter Cookies)

2¼ cups all-purpose flour
1¼ teaspoons baking powder
¼ teaspoon salt
½ cup sweet, unsalted butter, softened
1 cup powdered sugar
1 egg
2 tablespoons brandy or milk
1 teaspoon vanilla extract
1 egg yolk beaten with 1 tablespoon milk for glaze
3 tablespoons sesame seeds

Preheat oven to 375 degrees. Grease large cookie sheet. In a medium bowl, combine flour, baking powder, and salt; set aside. In a large mixing bowl, beat butter and sugar until fluffy. Add egg, brandy (or milk), and vanilla, beating well after each addition. Stir in flour mixture, ½ cup at a time, blending well after each addition.

Working with rounded teaspoons of dough, roll each piece back and forth on a lightly floured surface until it forms a 6-inch rope. Bring ends together to form a hairpin shape; gently twist hairpin 2 to 3 times. Lightly pinch ends together. Arrange 1 inch apart on cookie sheet. Brush with egg glaze and sprinkle with sesame seeds.

Bake 10 to 13 minutes until golden. Cool on wire racks. *Kali Orixi!*

DOLMATHAKIA (Stuffed Grape Leaves)

1 jar grape leaves
2 tablespoons olive oil
1 pound ground beef or lamb
2 medium red, Spanish onions, finely chopped
2 garlic cloves, finely chopped
1 cup rice
2 tablespoons fresh dill, chopped
½ teaspoon salt
Dash of pepper (or to taste)
2 cups water

Avgolemeno (Egg and Lemon) Sauce
3 eggs, separated
Juice from 2 lemons

Rinse the brine off the grape leaves in cold water. Drain in colander. Spread leaves out stem side up and snip off stems with a knife.

In a large bowl, mix remaining ingredients (except water and ingredients for the sauce). Place a full tablespoon of the mixture at the stem end of the leaf, fold the sides of the leaf in toward the center, then roll away from you. Use only intact leaves; reserve 2 to 4 leaves (torn are okay). Continue making rolls until you run out of leaves, mixture, or both.

Line the bottom of a large pan with the reserved grape leaves. Place each rolled leaf, seam-side down, on top of the lining so that they fit snugly. Add about two cups of water or enough to cover the rolls. Place a flat dish on top to keep the rolls intact while cooking. Cover. Bring to a boil, then reduce heat to simmer for approximately 45 minutes (until rice is cooked). Remove pot from heat.

Avgolemeno Sauce: Beat egg whites until frothy (about 5 minutes by hand, 2 with mixer). Slowly beat in yolks and lemon juice. Slowly stir 1 cup hot broth from the pan of grape leaves into mixture so it won't curdle when adding it to the pan. Make a kissing sound while pouring the sauce over the top of the rolls. You can serve the *dolmathakia* with or without the sauce and either cold as an appetizer or as a hot main dish. *Opa!*